CHRISTMAS NIGHTS AT THE STAR AND LANTERN

HERITAGE COVE SERIES - BOOK SIX

HELEN ROLFE

Boldwood

First published in Great Britain in 2023 by Boldwood Books Ltd.

Copyright © Helen Rolfe, 2023

Cover Design by Alexandra Allden

Cover Illustration: Shutterstock

A CIP catalogue record for this book is available from the British Library.

Paperback ISBN 978-1-80415-546-2

Large Print ISBN 978-1-80415-547-9

Hardback ISBN 978-1-80415-545-5

Ebook ISBN 978-1-80415-549-3

Kindle ISBN 978-1-80415-548-6

Audio CD ISBN 978-1-80415-540-0

MP3 CD ISBN 978-1-80415-541-7

Digital audio download ISBN 978-1-80415-542-4

Boldwood Books Ltd
23 Bowerdean Street
London SW6 3TN
www.boldwoodbooks.com

For my writing friends who share in the joy and the frustrations of being an author and without whom I would be lost.

1

Celeste drove back to Heritage Cove after making her delivery to the local school, and as she approached the bend in the road, she glanced over at the Copper Plough on the corner. Her heart sank. The pub was as much a part of the Cove as every business on the high street – but it was heading for a change and not one the locals were confident in. Any day now, its name would change and the people of Heritage Cove could only keep their fingers crossed that a new name wouldn't be the start of alterations that left their local pub unrecognisable.

She was about to continue around the bend, windscreen wipers swiping back and forth to disperse the November drizzle, when a man outside the pub caught her eye. It was only for a split second – any more than that and she would've careered into a car coming the other way – but it was enough to make her heart skip a beat.

She laughed at herself. *Don't be ridiculous.* She shook her head as she drove along The Street and pulled up behind the Twist and Turn Bakery, the business she owned and ran with her sister Jade. Whoever that man was, it couldn't possibly be Quinn

McLeod, the guy who'd visited here once upon a time a few summers ago and who she hadn't heard from since. But the man's build and the way he held himself were a sure reminder of Quinn and stirred something deep within her.

She grabbed the empty plastic containers from the boot of the car and made a run for it to the back of the bakery before she got soaked now the cold rain had started to come down even harder. And as she went into the warmth of the bakery's kitchen and put everything away, she allowed herself to reflect on a man who'd very much stolen her heart. Something that was never meant to happen.

The day they'd met, it was slow in the bakery. But slow days gave Celeste the chance to do what she usually did so well, creating different recipes to add new products to the shelves so their customers had even more choice. That day, she'd wanted to perfect a salted-caramel turnover and get it onto their menu. But one taste of her latest effort and she'd deemed the pastry too dry, the apple filling not cooked enough and the caramel sauce she'd tried to drizzle across it was too thick. It was her third failed attempt.

In the kitchen out the back of the bakery, she picked up one of the three turnovers she'd made and took another bite to try to really get a handle on what she needed to adjust for next time. But the pastry in her hand angered her, she hated to get it wrong, she hated wasted time and she didn't even think about it when she threw the turnover as hard as she could at the far wall with a curse she hoped hadn't carried into the main area of the bakery.

The problem was, Celeste had never been a very good aim. She'd been asked not to play darts at the pub unless it was under supervision and for good reason. Terry and Nola, the owners of the Copper Plough, had punters to protect. And when she heard a yelp from the bakery and saw Jade's face behind the counter, she knew she'd taken out one of their own customers.

She swore under her breath and went out to face the music and apologise.

What she didn't expect was to lock eyes with a drop-dead gorgeous guy not too dissimilar to her in age, tall and well-built with a crew cut. And she really didn't expect him to take her hand when she reached up to pull a piece of puff pastry from his hair either.

'Some might call this a classic meet-cute.' His mellifluous tone and enticing indigo eyes rendered her incapable of looking away as he pulled the offending piece of pastry from his hair without her help. 'I'm Quinn. Quinn McLeod.'

Celeste was a businesswoman, she had goals, aspirations, she didn't have time to fall for anyone. And yet standing here in front of this handsome stranger, she knew she was in trouble.

'Or perhaps it's fate,' he suggested when she didn't say anything.

She shook herself out of her trance. 'I apologise, I'm very sorry. Can I interest you in something on the house?'

'You most definitely can.' But his look suggested he wanted something that wasn't necessarily behind the glass-fronted cabinet or tucked on one of the shelves. 'Does it really taste so bad you had to throw it?' He looked at the pastry in his free hand, turning it over for better inspection.

She pulled her hand away from his slowly and took the pastry. 'To me, yes. It's not what I want to be serving my customers, put it that way.'

'And what do you like to give your customers?'

How could one person have this much effect on her? Usually calm and collected, professional to a tee, she found it hard to form a coherent sentence. 'My sister Jade will help you; I'd better get a dustpan and brush for the crumbs.' And she fled before either he or Jade had a choice in the matter.

She'd expected him to have chosen something and left but he was still there when she peered out into the bakery a few minutes later. And by the way he smiled back at her, he was waiting for her.

'Did you find something?' she asked in her best nonchalant voice as she emerged from her hiding place. Jade passed the other way and went out back, leaving her sister behind the counter this time.

'I did.' He held up a small bag. 'I've got the tastiest-looking doughnut in here, so thank you.'

'It's our pleasure.' And it was very much hers.

'I was hoping for something else.'

When he spoke with a cheekiness both in his voice and his expression, it made her want to laugh, but as a distraction she picked up the cloth and wiped down the counter.

He leaned closer in her direction, over the top of the till. 'You didn't tell me your name.'

'Do I need to?'

'Well, I usually like to know the name of the woman I'm going on a date with.'

Now that did make her laugh. 'You're confident. And nice try.'

'You're right. That was pretty lame. But give a guy a break.'

'All right. I'm Celeste.'

'That's a pretty name.'

'Thank you.'

'So Celeste, what time do you get out of here?'

'Late. I'm part owner so...'

'Brains as well as beauty.' He nodded, impressed. But his expression changed as he realised how he must sound. 'I'm not doing very well at this, am I? You can tell I spend most of my days at sea away from civilisation.'

'Kind of,' she teased. 'So, you're on leave?'

'I am, from the navy. I'm only here for a few days so I'm trying to make the most of it.'

Jade came through with a couple of poppy seed wholemeal loaves and pushed them onto the shelves behind the counter. 'She's off at six,' she said without preamble.

Celeste was about to argue that she could arrange her own love life, thank you very much, when Quinn saw his chance to stop her protest. He knocked once on the countertop in appreciation, thanked Jade, and left the bakery, calling over his shoulder, 'See you then.'

'What were you thinking?' she said to her sister the moment it was just the two of them again.

'I'm thinking you are both gooey eyed looking at each other and either you waste another half an hour debating whether to go out with him or you just go for it, arrange a time, and you can get out back and continue with your recipes. I know which is more useful for our business.'

Celeste grinned. And back in the kitchen, she perfected the turnover recipe on the next attempt.

They had dinner that evening down the coast, well away from the village and prying eyes, and in the days after that, whenever Celeste could get away from the bakery, they spent their time cocooned in each other's company, either at her cottage or walking along quiet stretches of beach. They'd both known exactly what it was, too: a holiday fling. They'd agreed from the first night that they wanted a no-strings-attached arrangement. It suited both of them – Celeste had the bakery, to which she gave her all and didn't want anything to distract her from, and she'd also learned a long time ago not to get attached because if you did, it came with a whole heap of hurt. And Quinn had the navy so he wouldn't be around for long. Before they knew it, he'd be back at sea, and so not making each other promises had been best all round.

At least that's what Celeste had thought. But when it came to the few hours before Quinn was due to leave Heritage Cove and go back to his own life, her emotions were all over the place.

'I can't believe you're leaving later today.' Curled up against him, she said it before she remembered what they'd agreed at dinner the very first night.

'Back to work for me soon, and at least you can get back to your bakery.' He was having a hard time keeping his eyes open and she took the opportunity to watch the way his lashes cast shadows below his eyes, the rise and fall of his broad chest.

'Hey, I've not left it.'

'Your sister has been doing the lion's share.' He opened one eye to tease her.

She smiled back at him. 'She's been really good to me.'

'Thank her on my behalf, won't you?'

'I will.' Although the pair had met, Celeste had done her very best to keep Quinn to herself since then, although there had been the odd awkward moment on the landing in the middle of the night. Not that Jade minded; she'd been all for it, probably glad her sister had a bit of a love life at long last.

'Back to our own lives before we know it,' Quinn sighed, satiated, his eyes heavy.

She crawled up the bed closer to him, their bodies pressed together beneath the sheets, and kissed him. 'Back to our own lives,' she repeated.

She settled down next to him again, her cheek resting against his chest, her fingers laced through his. 'You'll be off seeing more of the world soon.'

'Something like that, yeah. Not as glamorous as it sounds.'

'But it must have been part of the attraction.'

'It definitely was,' he murmured sleepily. 'You think you'll go travelling again some day?'

'Not sure. We did Europe at the right time.' She'd already told him all about her and Jade's trip around Europe: the places they'd been to, what they'd seen, what they'd experienced before they came back to England to run the bakery business they'd bought and left in the capable hands of the previous owner for a while so locals didn't have to face any period of closure.

'You could always take off again.'

'I'm not sure you understand what being a business owner means.' She laughed as they talked more about her bakery: what foods had been inspired from their travels, the seasons that brought various changes to her menu. 'I love it, Quinn.'

'I can tell.' He kissed her softly on the temple, barely a graze but enough to make her close her eyes and embrace it.

She told him how their Irish grandmother had looked after them every day after school and for something to occupy their hands and minds, they'd spent their time baking. 'We used to talk about having a cake shop, but that's really Jade's area of expertise so she deals with the made-to-order cake side of the business and it runs alongside the bakery.' Their hands were still entwined. 'It works for the both of us. It's very different to law too.'

He sat up in bed then and she clutched the sheets around her top half, embarrassed at being exposed without warning. 'You were a lawyer? How has it been three days and I never knew this?'

'There's a lot you don't know, Quinn,' she grinned. 'I was happy for a while as a lawyer in London. I'm glad I did it, I worked hard, but it wasn't too long before I realised deep down that I had a different dream. We both did, Jade and me. And so we followed it.'

'I can't imagine you in a suit as a lawyer.' He quirked an eyebrow and pulled her down next to him again. 'Although part of me wants to. Maybe in a short skirt, with heels.'

'I rarely wear heels these days.'

'Shame.' He trailed kisses up her jawline, the promise of more.

She basked in his attention. She wanted this moment to last forever.

'Any regrets at leaving it behind?'

'The job or the city?'

'Both.'

'Never. It feels as though I was always meant to have my own business, to spend my days baking. And at least I was used to working long hours. Those were a prerequisite of being a lawyer.' Her fingers caressed his chest, traced the skin up to the base of his neck, his chin, his jaw. 'What about you? Ever think of getting out of the navy?'

Lazily, he answered, 'When the time is right, I will.'

'That's a bit evasive.'

'I don't mean it to be. I love it, it's what I always wanted to do. But I also always said that if I felt the time was right then I'd leave, put down some roots, have more of a sense of family.'

The smile he couldn't see faded at the word *family*.

Because it was a reminder of Julian. The one and only serious relationship she'd had and it had ended up almost breaking her. To be so attached, content, and then to have it all fall apart around her produced a pain she had no control over and didn't ever want to have to go through again.

Celeste and Julian had met at work, hit it off straight away, and with them both in the same job, they had a strong connection, a way of understanding each other. But when they'd been together six months, enjoying their lives without much thought about the future, it had come to the fore that they might not want the same things long term.

The day had started off innocently enough. It was a normal morning in the office and they'd all gathered to give well wishes to Cate, a colleague about to embark on maternity leave. On the way back to their desks, Julian had made an offhand remark about Cate having to make a choice now between her career and her expanding family. 'Four kids is a lot,' he'd said and Celeste hadn't disagreed. What she had disagreed with was when he pondered the idea of how many they'd have themselves when the time came. When Celeste had said to Julian, 'I don't want to have kids; I don't really see them in my future,' he'd replied with, 'You might not now, but you'll change, you'll see.'

It would've been easy to assume Julian had forgotten all about their exchange but over the next month, there were hints left, right and centre. And it had broken her heart that she was letting him down so badly, that perhaps he'd thought she really would come around to the idea. In the end, it had been Celeste who ended the relationship because to Julian, the future had kids in it and to Celeste, it didn't. She wasn't being awkward, she was happy for others who did want that, but she wasn't one of them. And she'd known it was better to be honest from the start.

She'd heard a year later that he'd got married and already had a baby on the way. Celeste had cried that day because she'd been in love with him. And it didn't matter that it had been better to break up when they did. The pain still gnawed at her and ever since, she'd only gone for flings; she'd never let herself get as close to anyone again. If she did, she knew it would likely come with a whole lot of pain in the end.

She sat up in bed next to Quinn. 'I should get in the shower.'

He murmured an agreement, almost asleep now.

How had she let this happen? She'd fallen, or more like tumbled, head over heels and out of control. And he'd just told her that one day he might put down roots, concentrate on family.

It was happening again and Celeste tried to tell herself that it was a very good thing that he was leaving.

And yet, an hour later, when it was time to say goodbye outside the bakery, as they waited for his brother to come past in a car with all the gear from the holiday house, it pulled at her heart more than she'd expected.

'I'll always be glad we met.' Quinn held her face in his hands and kissed her. It wasn't a hungry kiss, one they'd shared plenty of times; it was a goodbye kiss. A firm press of their lips together. A gesture that said this was it, it was over.

And it had to be.

'I'm glad we met too.'

'We agreed not to stay in touch.' His forehead rested against hers.

'I think it's for the best.'

After a beat, he smiled. 'Yeah, it's for the best.'

'Thanks for a good few days,' she grinned.

His laughter was as bright as the sunshine bathing Heritage Cove in a summer glow. 'Good? I'd prefer to say wonderful, fantastic, amazing—'

She put a hand across his mouth to silence him. Even that had the power to make her feel weak at the knees. What had started off as a bit of fun had tugged at her heart. She was usually good at walking away, but Quinn had stirred something unexpected in her. A need for more.

When the car rolled up, both of them looked over at the same time and then back to one another.

'This is goodbye then,' he breathed into her hair. 'I won't ever forget you.'

'Or my salted-caramel turnovers.' She tried for a joke; it was easier than baring her soul.

'Yeah, and those.'

'You'd better go.'

When he opened his mouth to say more, she kissed him before he could and this time, she took his face in her hands. 'Goodbye, Quinn.'

And she turned and went into the bakery, past Jade at the counter and straight out the back, where she burst into tears.

It was a good five minutes later when Jade came through and wrapped her in a big hug. She'd been with a customer in the bakery and most likely kept up the same pretence Celeste had managed with her false smile as she breezed past them.

But now there was no pretence. Jade could see that for Celeste, this hadn't been a brief fling. This hadn't been a few days of fun before she went back to her normal life.

This had been so much more.

2

_____

The cosy warmth of the Copper Plough, Heritage Cove's 400-year-old pub, welcomed Celeste as she stepped inside out of the shivering November wind that evening. It felt like a comforting embrace coming in here, drawn along the narrow corridor and into the bar and all the chatter amongst locals. It had been a long day in the bakery with a big schedule of deliveries but she wouldn't miss this for anything. Tonight was the last night before landlord and landlady, Terry and Nola, handed the pub over to its new owners.

Nola had a collection of glasses expertly pinched between her fingers. She brought them over to the bar as Celeste peeled off her gloves. 'Early finish?' she smiled.

'Yep, it's my turn to escape before closing. Jade's finishing up.' Celeste pushed her gloves into her coat pockets and took off the claret, knitted hat that covered her ears nicely. The problem with having a pixie cut was that there was nothing to keep your neck or your ears warm in late autumn. The wind had whipped around her outside as she'd walked the short distance along The

Street to come here from the Twist and Turn Bakery but at least the rain had stopped.

'What can I get you, love?' Terry emerged from the kitchen and took his position behind the bar.

'Can't go wrong with a classic winter warmer,' she beamed.

'Well, 'tis the season. Almost. It's still technically autumn.'

'Technically,' she smiled, 'but it sure doesn't feel like it.'

He turned to the back of the bar and filled a glass with mulled wine from the urn, adding in a couple of orange slices and a cinnamon stick before handing it to Celeste. The alluring sensory symphony of warmed wine, cinnamon and cloves snaked into the air as Celeste clutched the glass between her palms, savouring the comfort.

She was about to ask Terry whether he'd had the new owners there today – perhaps that was who she'd seen and mistaken for someone very much in her past – but he was already serving somebody else and so instead she headed over to the group in the corner of the pub. Soon, she was seated in one of the cosy nooks made up of the same dark, almost black timber that filled the inside of the Copper Plough and also appeared on the pub's exterior. With her mulled wine in front of her, she listened to septuagenarian Barney regale the story of his first pub quiz here many moons ago.

'I expected the questions to be easy but what do I know about pop culture?' Barney cleared his throat and had another sip of whatever he was drinking – it didn't look like a pint of his usual Guinness. Barney was a permanent fixture in the Cove and, much like the pub, nobody could imagine the village without him.

'I'd have thought you knew quite a lot,' said Celeste, with the others agreeing.

Lucy, blacksmith in the Cove, tossed her long, blonde hair over one shoulder. 'Yes, you've usually got your ear to the ground, Barney; age is never a barrier for you picking up information here, there and everywhere.' Her blue eyes shone with mischief.

'Are you implying that I gossip?' Barney pretended to be offended. Celeste was sure in all his years he'd never met a crowd who didn't like him. 'Or maybe you're trying to say that I talk but I don't listen?'

'All she's saying,' put in Linc, Jade's boyfriend, 'is that she assumed you knew all there was to know about everything.'

'I went home after that quiz and brushed up a bit, watched some popular TV shows – not my taste – and picked up some magazines from the convenience store to catch up on celebrity gossip.'

'How did that go?' Celeste was sure she'd be getting a second mulled wine. It was going down a treat – it was festive and a good reminder they were in the run-up to another Christmas in the Cove.

'A lot of it was utter rubbish.'

Celeste laughed. 'At least you're honest. And you're right, I have to agree.' When she spotted Linc checking his watch, she told him, 'Jade's closing up at the bakery, she'll be here in a little while.'

'Aw, are you pining?' Lucy teased Linc but he took it well, with a smile and a shake of his head, his messy curls, which Jade was always complimenting, moving about of their own accord. Their baby daughter Phoebe, with her cherubic cheeks and cute smile, had inherited the same dark-brown curls as well as his blue eyes. She was simply gorgeous and Celeste was in love with being an auntie.

'And anyway,' Linc batted back, 'you're one to talk, Lucy. Don't think I haven't noticed you with one eye on the door to see whether Daniel is about to grace us with his presence.'

'I am not.'

But Celeste had seen her do it too and said as much. 'Is he heading this way?' she asked.

Daniel owned and ran the Little Waffle Shack, a gorgeous log cabin eatery that sat at the top of the green space that spread behind the local bus stop. The residents of Heritage Cove ate well between the pub, the waffle shack, Etna's tea rooms, the girls' bakery and the ice-cream shop.

'He said he'd try,' Lucy shrugged, 'but I suppose it all depends on whether the birthday party booking up there finishes at a reasonable time.'

'I love a good party,' Barney grinned mischievously. 'I'll bet it won't finish till late.' He coughed into a tissue, a cough that had Lucy lean across and rub him gently on the back and ask whether he was all right.

'I'm fine, don't fuss. It's a simple cold, that's all.'

'What is that you're drinking?' Celeste wondered.

'Nola made me a hot toddy.' He moved his chair back a bit. 'I don't want to pass this on to any of you lot.'

'Don't be daft,' Celeste told him, 'these things make their way around even when you do your utmost to avoid them. That's why it's called the common cold.'

'Well, I'll do my best to keep my germs to myself.'

'You make sure you rest, though,' Celeste encouraged.

'You sound like Lois.' Barney turned to make sure they wouldn't be overheard. 'And as I've told my better half, I'll rest when we've had the party.' He tapped the side of his nose conspiratorially.

It wasn't long before Celeste took off her rollneck, lambswool jumper. The mulled wine had warmed her right through. The fire was crackling in the hearth and heating the entire pub, not just those seated in the chairs right close to it. Even the dog that had been curled up on the rug had moved further away. She looked around and wondered – was it possible to keep falling in love with a place over and over again the more you visited? Sure, the Copper Plough was only a pub, but it was so much more than that for most of the folks who lived in the Cove. It was a hub, a place to meet, just like the tea rooms, the bakery, the waffle shack and the ice-creamery. Heritage Cove was a little community that was very hard to let go of.

Barney spotted Kenneth, good friend of Linc's Auntie Etna and star performer at the allotments by all accounts. 'Excuse me for a moment.' Kenneth was usually up for a good chat so Barney would be in good hands.

Linc, Lucy and Celeste talked business for a bit, bemoaning the busyness of the season but at the same time celebrating the boost it brought the bakery and the blacksmiths.

'Makes me glad of the school holidays,' Linc concluded, 'although the end of term will be manic before that even happens.' Linc taught music at the local school, a role that, according to Jade, he absolutely loved. Seeing her sister so happy with this man who was patient and kind was all Celeste wanted for Jade and now they had Phoebe, who was with Linc's Auntie Etna this evening, they were a happy, complete little unit.

'There she is,' Linc announced with a smile as Jade made an appearance. He got up, squeezed past chairs and weaved between tables to go over to her at the bar.

Lucy sighed as she looked over towards the door.

'It's good for Daniel to be busy,' Celeste said encouragingly when she saw Lucy's apparent disappointment.

'It's not that,' said Lucy. 'It's just that there isn't even a tree in here this year.'

'It's a bit early for a tree. Even for Heritage Cove, which is known for starting the festivities early,' she smiled.

'It's so dark outside, it makes me feel like there should be one. And what if the new owners don't have one at all?'

Celeste couldn't remember a time when the Copper Plough was bereft of a Christmas tree. She looked over at the position where the tree was usually placed. It was always by the section of wall nearest to the bar with just enough room for the staff to go back and forth behind as they served drinks. It certainly wouldn't be right come December if it was still missing the tree.

'Hopefully the new owners will carry on the tradition.'

'Thinking about the tree seems like such a small thing when we're all worried about what's going to happen to the Copper Plough,' Lucy fretted. 'And we won't be able to call it that for much longer either.'

The Copper Plough had been sold. And as yet nobody had any idea who the new owners were or what plans they might have. All they'd been informed of so far was that the new owners wanted to change the name of the pub, which Celeste could understand. She and Jade had wanted to put their own stamp on the bakery and had renamed it; other people in the village had done the same with their businesses. Terry and Nola had given their blessing for the name change at the pub and they'd insisted locals get a say before the process began. But even now Celeste wondered whether many had agreed to it because they all loved Terry and Nola so much, they'd not wanted to make things any harder for them.

'The Star and Lantern has a nice ring to it, don't you think?' Celeste pushed her cinnamon stick into the stained orange slices left in the bottom of her glass now she'd drunk all the liquid.

'I suppose it does have an appeal. It sounds cosy.'

'It does. So let's try to stay positive. Perhaps the new owners are like us: people who will fall in love with the village like we have and never want to leave.'

'I don't want this place to change.' Lucy looked around her.

'Me neither.'

'At least we still have twinkly lights.' She looked up at the lights wound around the beams.

'And mistletoe,' Celeste added good-spiritedly. 'I suppose we should appreciate the effort before it's even December. Terry and Nola have done their best. Shame that bunch on the beam over there is looking a bit tired.' Although what did that matter? It wasn't like she had anyone to kiss beneath it. Her bakery was her one true love and she couldn't very well kiss that, could she? Well, she could try, she supposed.

Barney had finished talking with Kenneth and came back over to claim his chair. 'Do you realise that this could be the last time we're all here like this?'

'Way to make us all extra cheerful, Barney,' Lucy moaned.

'Yeah, cheer up,' Celeste urged him. Although hadn't they been sitting here having similarly melancholy thoughts? She wouldn't admit it, though; that would only bring down the mood even more. 'The pub is changing hands. I think we should all remember that it doesn't mean it's closing its doors now or in the future.'

'Doesn't guarantee it won't either,' Barney said solemnly.

'But that was always the way even with Terry and Nola,' said Lucy. 'They're not invincible to pressures of the cost of living, consumer expenditure.'

'No, I suppose they're not.'

It was unusual for Barney to be quite so down in the dumps. Usually, he spun a situation and saw the positives, sometimes when most others couldn't see any at all.

Linc and Jade came back over in time to catch the tail end of the conversation. 'Unfortunately, a change of hands as good as kills a local pub.' Linc swigged from his pint of Guinness.

'Who are you? The bearer of doom?' Celeste asked.

'Sorry, don't mean to be.' Another sip of his pint left a slight creamy residue on his top lip. Jade reached out and wiped it away.

'When are you two going to get out of this sickly sweet, so in love phase?' Lucy asked.

'You and Daniel are no different,' Celeste laughed, glad of the lighter banter.

Terry appeared to gather up any empty glasses they'd accumulated; with six of them around the table this evening and discussions underway, they had a few. 'Why all the long faces, you lot?'

'You know why,' said Barney as though the landlord and landlady had done something terrible.

'I should point out,' said Terry, 'that we've sold up; we're not dying.'

A harrumph came from another punter not with their group who'd overheard.

'Honestly, you lot are going to be fine without us.' He cleared his throat. 'You all know that Nola had a health scare and we decided it was high time we retired. Life really is too short.' Wistfully, fingers clamped onto rims of glasses, he looked around him. 'I'll miss this place. My heart beat for it once, but it beats more for Nola and our marriage.'

'Can't argue with that,' said Barney.

Terry looked around at the expectant faces, at people who'd become their friends. 'We'll be back to visit; I'll come and see this place again.'

'It won't be the same.'

'Hang in there; change isn't always bad,' Terry assured them, although it didn't get quite the reaction he'd clearly expected.

'Change? What changes?'

'Calm down, I meant a change of hands.' He pulled a face in the girls' direction and Lucy put a hand on Barney's arm to placate him. 'Nola and I appreciate each and every one of you, you know. The Copper Plough – or rather the Star and Lantern as it will soon be – is still standing and with you lot as its customers I can't see anything changing too much anytime soon.'

'He has a point there,' Celeste put in. 'We're very generous with our custom.'

Nobody could disagree. Although Linc was still latching on to what he'd seen pan out before: 'A similar thing happened where I used to live and the local pub was never the same once it was taken over by a big chain. It ended up with no character, no personality.'

Barney seemed to collect himself. 'I apologise, Terry. None of us are being particularly helpful when you're as busy as ever.'

'I won't disagree,' Terry replied.

'Maybe we should all accept the situation and go with it.' As Barney spoke, Celeste knew he was giving himself a good talking to as well as everyone else here. 'We're just worried you've sold it to a big company who are going to change everything. And it doesn't need changing; it's wonderful, part of the Cove.'

'It's all happened quicker than we thought it would,' Terry explained. 'We thought we'd be waiting forever for a buyer but we didn't have to. The new owners are great; they were here earlier today and I think they'll fit right in. They're not part of a big chain and the pub will barely take a breath before it's open with them at the helm. The new sign will be up soon enough too.' His voice softened, showing his kindness, his understanding of what this meant for the community of Heritage Cove as well as

him and his wife. 'And I can tell you that the new own
assured me they understand the character this village ...,
vibe—'

'Vibe?' Barney raised a grey, bushy eyebrow.

'Their word, not mine,' chuckled Terry.

'The vibe is only created with a decent Christmas tree at this
time of year,' Lucy grumbled. 'I hope the new owners will
organise one. It won't feel like Christmas unless they do.'

'You'll have to take up the tree issue with them,' said Terry,
'and knowing you lot, you'll have no trouble doing that.'

Nola came to her husband's side, but it was Barney whose
shoulder she put a reassuring hand on. 'We honestly thought it
was too early for a tree even though I know you lot wouldn't have
objected. There's also the fact that all the decorations were
already packed up and with so much to do, unboxing them
would've been a nightmare, not to mention taking them all off a
tree afterwards and putting them away, ready for our big move.'

Lucy's shoulders slumped. 'I'm sorry for complaining.' She
got up and gave Nola a hug. 'We're all a bunch of miseries,
aren't we?'

'Well, I wouldn't say that.'

'You can and you should.' Lucy gave Nola's arm a squeeze
before excusing herself to use the ladies'. She promised she'd
come back with a bit more positivity than she'd had moments
ago.

Barney coughed again, and when he'd recovered and Terry
had brought him over a glass of water, he apologised himself.
'Lucy's right. We're miserable gits, the whole lot of us. And we
shouldn't be making this all about us.'

'Barney, you're making this about the Cove,' smiled Terry.
'And for that, I think I speak for everyone when I say it's a good
thing. You've always put Heritage Cove first.' Nobody disagreed.

Nola hugged the village's favourite resident. 'He's right, Barney. And it'll all work out, I have a feeling.' Compared with Terry's usual boom, especially when it came to last orders, Nola was softly spoken, tenderness in every word.

'We'll miss you both,' Jade told the couple.

'And we'll miss all of you. But this is our time; we need it.' The look he shared with his wife spoke of their reasons behind the decision. They'd had a scare, they'd seen uncertainty in front of them and they'd seized the opportunity to do something they'd always wanted to do. It had shaken their idea of the future, reminded them that the future might well be now, and they'd acted upon it.

Terry had Barney's attention again when he said, 'None of us get forever. Working late six or seven nights a week and falling into bed so exhausted we barely manage to say goodnight to one another isn't what we want any more. I want to take Nola back to Greece where we went on honeymoon, we want to sail, we want to eat seafood while the sun sets, swim in the sea and complain about how hot it is. And then we want to visit the Cove to see our daughter and our grandkids and enjoy them rather than snatching whatever moments we can.'

Everyone raised a glass, whether full or empty, and wished them well.

Celeste sighed and looked out of the window at the back of the pub, across the expansive beer garden abandoned in the colder months in favour of the cosy inside. 'It's hard to imagine talk of sunshine and being too hot when it's so cold. I'd love a bit of winter sun right now.'

'And avoid Christmas in Heritage Cove?' Jade was alert to her sister's words, having torn her attention away from Linc. 'There's nothing like it. You know that.'

Barney fiddled with the collar of his jumper as if it was too tight for him to breathe properly. 'Christmas in the Cove is a very special time.'

Terry and Nola headed over to the bar to serve eager customers and Celeste suspected that was where they wanted to be, embracing the last night as landlord and landlady before they embarked on a big change in their lives. They didn't want to be standing here, having to justify their choices.

'Where are Harvey and Melissa?' Celeste asked Barney. 'I thought they were coming along tonight? And Zara told me she might pop in once she finishes work.' Zara ran the ice-creamery and, contrary to popular belief, the ice-creamery wasn't only for the summer months. She came up with some out-of-this-world recipes for the winter, particularly during the festive season. Christmas Cake Crunch, Cranberry Orange and Christmas Pudding flavours were already grabbing customers' interest even before December hit.

In the Cove, there were plenty of independent business owners like Celeste and Jade, Lucy, and Zara. Daniel had the Little Waffle Shack, there was Lottie's convenience store, the Doyle family at Mistletoe Gate Farm supplying Christmas trees, Etna's tea rooms, and Tilly's Bits 'n' Pieces. Heritage Cove seemed the place to be if you were on a solo or family business venture. Most businesses in the Cove, including the bakery and the ice-creamery, did frequent late nights in the run-up to Christmas. Folks from far and wide came to see the village and the lights, the big tree on the green, to shop for individual items; some were guests at the Heritage Inn or maybe they'd visited the village for one of the carol concerts held at the quaint little chapel on the opposite side of the road to the bakery.

'I saw Zara before I came here,' Barney announced. 'She's got a delivery so had to head home first and if it arrives on time, she'll be here. As for Harvey and Melissa, I don't know what's going on with them. I was rather hoping you could tell me.'

Celeste shrugged. 'Melissa was in the bakery the other day and she did seem a bit preoccupied now you mention it.' She sipped the second mulled wine Linc had brought over for her.

'See...' He shook his head. 'I thought it was my imagination. I thought she was getting frustrated with an old fossil like me, not being her usual patient self.'

'She'll never be frustrated with you, Barney. You're family to her and Harvey, you know that as well as I do.'

'I do know that. But I also know that there's something going on. She's keeping something quiet.'

Celeste hadn't thought about it too much since she saw Melissa but now Barney had mentioned it, she suspected he was right. He might not be Melissa's parent but he was the closest thing she had to one, with her parents sadly gone, and he had an intuition about Melissa like any father would his daughter.

When Melissa had come into the bakery and ordered three baguettes the other day, Celeste had bagged them up and when she'd passed them over the counter, Melissa had closed her eyes in realisation of her mistake. 'I meant baps, rolls, whatever. Sorry.' Celeste had laughed and simply put the baguettes back and got a bag in which to put three baps. She'd thought then that Melissa seemed to have a lot on her mind but another customer was right behind her and hadn't been quite so understanding about the mistake and in a rush, so Celeste had had to serve her rather than ask her friend if she needed to talk.

'Keep your ear to the ground,' said Barney now.

'I'm not your spy.'

'I know, but I'm worried.'

'Try not to be. She has Harvey, remember, and I'm sure if there's anything terrible going on, they'd come to you.' A change of subject might stop him from fretting. 'Is everything set for tomorrow afternoon?'

Barney turned to make sure that Nola and Terry were safely tucked behind the bar and wouldn't hear them. 'All set. I think they'll be surprised. And I know they said no fuss so turned down a party here but there's no way we could let them leave the Cove without a proper send-off.'

'Agreed.'

The following afternoon, the residents of Heritage Cove were having a going-away party for their favourite publicans. It was to be held in Barney's barn, which was situated adjacent to his cottage that sat around the bend as you drove on out of the village after passing along The Street. The barn was the setting for the summer Wedding Dress Ball every year and for big occasions. It was sometimes hired for celebrations and it was perfect for a farewell party.

'He thinks he and Nola are coming for cream tea with me and Lois,' Barney explained.

'Do you think he'll mind?'

'He's used to crowds and noise in this place. I think he only said we shouldn't make a fuss about their departure because they both feel guilty about letting everyone down and having us all worried.' Barney frowned. 'I shouldn't have moaned so much, should I?'

Celeste put her hand over his. 'He knows it comes from a place of caring.'

'That it does.' He whisked his hand away to cover his mouth as a cough took hold, only dampened down by the hot toddy he drank from.

'You should get yourself home after this, go take it easy.'

'You're probably right, Celeste. I don't want to be laid up with the lurgy tomorrow for the party.'

Benjamin, chef at the pub, delivered a bowl of hot, golden chips to the table for Linc, who immediately requested another three as eyes around the table widened and Linc couldn't do anything other than offer them around.

'What's happening with your job, Benjamin?' Barney asked.

'I've spoken to the new owners and my job is safe when they reopen.'

Barney expressed his relief. 'I'm glad to hear it.'

Celeste left everyone at the pub after another hour or so, given the early start the next morning at the bakery. Daniel had shown up for Lucy, her sister and Linc were happily ensconced in the booth in the pub, making the most of Linc's Auntie Etna babysitting Phoebe. Sometimes it was as though any gatherings were peppered with reminders that almost everyone was in a relationship except her these days. Even Kenneth who waved goodbye to her as she left was growing closer to Etna, not that either of them would admit to a romance if they were asked.

Her breath came out cold as soon as she stepped outside the Copper Plough. She pulled on her hat and matching gloves, buttoned up her coat and set off along The Street. Barney was right; Christmas in Heritage Cove was special. It wasn't even December yet but soon there would be a sense of festive revelry in the air with all the decorations, with the temperatures dropping even more, with the lights along The Street which were due to go up tomorrow morning, with eateries bringing out their festive favourites. And the Copper Plough was a very big part of that.

She hunched her shoulders against the cold and buried her face in the collar of her coat as she made her way home to the cottage behind the Twist and Turn Bakery.

Celeste and the rest of the Cove were anxiously awaiting the arrival of the new owners of the pub. And all they could do for now was hope that apart from becoming the Star and Lantern, the Copper Plough didn't change too much with its new owner-ship, that it retained its character, that it stayed as much a part of the village as it always had been.

Was that too much to wish for?

3

Barney came into the bakery the next morning to collect the cake Jade had made for the farewell party.

'I told you I'd deliver the cake, Barney.' Jade closed the door behind him and ushered him inside out of the cold.

His shook his head at his mistake. 'It totally slipped my mind you'd said you would.'

'Ah well, no harm done. I'll take you back to your place too; you can be the cake's escort, make sure nothing happens to it on the way. Give me a sec and I'll box it up.'

As she went to do that, Barney waited for Celeste to finish with her customer. 'I've met the new owners, you know,' he told her when it was just the two of them. He turned away before he coughed, and when he turned back, he told her, 'I had to. Curiosity was getting the better of me.'

'Now why doesn't that surprise me?' she grinned.

'I tried not to get in the way so I pretended I was reminding Terry and Nola of the time they're due at our place. I think Terry was onto me because he asked whether my phone had stopped working.' When Celeste smiled, he informed her that the new sign for the local pub was going up already.

'That was quick. Out with the old...'

'It'll take some getting used to. The Star and Lantern.' He said the name as though trying to get used to the words rolling off his tongue.

'It's a great name.'

'I admit I quite like it.'

'Did you quiz the new owners?'

'Not really. I want them to feel welcome. As much as we'll miss Terry and Nola, they deserve a chance, don't they? And Terry and Nola assure me that they sold to people they felt would fit in.'

'That's very considerate.'

'I told the new owners if there's anything they need to know about the Cove then don't hesitate to ask. I couldn't really invite them to the party given Terry and Nola don't think it's anything of the sort, but I got a good feeling about them. I want them to feel at home.'

'I know you do, Barney. You're kind-hearted; it's why we all love you.'

He waved a hand to dismiss the notion but he said nothing because he was too busy coughing and mumbling his apologies.

'Don't say sorry; you go and get better.'

'After the party, I will.'

'Good. Now, tell me more about these new owners?'

Right on cue, the bell above the door tinkled to announce another customer arrival at the same time as Jade called out to Barney that it was time to go.

'We'll talk more later,' he assured her before hurrying out back. 'I've got a party to put on.'

The morning went by at its usual pace and the time to get ready crept up on Jade and Celeste, who both took turns to run out to the cottage to get changed for the party. The cottage was only occupied by Celeste since Jade moved in with Linc and it was approximately thirty steps along the stepping-stone footpath that ran alongside a small patch of lawn to commute from the back entrance of the bakery to the cottage, depending on how long your stride was.

When the time came for them to leave, Jade turned the sign on the door of the bakery to *Closed*. 'I hate closing up unexpectedly. Does that make me a control freak?'

Celeste added a piece of paper beneath the sign that would let any hopeful customers know the time they'd reopen. 'No, it makes you a businesswoman.' Neither of them wanted to miss Terry and Nola's send-off and so they'd agreed on shutting the bakery for an hour and then one of them would return, the other not long afterwards. 'And besides, I feel the same, but it's for a good cause. Let's give Terry and Nola the send-off they deserve. I feel like they've been given a raw deal with everyone whingeing and whining about a change coming our way.'

Celeste smiled at her sister, similar to her in so many ways with their pale, Irish complexion and dark hair and the freckles that ran across the bridges of their noses. Both were tall and willowy, although Jade had filled out more since she'd had Phoebe and she looked better for it. Some glowed during pregnancy and Jade sure had, but more so, she glowed with motherhood and sometimes Celeste found herself staring, wrapped up in the pleasure of her sister's happiness. She deserved it and having Linc in her life had been unexpected but perfectly timed. They were a good match.

'You look gorgeous, by the way,' Celeste remarked as she watched Jade take off the apron that had been covering the emerald-green dress she wore with tights and high boots. She hung the apron on the hook on the wall you had to pass by to go from the customer area to the kitchen. Unlike Celeste with her pixie cut, Jade wore her hair long and she'd twisted it up into a chignon fixed with a sparkly clip that felt right at home with the Christmas decorations in the window and the fact they were off to a party.

'Right back at you.' Jade took out a red lipstick and, using a hand mirror, applied a nice shiny coat.

Celeste straightened the elf in mint-green and white and red stockings climbing up the wooden shelves against the walls. Yesterday, he'd been in the window; today, they'd moved him between the bloomer loaves and the sourdough. Kids coming in here loved seeing what he was getting up to and Celeste had to admit she had fun shifting him around.

Jade, ready now, admired Celeste's jumper. 'Where's it from? It's gorgeous.'

Rather than a dress, Celeste had gone for a fluffy-knit, smoky-grey jumper with ink jeans and heeled ankle boots. Not practical when the winter began in earnest with icy pavements and slippery roadsides but great for today and a party. 'I ordered it online last week. I'll send you the link if you like; they've got some great stuff.' She'd already done her make-up but held a hand out for Jade's little mirror to check it over.

Jade picked up a bauble that had fallen off from the miniature artificial Christmas tree they'd placed in the bakery window. It was tiny – they had way too many things to show off on display as it was – but they'd fitted that in, garlands with red and gold baubles amongst frost-sparkling greenery along the front away from edibles, and they'd stuck plenty of bright white snowflakes to the inside of the latticed windows as well as twinkly lights at intervals.

'Is Linc bringing Phoebe along today?' Celeste wondered.

'He said he'll try to but she has her baby music class. I think she'll get more out of that than a party for Terry and Nola and I don't want her to be a nuisance.'

'Nobody would ever think that, you know they wouldn't. People would be lining up to cuddle her if anything.'

'She loves those classes,' Jade smiled proudly. Phoebe might only be seven months old but Celeste suspected she might well follow in her father's footsteps. As well as being a music teacher, Linc had a real talent for singing and playing the guitar. He'd played at the pub more times than Celeste could remember and everyone loved him.

They pulled on their coats and locked up the bakery behind them. 'I wonder what instrument Phoebe will ask for first. A guitar?'

Jade laughed as they reached Etna, who was about to close up the tea rooms and join the party. She refused their offer to help her take the blackboard detailing her menu items inside for her. She told them they'd be her first port of call when she was too old but that wouldn't be for some time yet.

'I don't think guitar,' said Jade as they walked on. 'I'm thinking more like a xylophone. Her eyes light up when she gets to bang away at it with the little mallet.'

'I can only imagine how noisy those classes are,' Celeste laughed.

Tilly had already closed up Tilly's Bits 'n' Pieces but the girls couldn't resist a peek at the festive window display as they passed by. Her excuse for starting even earlier every year was that she wanted to sell decorations, so really she was doing everyone a favour. She had a bigger tree than the girls and on it were old-fashioned baubles, hand-painted, the sort you'd expect from the Victorian era. There was an enormous candelabra with alternating red and gold pillar candles and red berry foliage all around its base, an old brown leather trunk with a big leather label hanging from its handle, and a set of Nordic decorations displayed in a wooden square.

Celeste breathed in the cold air as she linked her sister's arm. 'Heritage Cove is getting ready for Christmas. And it's only November.'

'I like that we do it so early here.'

'Some people must think we're crazy to get into Christmas so far in advance.'

'Crazy or not, I still love it; we get longer to appreciate the season before the gloomy days of January and February.'

The lights were being strung up along The Street right now and it made Celeste smile as she watched the work going in to making this season as wonderful as any that had gone before. Soon they'd be illuminated, soon all the businesses in the Cove would be full of seasonal joy, and the bakery would become filled with the smells of drunken fruit cake and mince pies.

As they passed the pub, Celeste felt a sense of sadness. Closed right now, in the process of being handed over, it had everyone on tenterhooks as to what it would be like when it reopened. The new sign was partially up, its first word a shining gold, ready for the remaining lettering to join it, and she tried to envisage what the wording would look like when it was finished. What would it feel like to nip into the Star and Lantern rather than the Copper Plough?

Lottie, who'd just closed the convenience store, caught up with them. It seemed she was thinking much the same when she nodded in the pub's direction. 'I can't believe it's changing its name.' She unhooked her hair from beneath the collar of a smart, chocolate-brown, wool coat and the cream scarf she'd wound around her neck. In her late twenties, she had tight-ringleted chestnut hair and dimpled cheeks that gave her the air

of eternal youth, but she fooled nobody; she was an astute businesswoman. She knew how to treat customers, respond to
changing demand, and she worked hard. 'The Copper Plough is
an institution.'

'Let's hope the Star and Lantern will be too,' said Celeste.

Jade warned the others, 'We mustn't make Terry and Nola
feel bad today.'

'I went in before last orders last night,' said Lottie. 'I was
exhausted but I thought... well, I thought, you know, this might
be the last time.'

'The pub isn't closing,' Celeste and Jade said at the same time.

'I know,' Lottie sighed.

Change wasn't something the locals in the Cove resisted, but
what they did battle against was the thought that anything might
take away from the character of the village. It was why when the
sisters had refurbished the bakery, they'd done so sympatheti-
cally, retaining the years-gone-by appearance out front apart
from the signage, it was why the waffle shack up on the green
wasn't a dull concrete building with neon signs but rather it
looked like it had always been there. It was why Lucy's Blacksmithing and Tilly's Bits 'n' Pieces worked too because they
looked like they'd existed in that way for years.

They spotted Tilly walking ahead with Benjamin and upped
the pace to catch up with them. And by the time they reached
Barney's cottage, Lois was standing guard at the front door and
ushered them past the neat front garden and through the
archway formed by hardy juniper trees, across the courtyard and
into the barn. With it being almost winter, the double doors
weren't flung open the way they were in the summer months for
the ball or lunch events. The right-hand side welcomed them in
to a winter wonderland: fairy lights wound around the beams up
high and those going up from the floor, other beams had

garlands of green and red, there was a beautifully adorned Christmas tree to the side of the stage where the band usually played when it was the Wedding Dress Ball. Apparently, Barney had insisted on having a tree in the barn if there was going to be a party. He didn't care how early it was, not for this, because Terry and Nola deserved the full works, he'd said. And he'd always been a man keen to please everyone else.

'Are they here already?' Celeste asked Barney, who looked as though the cold he had in his system was letting him know that it might well win the battle.

'Sitting inside my cottage as we speak.' He tapped the side of his nose. 'None the wiser.'

'Are you sure you're up to this?' He really didn't seem well but the look he gave Celeste suggested he might have heard the sentiment one or two times before and would appreciate her giving it a rest. 'You're clutching your chest.'

'I am not.' He removed his hand. 'I was rubbing it. I've been lifting bags and boxes – online shopping delivery, you know how it is.'

'Very modern.' She wasn't sure she believed him because he seemed to have significant discomfort, but she wouldn't go on or it could get him all het up and nobody wanted that.

'Modern and necessary,' he answered. 'Everything is online these days.' Despite his protests, he sat down on the chair behind him. There were hay bales aplenty but chairs too for anyone who needed. Barney had always known how to throw a good party and cater for the masses. 'There's not enough variety in the shops these days so if I need anything other than what I can buy locally then it has to be online. As well as food shopping and bits and pieces, I ordered my Lois one of those foot spa things... for Christmas.' He finished with a cough Celeste felt sure he should get checked out.

'She'll love it,' Celeste managed, knowing Lois would love it more if she felt sure the man she loved was taking as much care of himself as everyone else.

'I smuggled it out of sight as soon as I could.' He swigged some water Melissa brought over for him. She'd probably been watching him closely as well. 'It does massage and all those bubbles and warm water will do wonders. She suffers with her feet these days. We're getting old.' A smile broke out on a face that had enough cheekiness to hint that a younger Barney might well have had the very same expression. 'But we're getting old together. She can use it while we cosy up and watch *It's a Wonderful Life* with a glass of whisky.'

'The foot spa and the movie sound perfect to me,' said Celeste.

Melissa put a hand on Barney's shoulder when he moved to stand up. 'They'll be here soon; save your energy for when they come in.' She went off to resume hostess duties and take trays of drinks around the barn to make sure everyone was happy and in party mode as they lay in wait for the guests of honour.

It wasn't long before Melissa came back to Barney's side. 'Promise me you will rest as soon as the farewells are finished.'

'Lois has been at me all morning. This one now too.' He indicated Celeste at his side before coughing and muttering something about a moment's peace. 'I promise I'll rest soon enough.'

He coughed again and moved away before either of them had a chance to instruct him to stay put.

'He must be sick to admit defeat,' Melissa said quietly to Celeste. 'And he never mumbles like that.'

'It's out of character for sure.' But she knew Lois was on the case as much as they were.

Harvey had been keeping watch at the barn doors and he held up his hands, shushing everyone. It meant he'd had the signal from Lois to tell them the guests of honour were heading over. It wasn't unusual for Barney and Lois to serve festive meals and gatherings in the barn so this wouldn't be that out of the ordinary from Terry and Nola's point of view.

Everyone fanned out to the edges of the barn and quietened down so much that they could hear voices approaching. It was Nola who came inside the barn first, followed by Terry and as everyone chorused, 'Surprise!' they registered that this wasn't the cosy occasion as a foursome that they had predicted.

Nola put a hand against her chest, Terry stood there stunned, and the emotion in the room, coupled with their own as people rushed forth to hug them, tugged at everyone's heartstrings. Celeste wondered how many tears would be shed today because no doubt about it, the Cove's favourite publicans would be missed.

As Nola and Terry brought themselves back down to earth, Lois and Melissa did the rounds with enormous trays of canapes for the guests – turkey and cranberry roll-ups, sausage rolls, chilli-and-marmalade-glazed pork belly skewers, halloumi wrapped in bacon – and Harvey was in charge of making sure everyone had drinks.

'Are you annoyed we did all this?' Lois asked Terry.

Terry put an arm around Nola's shoulders. 'Annoyed? Never.'

'We didn't want a fuss,' said Nola, 'but this is perfect. We both feel very special.'

'I'm going to say a few words.' Terry kissed his wife's forehead and went over to the stage, clearing his throat more than once as the crowd quietened. His voice was thick with emotion as he began. 'What can I say?'

'Lost for words?' Lottie asked with a giggle. 'That's a first, Terry!'

Terry laughed, amongst friends. 'You are all the most remarkable people, the very best, and I'm sorry we're letting you all down.'

'Stop that,' Barney called over although his voice wasn't too clear, his suffering apparent. 'You've run the Copper Plough like a dream for years and we've loved every minute. Now it's time for you both to go live your lives,' he added, just about, patting his chest as though to ease it of any congestion.

'We will do our best. And I promise you, the new owners of the Copper Plough which from today is otherwise known as the Star and Lantern, will fit right in.' A sigh of relief sounded around the barn. Etna, who ran the tea rooms, looked so happy, she sat down on one of the hay bales dotted around to enjoy her cup of tea. 'The new owners have the same vision Nola and I did; they want the pub to remain unique, a true part of the village.'

'Who are they?' someone else called out. Celeste was sure it was Patricia who worked alongside Etna in the tea rooms and her question had been the one on everyone's lips.

'What can you tell us about them?' Tilly queried.

'Their names are—'

But Terry didn't get any more words out about the new owners or anything else because there was a panicked gasp from the middle of the crowd and then all of a sudden Celeste saw what the commotion was as people made space and Melissa rushed to Barney's side.

Barney was lying on the ground, and he wasn't moving.

Celeste saw the look of utter devastation on Melissa's face as she crouched at the side of the man who was like a father to her and Harvey. She shrieked for someone to call an ambulance, she grasped his hand and pleaded with him not to go anywhere.

And what had been a party soon became a living nightmare.

4

Celeste stood at the front door to the bakery for a brief respite. It was amazing how quickly you could warm up inside when you were busy baking and getting everything ready, even when it was this cold outside. She thought of Barney and knew how much he would've loved to be here right now, embracing the frost glistening on the rooftops, the prettiness of the village that came to life in every season. It was impossible not to drink in the sight now of the main road that ran through the quaint village of Heritage Cove, nestled on the east coast of England. Businesses had their windows decorated and ready even though they weren't out of November yet, the nativity display would soon be set up at the front of the chapel, illuminated for all to see. On either side of the main street, bright decorations were strung between lampposts, from one side of the road to the other, setting the scene and serving as a reminder that Christmas was coming. And soon, the finishing touch – an enormous Christmas tree – would be erected on the grass area beyond the bus stop that led out of the village.

By mid-morning, Celeste was hard pushed to take another

break they were so busy but between them, the sisters had every-thing in hand.

'Here we are.' Jade delivered a big tray of glazed doughnuts from the kitchen at the back of the bakery to the front of the shop. 'Sorry about the wait.'

Celeste used tongs to put three of them into a bag emblazoned with the Twist and Turn Bakery logo and handed them to her customer, who had already paid. Jade, meanwhile, put the rest of the doughnuts into the glass-fronted display cabinet. They were usually a lot more organised but after the dramas of the party earlier that week, their heads had had to fight to really be in the game. As if she knew about the commotion, Phoebe hadn't slept for the last few nights either, which meant Jade was permanently exhausted and today had arrived less than ready for a full day at the bakery. With them both still worrying about everyone's favourite resident now he was in the hospital, it was hardly the recipe for a smooth working day. But a working day it was, and as owners of the business, they couldn't afford to drop the ball.

'What time are you delivering the sandwiches to Aubrey House?' Jade brought the iced buns out from the kitchen.

'Soon.' Celeste had already swept the floor behind the counter and wiped around the till, jobs that had to be done repeatedly given the products they handled. 'I'll take the rolls over to the Heritage Inn while I'm at it.'

'I forgot they had a delivery today too.' Jade checked her watch. 'Why don't I go now to make my cake delivery – it's not too far away – and you go as soon as I'm back?'

'Sounds like a plan.'

Out in the kitchen, Celeste had a peek in Jade's cake corner. 'You did really well to get it finished.' She'd seen her sister icing it this morning, piping the pale-yellow and cerise-pink roses on top of the yellow buttercream, the leaves around the edge. The sisters had started the bakery together but Jade had a passion and a talent for spectacular cake baking and so when this place was refurbished, they added in a special area complete with dedicated cupboards, a separate oven and a blind-corner storage unit with metal baskets that swung out smoothly to store all Jade's equipment.

'I was thinking about Barney the whole time,' said Jade. Tears sprang into her eyes and she used the heels of her hands to stem them. 'Being extra tired makes me really emotional, I'm sorry.'

'I'm sure it does but don't apologise. We're all feeling it.' Lois had got word around the Cove about how Barney was doing. He had pneumonia but all they'd heard since he'd gone into hospital was that he was stable.

'I kept wondering whether I would get to make him a birthday cake again.'

Celeste pulled her sister into a hug. 'I'm sure we'll hear something more soon. Now don't cry all over this cake or it'll be ruined.'

With a deep breath, Jade pulled herself together. 'Now I just need to get it into the special carrier and not fall flat on my face on my way to the car.'

'You get it ready to transport; I'll hold the door.' She had a brief look out into the bakery's main area to be sure nobody was waiting to be served and that she didn't have a customer sitting at the little bench against the far wall on one of the stools they tucked beneath when they weren't in use. Customers could choose to enjoy their cake or pastry at the bench if they liked and often people sat there to have a think about what they wanted to go for if there was too much of a selection at first glance. Barney had done it often and the memory left Celeste even more worried about the Cove's favourite local.

Celeste picked up Jade's car keys and after holding the door open for her sister, she went over to the car to undo the boot. Jade had put a large, fairly flat cardboard box with bean bag inserts in here exactly for this, to keep containers still during transportation and able to withstand any sharp turns.

'Text me if you hear about Barney.' Jade closed the boot. 'Tilly didn't know much this morning when she came in with the coffees; I thought she would've heard something.'

Tilly was close to Barney as well. He really had that effect on people, especially if their family were either no longer around or dispersed around the country and not on hand. It was as though he had enormous wings capable of taking anyone under them should they need it.

'I tell you what,' said Celeste, 'after my own deliveries, if we still haven't heard anything, I'll drop in on Tilly or perhaps Melissa, see what I can find out.'

Back in the bakery solo, Celeste went through to the front to serve the woman waiting for two wholemeal baguettes and a dozen rolls of the same variety. And when she saw Melissa coming in through the front door, she held her breath because she couldn't read the look on her friend's face at all. Melissa's cheeks had no colour, her auburn hair fell in disarray around her shoulders as though she'd had a fitful sleep and not managed to pay her appearance any attention in the wake of more serious things on her mind.

Celeste's mouth went dry. She felt tension in her body rise as she handed her customer her change and did her best to keep a smile on her face as she thanked the woman for her custom.

Surely not. Not Barney.

When Barney collapsed in the barn, the world had stood still for most of the people gathered. They'd been there to give Terry and Nola a true send-off and instead, the gathering had ended in the worst way possible, with nobody knowing whether Barney was going to pull through or not. The paramedics had come quickly, a blessing at a time when that wasn't necessarily guaranteed. Waiting times for ambulances had been the topic in news reports for months and Celeste bet she hadn't been the only one to think that when they called, they might not even get the help they needed, let alone before it was too late. But the ambulance had arrived, sirens wailing, a harsh bringing back to reality against the backdrop of twinkly lights and a tree that smelt of the season, the garlands, the decorations along The Street, all of it the complete opposite sentiment of how everyone in that barn had to be feeling. They'd got him into the ambulance quickly but not before Celeste saw the look of fear in his eyes, a look that suggested he might well be wondering if he'd ever be back in his beloved Heritage Cove again.

Celeste came out from the behind the counter as the customer left and Melissa closed the door to the bakery behind her, shutting out the drizzle that had just started.

'Well...?' Celeste bit down on her lower lip.

'He's improving, albeit slowly.' Melissa divulged a few more details about Barney's last few days at the hospital: how he'd responded to fluids and antibiotics and how positive the medical staff seemed.

'Thank goodness for some good news.' She tutted. 'We all kept telling him he was sick and needed to rest, he wouldn't have it.'

'He's too stubborn for his own good.' Melissa's own relief was evident but she still looked as though she was in shock.

'Have you slept at all?' Her hazel eyes didn't have their usual mascara on them. Instead, they were underlined with dark circles.

'What do you think?'

Celeste indicated to the stools at the bench. 'Come on, sit

down.' The news was semi-positive but if Melissa was this worried, so was Celeste. 'Tell me more about what's going on.'

'Pneumonia can be really serious, especially at Barney's age.' Her voice broke and she pulled a bottle of water from her bag.

Celeste went and grabbed a mince pie from the selection in the glass-fronted display cabinet. Both she and Jade made them and although their recipes had differed once upon a time and they'd often pitted against each other in jest, they'd agreed on one recipe for the bakery and stuck to it these days.

She handed Melissa a mince pie on top of a napkin. 'You need something sweet: have this. I insist,' she said before Melissa could refuse her.

'He should've got help sooner. I should've made him.' She took the mince pie.

'You and I both tried and so did Lois. And this is Barney we are talking about. Since when has he been one to heed a warning like *rest,* or *take it easy*?'

'I'd say pretty much never. He's a terrible patient,' Melissa said after a nibble of mince pie.

'Is he talking much?'

Tears filled Melissa's eyes. 'Not really. That's the hardest thing. He's the one who's never quiet, who never shuts up, and we all love him for it.'

The bell above the door tinkled and Celeste put a hand over Melissa's with the assurance she'd only be a moment. She wrapped a dozen gingerbread cookies in a paper bag and when the customer went on their way, she was back with her friend. They'd only known one another a few years, meeting here in the Cove, but it felt much more like an enduring friendship to Celeste. That was what she loved about Heritage Cove; you didn't need to have lived here all your life to feel as though you had.

'I was so worried he'd had a heart attack when he collapsed,'

Melissa admitted. 'The way his hand was against his chest, I thought—' Melissa found a tissue from her pocket. 'I keep having to remind myself of what is actually going on rather than catastrophising.'

'He's lucky he doesn't have much else to worry about healthwise.' At least that was what Celeste thought. Unless he'd been keeping his troubles to himself.

'Lois told me he hasn't.'

'That's a relief. He's strong too; we all know that. And he has Lois by his side. How's she holding up?'

'Better now he's in bed and she doesn't have to nag him about resting. Her words, not mine,' Melissa smiled.

'He's going to be fine, I just know it.' He had to be. The residents of Heritage Cove weren't ready to lose Barney. She prayed inwardly that they'd have many more years of his company in the Cove. It made all the fuss they'd made about a change of ownership at the Copper Plough seem so trivial now.

The bell above the door tinkled again, announcing Hazel's arrival. Hazel co-owned the Heritage View riding stables with her brother Arnold and she was all wrapped up in her winter riding gear – a quilted navy gilet over what looked like a very warm waterproof top, fleece ear warmers beneath her riding hat and her long, blonde, wavy hair tied back in a low ponytail.

Hazel enveloped Melissa in a hug, apologising if she smelt of horses.

'Don't be ridiculous,' said Melissa. 'I'll take the hug whatever you smell like.'

Hazel pulled off her thermal riding gloves. 'What's the news?'

Melissa reiterated what she'd told Celeste while Celeste served a couple of elderly ladies.

When the collapse had happened, most of the residents had been in that barn to witness it, but respectful and with their own lives to return to and businesses to run, they'd kept their distance from Lois, Melissa and the hospital. But all bets were off as soon as they saw those closest to Barney. And Hazel was no exception.

'How can you hear through those things?' Celeste asked Hazel, trying to lighten the mood a little, after opening the door for the ladies who left with their festive treats in paper bags.

Hazel grinned, her hands patting her ear warmers. 'Not always easy but I'm used to it. And I can't be bothered to take them off right now. Why, am I shouting?'

'No, not shouting,' Melissa assured her.

'Give Barney my love, won't you,' Hazel said.

'Where did you park your horse?' Melissa wondered.

'I'm riding Cinnamon today and he's parked outside. Translation: Gus is holding the reins on the proviso that I come in here and get us a mince pie each.' Local vet, Gus, was Hazel's boyfriend and they'd been together since the summer.

Celeste went behind the counter and shook out a paper bag before picking up the tongs to grab the sweet treats. 'And for Cinnamon?'

Hazel patted her pocket. 'I don't think baked goods are good for Cinnamon but don't worry, I've got some carrots right here.' She used her card to pay and took the bag. 'I'd better go. See you both later and remember… send my love to Barney and tell him I hope he's back soon. I miss having him wander down to the stables to say hello.' She opened the door but stopped before she took the mince pies out to Gus. 'I meant to say, I saw the new owners of the pub earlier.'

'You did?' Celeste and Melissa asked almost at the same time.

'I said a quick hello when I rode past and might I say…' She puffed out her cheeks.

'See, I have no idea what that means,' Melissa giggled.

'Me neither,' Celeste laughed. 'Please translate.'

'Two men, both rather gorgeous – if I was looking, which of course I'm not because I'm in love with Gus.'

'We know,' they chorused as Hazel waved her goodbyes and headed out into the cold.

Hazel's recent romance with the local vet was yet another happy ever after. There were plenty in the Cove, a village that seemed to bring romance along with picturesque, beautiful streets and character with barely any effort at all. Celeste's interlude with Quinn was a perfect example and at least she had the memories to keep forever, although she couldn't help wondering how it worked out so well for everyone else but not her. Was it because she hadn't really been open to anything serious? Maybe she'd made her own luck and had nobody else to blame.

Still, she was surprised they didn't get more people coming here thinking they could find true love just because of the location, given how many love stories they had under their belt, something Barney had suggested he might float to a local newspaper for an article idea. He'd thought it could bring more tourism to the area, before he'd realised perhaps things were fine just as they were. The village had enough visitors for the locals to keep their businesses thriving; they didn't want to be overrun, they didn't want their community to lose any of its closeness and friendliness because it was diluted by too many outsiders. Not that they weren't welcoming, quite the opposite; it was just that they all closely guarded Heritage Cove for what it was. A small village on the east coast of England that wasn't always on everyone's radar and that suited them just fine.

'I'd better get going.' Melissa picked up the napkin that had cradled her mince pie and took it over to the bin just past the bench and the stools. 'Thank you for the mince pie; I needed it.'

'I know you did.' Celeste thought about her conversation with

Barney; how he'd told her he was worried about Melissa. 'You'd tell me if there's anything else on your mind, wouldn't you?'

'What do you mean?'

'Is there something else going on with you? Something you need to talk about? Apart from Barney, I mean.'

Melissa looked about to say more when Jade came through the back door and into the bakery. She pasted a smile on her face instead and looked at Jade. 'Celeste will give you the update but it's looking positive.'

Celeste's question unanswered, she filled Jade in on Barney's condition and then went outside to load up her own car with Tupperware containers of sandwiches and bags with the rolls for Aubrey House and the inn so she could do the rounds.

She quickly dropped the rolls at the inn first seeing as it was so close and then headed out to Aubrey House, the residential care home, situated on the outskirts of the village beyond Barney's place. She had a good chat with the staff, ran through the list of fillings in the sandwiches – double egg and cress this time as requested – and told them she'd added in some Danish pastries as well, all with apple, raisin and cinnamon filling. The manager checked in about the three Christmas cakes on order and Celeste assured her that they would be ready in time with Jade in charge.

She drove back to Heritage Cove, past Barney's cottage and the barn, and around the bend. At the Star and Lantern on her right-hand side, a guy was washing the windows out front. *Crazy.* It was freezing! And he only had a long-sleeved top on rather than the layers everyone else out and about seemed to be dressed in today.

Hazel was right; he looked easy on the eye, or at least his physique from a distance did. In combat trousers with a dark top that hugged a muscular torso, she could safely say it wasn't Quinn either.

She chuckled to herself. Perhaps her imagination had gone into overdrive the other day because she hadn't had a whiff of a love life in forever.

She parked up next to the cottage and back inside the bakery she washed her hands and found her apron again.

Out front, she smiled at Daniel as he took a filled focaccia across the counter from Jade.

'Careful,' Jade warned him. 'You told me to stack it high and I have.'

'Wow, how much filling did you put in there?' Celeste finished tying her apron behind her back.

'Lots, I hope,' Daniel said before her sister could. 'Now all I have to do is safely deliver it to Lucy.'

'Let me get the door,' said Jade. 'And thanks for the intel.'

'What intel?' Celeste asked as Jade closed the door behind him.

'Daniel met the new owners of the pub yesterday. Word has it they're not having a Christmas tree this year.'

Celeste started to laugh until reality dawned. 'Oh, you're not joking. Talk about the Grinches who want to steal Christmas.'

Jade shrugged. 'According to Daniel, the new owners are well aware that the pub is struggling as much as any other and apparently they don't have decorations already so right now, it's an expense they don't need.'

'I kind of understand the need to cut costs, especially early on. But I can't help thinking that this small thing is an indication of things to come.'

'Well let's hope not. And to give them their due, they promised they'd have a tree next year.'

'Not much good *this* year, is it?'

'Not really, no.'

'For goodness' sake, don't let anyone tell Barney. It'll really upset him.' With a sigh, she conceded, 'At least we'll have the village tree soon enough and numerous other trees to look at, including ours.' Celeste smiled at their own festive window, thinking what a shame it was that the new owners wouldn't be joining the rest of the Cove with the decorations this year. It was a cost, sure, but it was also an investment. If the customers were happy, it would be good for their business.

'As it's quiet,' said Jade, 'I'm going out back to feed my babies.'

Celeste knew she didn't mean Phoebe. She followed her sister out to the kitchen and while Jade went to the cake corner, sliced a few more of the wholemeal loaves they'd kept back here until the shelves needed replenishing, running each one through the bread slicing machine to produce thick slices. She put each loaf into a bag in turn, twisting the top afterwards before securing it with a tie each time.

'I'll do all of them now if that's all right with you.' Jade got organised in her cake corner.

'Fine by me.' Celeste went over to inspect the process. 'I'll be out front and call you if I need you. The cakes need your love and attention. Who's that one for?' She nodded to the first fruit cake Jade had unwrapped, releasing the rich aroma into the air. It already smelled and looked delicious, no matter that it wasn't quite ready yet.

'This one is ours.'

Celeste looked at the label on the bottle Jade had next to the cake she'd set down. 'Orange liqueur. Wow, my mouth is literally watering right now.' She watched her sister poke holes in the cake's surface before she measured out the liqueur and began to drizzle it over the cake. Once that was done, the cake would need to be rewrapped to let the alcohol work its magic for a while longer.

When the bell in the shop tinkled, Celeste instructed her sister to be generous with the liqueur. And armed with the wrapped loaves, she left Jade to it and went through to the front of the bakery. Without looking up, she hurriedly crouched down to slot the loaves onto the shelves. 'Won't be a sec,' she called out to whoever was waiting.

'Take your time,' a deep voice urged her as she pushed the last of the loaves onto the wooden shelf. Something about the smoothness and depth of the man's tone made her heart beat faster.

Celeste knew who it was before she'd even turned around.

She swallowed, stood up, hands brushing against her apron and suddenly clammy and when she turned, it was as though the rewind button was pressed and whizzed her back in time.

'We meet again.' He spoke calmly, his deep, velvety voice like a whisper on a breeze that made her shiver all over and rendered her speechless. It had been the same when they'd met for the first time: him calm and collected, her all of a dither.

Quinn McLeod.

Here in the village.

So her eyes hadn't been playing tricks on her.

She thought about the last time he'd been here, the days and the nights they'd spent together in each other's arms. But she'd thought that was it from both of their perspectives.

What was he doing here now? Did this mean he was here for round two?

The way he was looking at her, his almost indigo-blue eyes dancing with mischief, suggested he might well be.

5

Quinn had been attracted to Celeste from the minute she threw that pastry at his head the summer they first met. He'd been in Heritage Cove for a holiday while on leave from the navy a few years back and happened to walk into the bakery, although it had had a different name then. He'd been looking at the menu behind the counter when a pastry came from the direction of the kitchen and slapped him on the head. From the moment she appeared to apologise, he'd fallen for her, and although they'd both told themselves it was a brief fling, a few days of no strings attached, she'd been the only woman he hadn't been able to get out of his mind. There'd been other women along the way but nobody had ever had quite the same effect on him. And he'd be lying if he said the reason why Heritage Cove had appealed this time round had nothing to do with a certain baker. He'd hoped she'd still be here and, more so, hoped she was unattached.

Seeing her again now, all the feelings came rushing back. Especially when she hurtled around from the other side of the counter and flung her arms around him.

Her body felt so good against his. Already he didn't want to let her go.

'What are you doing here?' When she pulled back, her green eyes danced and he was reminded of their bodies, tangled between sheets, the fun they'd had before that he wouldn't mind repeating if that was what she wanted and if he ever managed to sort himself out. 'It's great to see you, but I thought—'

'You thought you'd never see me again,' he said for her.

He loved the way she tried to talk but stammered as though she didn't want her words to suggest that wasn't what she thought at all. Eventually she settled with, 'It's really good to see you.'

He couldn't help himself; he moved closer, so close he could feel the heat coming from her body. Or was it his? Or both of them? 'How good?'

'So good,' she repeated but then pulled away. 'I should behave; I'm working.' And the pale, Irish complexion couldn't hide her blush as she ran her hands down the front of her apron as though straightening herself out. She had on jeans and a roll-neck, navy jumper beneath that hugged her body.

'This place has had a facelift.'

'Sure has.'

'I like the name.'

'Thank you.'

'You must be really pleased with it.' Small talk was overrated when he wanted to do so much more. But were they ever going to be in that place again? She could easily be with someone else by now. He peered into the fancy new glass-fronted cabinet that looked high tech with lighting and temperature controls and began to smile. 'You're still serving them.' He pointed at the salted-caramel turnovers, their identity in no doubt with the label written there to tell the world.

'Want one? On the house.'

'Not going to say no to that.' Those pastries had, after all, been responsible for the way they met. He wondered how they would've reacted to each other had he been just a regular customer and hadn't had a collision with a baking effort she'd deemed terrible, the reason she'd thrown the pastry out of sheer frustration. He liked to think he would've still asked her out. But it might have been a lot harder to get her attention.

She took out the pastry and handed it to him on a napkin. 'Let me know what you think.' She indicated she was going to serve her latest customer to push open the door and he moved to the side to enjoy the pastry, which was perfection. Sweet, flaky, and just the right amount of stickiness, he didn't take long to polish it off.

'Well?' she asked when her customer left them to it.

'Perfect. Just like I remember.' The day after their first date, she'd given him one of the turnovers from the batch she was more than satisfied with.

'I'm happy with them these days. Not like my first few attempts, which were terrible and kind of the reason why I threw one at the wall.'

'You threw it at *me*.' He'd inched towards her again but they sprang apart when she got another customer, a lady with a couple of kids whose immediate concern was where the elf was hiding today. The children spotted him perched on top of the architrave surrounding the wall that led through to the kitchen.

The woman bought a dozen doughnuts, looking Quinn's way more than once and then back to Celeste, but Celeste was giving nothing away. Either that meant she was attached or she was the way she'd been the last time: simply determined to keep her private life just that. Private.

Celeste boxed up the doughnuts and took the payment. She'd always had a certain confidence; it was something he admired.

But he also liked that she wasn't so confident, her emotions always did as they were told. He was glad he'd surprised her today. He wasn't sure, if she'd known he was coming, that he would've got quite such an honest reaction. No matter her circumstances, he could tell she was happy he was here.

When they were alone again, he said, 'It's a bit early for elf on the shelf, isn't it?'

'What can I say? Heritage Cove likes to start Christmas before everyone else.'

'How does the elf stay up there?'

'Jade used a few clumps of Blu-Tack; they're holding firm so far. I had my doubts.'

'Those kids were quite taken with him.'

'We like to keep our customers happy.'

'Your customers are very lucky.' He reached for her hand and she let him take it again, although judging by her expression, she hadn't quite expected the familiar bolt of electricity either, the insane connection they'd both felt the last time evident once again. 'Is this okay?' Surely if she was with someone, it wouldn't be and she'd tell him.

He had his answer when she moved closer to him, her body up against his. 'More than okay.' She was nervous; he could tell by the way she kept curling her lips inwards as she thought of something to say or do, as though she was torn between him and the workplace. It had been a long time since he was last here and yet it felt like no time at all.

She smiled up at him. 'You let your hair grow.'

He put a hand to hair that had once been strictly shaved very short. Sometimes he forgot that it did its own thing now, the floppy-on-top style that didn't fall the same way every day. 'Yeah, it's weird, although I've had it like this for a while.'

'You have?'

He nodded. 'Listen, can I see you, soon, when you're not at work?'

'How long are you here for? I finish around 5 p.m. tonight.'

His smile and his desire ramped up. 'Good to know. But I can't do 5 p.m.'

Her soft breath against his neck as she leaned in sent a shiver all the way up his body and to regions that were on high alert with her proximity. He'd thought about this moment before he'd arrived in the Cove, hoped she'd be the same woman he remembered, and he wasn't disappointed. Seeing Celeste again was 100 per cent first class.

'Why, do you have another date?' she joked.

'Not a chance.' He rested his forehead against hers and she didn't pull away. She was single, he knew it, and that made him happier than he'd be prepared to admit to anyone else. 'I've got another commitment.'

'Are you trying to play hard to get?'

'I have work.'

'You're setting sail at 5 p.m.?' She was teasing and he didn't mind in the slightest. 'Doesn't give you long to get your uniform and sort this hair of yours out.' She'd reached up and when she ran her fingers through one side, he felt his knees weaken at the power of her touch.

'I'm not setting sail. I left the navy.'

She stepped back. 'You did?'

'Getting on for two years ago now. It was time.'

Before, when they'd talked, lying next to one another in the still of the night, he'd admitted that while he loved the job, he wouldn't do it forever, that he'd know the right time to come ashore for good, and that that time would be when he wanted to put down roots. For now, he didn't need to elaborate.

'When you say you can't do 5 p.m., does that mean you're

leaving the Cove already?' She was smiling but in that way you smiled when you were forcing yourself to look pleased.

'Not exactly.'

'You're being very cagey. How long are you here for?'

'I actually don't know.'

'Seriously, how long are you in the Cove? I'd like to see you but time off is difficult in the run-up to Christmas.' Her frown deepened as she put a hand against his chest.

He wished there weren't the layers of his coat and his fisherman's jumper between them. But he liked teasing her. She looked so serious now she thought they might not get the chance to be together properly. 'I want to see you, Celeste. And we'll see lots of each other, I hope.'

'Ah, so you're in the Cove for Christmas?' Her confusion was an attractive quality in someone who barely let her guard slip, usually so in control of everything.

'You could say that.'

'Quinn...'

'All right, I'll stop winding you up. I'm here with my brother Eddie.'

'Are you staying at the Heritage Inn?'

'No, we're embarking on a new venture.'

She puffed out her cheeks in frustration as another customer came in and the moment they left with their mince pies, she demanded, 'Out with it, I'm too busy in here to play games.'

'All right. I apologise, it was just a bit of fun; I enjoy it with you.' She was trying not to smile; he knew she liked it too. He took her hand in both of his, held it against his chest. 'We've bought a business, the two of us. We bought the pub.'

'You bought a pub? Where?'

'Here. We bought *the* pub. The Copper Plough. Or rather the Star and Lantern as it's called now.'

He'd felt her hand begin to pull away well before she managed to do it properly and step back behind the counter even though she didn't have another customer. It was just the two of them, although he was well aware of sounds coming from the kitchen.

'You bought the Copper Plough.' She repeated it as though she might not have heard him correctly the first time. 'Well, that's great, I'm happy for you. For us all. For the village. We wanted to know who the new owners were and now we do.'

'So you're pleased?'

'It's great news.' The smile wasn't quite reaching her eyes, not in the way it had when she'd first laid eyes on him today. 'Although I have a bit of a complaint already.'

'Yeah?'

'I hear there won't be a Christmas tree this year.'

He whistled. 'Wow, word travels fast in the village.' And that was her first thought about him being here long term? 'Are we in trouble?' He couldn't read her expression.

'There's always a tree in the pub. Same position every year. Kind of a tradition, a bit like Christmas itself.'

They really were in trouble. And she was acting differently towards him now, as though they didn't have those memories between them.

'We were cutting costs,' he said matter-of-factly. 'We didn't mean to upset anyone. We heard there's an enormous village tree every year, we thought that would be enough.'

Celeste didn't say anything.

'You seem shocked – at my announcement about the pub, not the tree. At least I don't think it's only about the tree...' The truth was, he had no idea how to work out what she was thinking right now.

'I haven't seen you in a long time, Quinn.' His name on her

lips sounded firm, like a full stop, although she carried on. 'The last I knew, you were in the navy so taking on a pub, and one right here in the village, has come a bit out of nowhere.'

'It means I'll be close by,' he tried. 'It means we'll get time with each other. If that's what you want.' Oh, God, maybe it wasn't.

'Yes, definitely. We should get together soon.' But the counter was well and truly separating them both now: her on one side, him on the other. 'Business is crazy, though, so I'm not sure when.'

Quinn had a sinking feeling as though he was one of those men who became obsessed with a woman who actually didn't want anything more than what they'd once had. A fling. It had suited them both at the time with his job, with her business-savvy head and career-minded goals. Both of them had been very open about it.

He thought of the guys who went ashore and picked up women who said they wanted no strings attached, a bit of fun, a fling with a sailor and then turned up the next time they docked declaring the relationship had meant far more to them. The crew on board his vessel had seen it happen more than once. One guy had had a two-day affair with a woman who'd got down on one knee and proposed before he went back to sea. They'd all laughed about it then but was that what Quinn was doing now by turning up unexpectedly and hinting he might want Celeste to pick up where they'd left off and carry it into a relationship she'd never wanted in the first place? When they'd got together before, it had been a bit of holiday fun for both of them. He just had this feeling that Celeste could be more. But that wasn't much good if she didn't share the feeling.

'Quinn, it's great to see you, but...' She tilted her head towards the door to the bakery again as a group of four people filed in, followed by another couple who were giggling about something or other.

'I can see you're busy.'

'We'll catch up soon,' she said again, but she wasn't quite meeting his eye now. She might well pretend it was because she was focused on her customers, but he knew the brush off when he saw it.

And when he stepped outside, pulling the door to the bakery shut with a little tinkle of its bell, he looked back through the latticed window at her, past all the festive decorations and the snowflakes. He expected her to look at him at least briefly, that smile of hers suggesting she was still very interested.

But she didn't look at him at all. She kept her mind and her gaze firmly on her customers in the bakery and Quinn headed back to the Star and Lantern, disappointed that their ecstatic reunion as well as the undeniable chemistry between them had fizzled out the moment he told her he'd left the navy and bought the pub with his brother.

Was that what had done it? Did she have a picture in her mind of the man he was, in his uniform – not that she'd ever seen it for real – and now he was different?

It almost made his legs buckle to think that – that she thought he was anything less than he'd once been. Because he'd been telling himself that for a long time.

6

The day after he'd been into the bakery, Quinn tried to get his mind away from Celeste and back to being a part owner of a pub, a pub that was reasonably successful and definitely not going under, but a pub which still had the same challenges as most others in England. It was a tough industry to be in, but the brothers were determined to make this work.

He was doing okay until he went outside to grit the front path that led up to the entrance of the Star and Lantern and saw Celeste walking past. He would've run over to see her but she waved and may as well have broken into a sprint the way she moved so fast away from him.

He sighed. *Focus.* Maybe she'd come round in time.

He sprinkled a bit more grit. Terry had told them the path would need doing often when the temperatures fell and with so much ice this morning and on the weather forecast for the coming days, Quinn had wanted to get it done sooner rather than later. And now he knew they'd likely already upset people before they even reopened, given their choice about not having a tree, they'd better not do anything else to annoy the locals. Which included not letting anyone slip over on their watch.

He went in through the door that still had the sign on the front stating the pub was *Closed* and the additional sign he'd made earlier to say what time they'd reopen tonight. He hadn't had a chance to tell Celeste that what he meant by another commitment was that he had work this evening. It would've been the perfect opportunity to have a local spread the word. Instead, they'd have to rely on the board his brother suggested they place beneath one of the iron lamp-posts on the grass area out front of the pub come opening time.

He wondered whether this evening, a decent segment of his brain would be thinking about the girl at the bakery as she finished work: the girl he could've been spending time with, rather than opening up a pub, something he'd known might possibly be in his long-term future but something he hadn't expected to come along quite so soon. He'd thought his career as a sailor in the Royal Navy would go on for a lot longer than it had.

Since he left the navy, Quinn had divided his time between the pub his brother was in charge of in Nottingham and the old pub – not its official name – their parents owned in the Peak District. Eddie had needed him, part of his official reason for retiring from the navy – family commitments. Eddie had been in a bad place and helping him get his life together had taken iron will and persistence, but it had also given Quinn a reason to be there, a focus. And shifting from one home to another kept him from getting bored, from having too many questions thrown his way about his real need to leave his navy career behind. When the inquisitions started, that was when he usually made himself physically move on. It had taken Quinn a long time to admit to anyone that Eddie wasn't the only one who might need help. And even then, he'd only confided in his brother, who had been glad his own life wasn't the only shitshow. He'd said it mockingly and Quinn had appreciated the sibling normality rather than a dramatic reaction.

The floorboards creaked beneath his tread as he made his way along the narrow corridor, past the toilet facilities and into the bar area, and when Eddie popped up from the serving side of the wooden-topped bar, Quinn jumped.

'Whoa, you scare easy,' Eddie bellowed, his voice well-trained for this job, having had a couple of pub tenancies with his ex-wife Claire before the marriage fell apart. Quinn was familiar with the trade but Eddie was almost born for it, like he'd been produced in a certain shape that slotted into the pub life just like that. He had a drive for this business, whereas Quinn was doing it more because it was decent work, he needed something, and seeing as the navy was no longer an option, this was a good alternative.

Quinn cursed at his brother for scaring him. 'For your information, I only jumped a mile because you were like a jack-in-the-box coming up from behind there. Don't do that to the punters later on, will you?' Quinn took off his jacket and put it on the back of one of the chairs at the tables which tonight would hopefully be home to enthusiastic customers with nice deep wallets.

'I won't. But what if nobody comes?' His brother was a good inch taller than Quinn, who wasn't short at six foot, and along with the fit-for-purpose landlord voice and muscular build, Eddie's doubts didn't fit with a man who looked like he could handle anything.

'I hardly think we'll have an empty pub on our hands tonight or any night.'

'What if the locals boycott? We've already upset them by not having a tree. And we've changed the name of their local.'

'Which they approved. And don't forget it's a bit of a distance to any other pub and I don't see a taxi rank anywhere, so walking to the nearest watering hole seems like a good option, don't you think?'

'They might be pissed off that Terry and Nola left and decide they don't want to give us their custom. Whatever the pub is called, tree or no tree. And talking of trees, I might have a solution to that...' He showed Quinn a piece of paper with the name of a Christmas tree farm at the top. 'A guy from this place came and asked whether we'd sell trees out front, said that this would be a great position to do it from as people driving past impulse buy. And I thought they might get out of the car, nab a tree, then come in and give us their custom. I'm getting twenty delivered in a few days.'

'I'm impressed.'

'We don't have any decorations so I won't get one for the inside, too much hassle, but you can't complain with a bank of them outside, can you? Imagine the scent, the smell of Christmas. I can't see how anyone can moan at us.'

'I hope you're right.'

'Well, Terry and Nola did say this was a local hub.'

They had and from what Quinn had seen, so was the local bakery. He and Celeste had been interrupted enough times. He wondered what more they might have said if they hadn't been. 'People will come, you wait and see.'

'Cocky,' Eddie concluded, 'but I like it. And I admire the optimism.'

It was the only way he could be. This had to work, for both of them. They'd committed, bought the place, and there was no turning back.

Quinn went around the other side of the bar to help put away the rest of the glasses: the last batch to go through a glasswasher cycle. On takeover day earlier that week, the boys had got the keys first thing in the morning so that they could at least move personal effects inside. The pub had a flat above with three bedrooms, so Terry and Nola left them to it while they went to visit friends. The afternoon they'd earmarked for the business part of the handover, the hardest part to get to grips with. Quinn had been nervous about that part but Eddie right from the get-go seemed to be taking it in his stride and that had had a calming effect on Quinn. They'd never seen themselves as a partnership in their earlier years, especially when Eddie got married; it had been him and Claire who had run pubs together. But the brothers were already taking to it well and seemed to complement one another. Whereas Eddie was the louder and more decisive one, Quinn was the brother who thought things through more carefully and as ridiculous as it sounded to Quinn sometimes, given his own problems, he tended to be the voice of reason when Eddie couldn't see clearly enough.

Terry and Nola had returned from their friends' house that day, ready to do the business part of the handover, and Terry had started by running through the seemingly never-ending to-do list he had for the pub. But as the former landlord had tried to convey all the knowledge he needed to, both Eddie and Quinn had picked up on a problem. They'd thought the couple was emotional about wrenching themselves away from their home and the business they'd built up, the community they'd served, but Nola's voice had wobbled when she told the boys what had happened with their very good friend and local favourite, Barney. Apparently, the locals had thrown a surprise going-away party for Terry and Nola, and Barney, the host, had collapsed. Terry and Nola were so distraught as they shared the story that Eddie had immediately leapt into his role as the new publican, gone behind the bar, found two glasses, and brought them both back a measure of single-malt Scotch whisky for the shock.

The rest of the afternoon, Terry and Nola had gone into business mode once they'd calmed down. Both former and current publicans had been in communication for a number of weeks already, with all parties keen that this transition go smoothly. The handover had been manic – Terry and Nola had given the boys bunches of keys for this, that and the other, they'd gone through inventory of stock, they'd recapped on insurances that were needed so Quinn and Eddie knew what was required. Nola had shown them how the computer system worked when it came to payroll once Eddie had his laptop set up. Terry had taken them into the cellar as a reminder and gone through the reordering system. He'd also shared the workings of the safe, the till, the card machine. The couple had taken them through where fire equipment was, how to work alarm systems, paperwork of contracts in place, current employee details including those of the chef, who would continue to work here. Because Terry and Nola weren't going to another premises, both parties had agreed that it was mutually beneficial for them to leave things like crockery, glasses, equipment all as part of the sale which worked out well for Eddie and Quinn, who'd almost bitten their arms off to leave as much as they wanted to. It meant the Star and Lantern was ready to go and they wouldn't have to close for long at all.

Quinn stacked pint glasses upside down onto the racks high up at the back of the bar behind a thin, brass rail that ran across the shelves set in dark wood, the same brass that ran around the outside of the bar that punters could lean against and added to the traditional feel of the Star and Lantern. He looked across at Eddie, who was going through the folder filled with paperwork on equipment in the pub – service agreements for the ovens, the dishwasher, glasswasher, instructions on how to run the pumps at the bar and how to keep them working properly. There were a lot of similarities to what they were used to, what they'd seen before, but a few unknowns they had to get on top of.

As Quinn watched his brother, he hoped Eddie was viewing this in the way they'd discussed and that he'd continue to do so. With pub tenancies he'd shared with his ex-wife, they hadn't been long term; they'd been to get the pubs turning over a decent profit and then they'd moved to another project. Eddie had said he didn't want to keep moving but Quinn still had it in the back of his mind that Eddie might lose interest, decide it was time to do just that.

Eddie's marriage breakdown had happened right before Quinn left the navy. Eddie took the split hard because there was another party involved – the man Claire ran off with had been Eddie's so-called best mate, who he'd been at school with, and it was a hell of a stab in the back. Eddie had spiralled, drinking, gambling, and with their parents Keely and Grant in the process of giving up their own pub and retiring down to Penzance, as they'd intended to do for many years – much in the same way as the previous owners of this place – Quinn hadn't wanted them to be the ones to deal with Eddie and his troubles. And he definitely hadn't wanted to burden them with his either. And so Quinn had leapt on Eddie's problems to give him a reason to have to be home sooner. It was all he'd needed to take the final step to leaving life in the navy behind. He'd wanted to for a while but had never had the guts to do it for fear he'd be asked for a reason, a reason he couldn't really give, and didn't want to either. Because his real reason for getting out was something he was ashamed of, embarrassed of. Something that plagued him with an overwhelming sense of failure.

Eddie hadn't taken long to turn himself around. And Quinn was proud of him for doing so. Within a couple of months of

Quinn being out of the navy and at his brother's side as often as he needed, Eddie had accepted that Claire wasn't coming back, that he had to let go of his anger and forget about her and her new partner. His life wasn't over; he may have lost his wife but he wasn't going to let it break him. Eddie's mindset had changed quicker than Quinn expected it to and he was partly envious his brother had managed it; he wished he could do the same. And almost as soon as Eddie was on the road to a normal life again, it was as though it gave Quinn permission to let it all out, let what he was bottling up go, be truthful with Eddie. And Eddie had been there every step of the way.

Quinn took the big tray out to the kitchen and brought back the remaining few wine glasses between his fingers. 'Do you think we were both born with a pub gene?' he asked his brother.

'Hey, I think I was born knowing how to pull a pint... remember the shed at the bottom of the garden?'

Quinn began to laugh. 'Do I remember it? Course I do. We made pretend drinks up until we were in our teens and got our hands on the real stuff.'

'Still don't know how we did that. Mum and Dad certainly never let us drink, much less pass it around our mates.'

'You don't remember?'

'Nope.'

'We nicked a crate of beer cans from the cellar, a couple of bottles of wine.'

Eddie pulled a face. 'We were little shits.' They'd bought a load of plastic glasses and served beers from the shed with their parents none the wiser at the time, tucked behind the bar and the boys cleverly serving beverages from the back of the shed at the little window rather than the front.

'We were boys, messing about.'

'Boys making a bit of extra cash,' Eddie laughed. 'I remember selling the beers – it was profitable until Mum and Dad shut it down and we got a bollocking.'

'I won't ever forget that,' Quinn grinned. 'Working for no money really drove the point home.' They'd both been grounded for a month and when they weren't at school or doing homework, they were glass collectors and cleaners in the pub, foregoing any financial compensation. It had felt brutal at the time.

'It was slave labour.'

'Or teaching us a lesson. We never did it again after that and after word got around.'

'And after Dad started checking the shed every five minutes.'

'Mum and Dad say they'll visit this place once we're on our feet.' Eddie screwed the top back onto his bottle of water and set it down beside the laptop.

'Sounds good to me.'

And they'd be proud to see how far Eddie had come because as much as Quinn had tried to shield them from Eddie's problems, any fool could've seen he was a mess when Claire walked out on him for his best mate.

When Quinn had been out of the navy for a while and Eddie in a better place, Eddie started making murmurings about taking on another pub. Quinn had been applying for security guard jobs and had an interview lined up but while Eddie had originally been thinking of a solo pub venture, he floated the idea to Quinn that they do it together. 'Why not?' he'd asked Quinn. And Quinn hadn't needed it pointing out to him that working security had never been a dream of his; he was doing it because he needed a job and had no idea what else to do. It had seemed good enough. But the more Eddie talked about taking on a pub, the more Quinn began to see a promise of a different future away from the life he'd known in the navy, something new he could get excited about for the first time in a long while. They both knew enough

about life in a pub; admittedly, Eddie knew more, but Quinn
knew the basics and had experience. As soon as he was old
enough, Quinn had worked in their parents' pub – a paid position – as a glass collector and then behind the bar. It was that or
work in a local supermarket or pizza joint and he'd known all
along which one he preferred. It paid well enough, he could
adjust hours as and when needed, and during that time, he'd
picked up bits here and there about the daily running of the
place.

Eddie's idle chatter about leasing and running another pub
had soon turned into something more serious. He began trawling
the online ads for jobs as a landlord, for leases and then for pubs
to buy. Buying was risky, more expensive, but would be worth it
in the long run. Eddie had come up with most of the capital –
this had been his dream for a while – and once he grabbed a hold
of the possibility, not much could've stopped him, especially with
his brother alongside him. Quinn cashed in all of his savings, and
the rest they'd taken in a loan. Their experience had served them
well with the bank manager, their backgrounds too, and when a
pub came up for sale in Heritage Cove of all places, it was like
Quinn had been given a sign. He'd come on holiday to the Cove –
the name locals used for the village – once before, expecting to
leave at the end of his stay and never give it another thought, but
thanks to a certain girl at a little bakery on a traditional high
street, that had changed.

And the feelings were still there. At least, for him they were.

'Where's your head at, bro?' Eddie asked as he closed up one
folder and flipped through the manual for the till yet again. He
came and shifted the wine glasses Quinn had stacked on the far
left over to the shelf on the far right where the rest of that type of
vessel were. 'Come on, we open in a few hours.' As far as Eddie
knew, their holiday here previously had been just that. A holiday.

He knew Quinn had been involved with a woman but he didn't know she was a local or that Quinn had never forgotten about her. Navy men had a reputation for being more than happy to move from one lover to the next and he'd never said anything to change people's perception. It was easier that way than sharing true feelings half the time. *Let them believe what they like*, he'd always thought.

'Get your head in the game,' Eddie urged. 'Did you sleep okay?'

'Yes, Dad.' Quinn began to put the pint glasses on the shelf he'd populated with the wine glasses now they were shifted out of the way.

'I'm being serious. You looked like you were ready for tonight earlier on, but now...'

'I slept okay. Thanks for asking.'

Eddie put a hand on his shoulder. 'You let me know if you need to talk.'

'I've talked too much already.'

'No, you haven't.'

Quinn checked his watch. 'What time is the chef due?'

His brother ignored Quinn's usual way of deflecting and answered, 'He's due an hour or two before we open.'

'The menu sounds great; do you think we need to make any changes?'

Eddie thought about it. 'Wouldn't mind talking with Benjamin at some point, perhaps think about pastries, coffees, teas, you know, faster snacks as well as food that has you in the pub for a sit-down meal.'

'All good ideas but maybe we wait, get a feel for what's going on here first.'

'You're probably right.'

'You know I am,' he grinned. 'And it sounds as though this

guy Benjamin is switched on, so I say cross it off our worry list right now.'

'I guess we've got enough to contend with opening up for the first time.'

'Let's try to remember this is the local and people will want us to succeed.'

'You trying to convince me or yourself?'

'Both.'

'Did the coffee machine arrive while I was out, by the way?' Quinn could use a big injection of caffeine right now.

'Sure did. It's in the hallway near the bottom of the stairs; we'll set it up later on or tomorrow.'

Quinn groaned. 'I should've grabbed a couple when I was out.'

'Yeah. Where were you anyway?'

'Just wandering, exploring, getting a bit of fresh air.'

'Well, soon enough we'll have coffees at our fingertips,' Eddie announced triumphantly.

Eddie stood back at the bar now all the glasses were in place. He had a beer towel in his hand and polished the pumps even though they already gleamed. Terry and Nola had had professional cleaners in at what must have been the crack of dawn today and left this place more pristine than they'd ever thought a pub could be. It still had that pub smell, thankfully no longer inclusive of stale cigarette smoke, and the looked-after interior didn't have yellowing walls but rather bright-enough paint in the areas it needed contrasting with the classic appearance of the wooden beams and fittings. The cosy nooks added even more and the fireplace was ready to go, the grate cleaned out and refilled with kindling and logs waiting to be lit. Nola had tried to do that on handover day in the absence of customers and just the four of them going through everything that needed to be covered, but Quinn had refused to let her. What he had done was got the fire going himself and had her pass him the pieces of wood and the logs. She wanted to be involved and he hadn't minded one bit. The brothers had seen the same reaction with their parents. The pub they'd run had become so much more than a business and despite wanting retirement, leaving all that behind hadn't been easy. It had been their living, their home, their way of life for so long.

Eddie put his arm around Quinn's shoulders. 'This is it. We're here, we're in, we're gonna open. Me and you, the McLeod brothers, back in business.' He put up a hand to meet his brother's mid-air and clasped his palm.

'Back in business,' smiled Quinn.

And he wondered how long it would take Celeste to show up in the pub, at their business, their new home. He hoped it wouldn't be long. But already, he knew she wasn't as pleased to see him as he'd first thought, and he'd be lying if he said he wasn't gutted.

7

'Are you sure you won't come?' Jade nagged yet again as Celeste bagged up a doughnut for Sandy, daughter of Tracy and Giles who ran the Heritage Inn on the corner past the bus stop.

'There you go.' Celeste handed the bag to Sandy, along with her change.

'Call me if you need me,' Sandy said in Jade's direction, giving Phoebe a little wave as she departed.

Phoebe gurgled and waved back; she liked Sandy, who was a reliable babysitter for plenty of residents in the Cove.

Celeste focused on her niece in her sister's arms. 'Yes, Jade, I'm sure I won't come because I'm looking after this one tonight. I offered because I'm exhausted.' She clutched the little girl's fingers and kissed them. She also couldn't face Quinn just yet. She'd avoided him when he saw her walk past the pub but she couldn't very well do that if she went in. Jade had no idea that he was in the Cove yet – Celeste had been trying too hard to get her own head around it before she told her sister – but soon she'd find out for herself.

'Sandy would've babysat, she just said as much,' Jade went on.

'No need.'

'Or Etna would've leapt at the chance; we've plenty of options. Come on, I know you're tired but it's the first night of the pub being the Star and Lantern. Don't you want to see who the new owners are?'

'I do, but I also need to relax a bit tonight.'

'So you want to babysit a baby? Well, that makes no sense at all.' Jade adjusted her daughter on her hip.

'You know what I mean. Just me and Phoebe rather than a bar full of people will be perfect. I'm sure I'll have plenty of nights at the Star and Lantern.'

'Well, if you're sure.' Her sister didn't look convinced. 'You're not coming down with something, are you?'

'Stop stressing. All I want is a night in.'

'O-kay,' she said, eyes wide. She kissed Phoebe on the temple. 'I'll take her to your place. I've already brought over the change bag and some toys.'

'I'm almost finished up here. I'll be over in thirty minutes; you get her settled and sort the travel cot. You know I'm useless with that thing.'

'Will do,' Jade grinned.

It was Celeste's turn for the solo finish at the bakery this evening and what she could really do with was a night alone, at home, but being with Phoebe was the next best thing. Phoebe wouldn't talk about the pub or its new owners, Phoebe wouldn't ask why Celeste was so adamant she wasn't going to go, Phoebe wouldn't work out that there was something else going on other than she just didn't feel like it tonight.

But it was only delaying the inevitable because the moment

Jade came to collect her daughter this evening, the questions would start. She just wanted to put it off as long as she could. Or maybe, if she was lucky, Jade wouldn't recognise Quinn. I mean, he did have a new hairstyle, after all. The crew cut was gone, replaced by longer, dirty-blond hair that suited him and gave him a softer edge.

She got the broom to sweep up behind the counter. Who was she kidding? Her sister had seen enough of Quinn when he was in the Cove before to recognise him. She'd also seen Celeste ogling the photograph of Quinn in navy uniform. They may have only had a few days together but at Celeste's request, Quinn had scrolled through photographs on his phone and he'd sent her the one she absolutely adored. He looked hot and she'd told him as much. He was wearing his uniform, the ship having just returned to shore. Despite the professional, serious expression on his face, you could just about see beneath the shiny peak of his navy and white cap that he was elated and buzzing. It was a beautiful picture, him in full uniform; the dark navy with gold rank slides on the upper arms suited him. Jade had seen the picture plenty of times, although not recently, and all it would take tonight at the pub was one look into those near-indigo eyes and it wouldn't matter that Quinn's dirty-blond hair wasn't cut as short or that he wasn't wearing a uniform; her sister would know exactly who he was and then she'd have something to say to Celeste.

Celeste and Jade had both done a lot of the cleaning up already so it wasn't long before Celeste switched out all the lights, set the alarm by the back door and took the path to the cottage. She ushered Jade out the door less than twenty minutes later.

Celeste loved being an auntie; it came naturally to her. She adored Phoebe and wanted to be in her life for always but even as Phoebe's chubby hands grabbed for her hair after she'd wrapped her in a towel following a calming bath time, she knew she still didn't want children of her own. She never had. Sometimes she thought that made her a monster, an oddity, an unacceptable part of society, and for that reason, she didn't voice it out loud. Maybe in the odd drunken moment with her sister, it got a mention, but usually she made sure she was very vocal about her career aspirations. While both sisters had had the same career goal, it was Celeste who'd made sure to shout the loudest about it so it would dim down any questions, well-meaning or otherwise, from outsiders about what she wanted out of life.

'Are you holding Snuggles nice and tight?' Celeste had Phoebe on her lap and she'd been cuddling her niece and her toy bunny rabbit on the sofa for a good half an hour after her bath time. She'd read *Goodnight Moon* twice because Phoebe seemed to be content to listen and gradually her eyes had grown heavy. And right now, the little girl was fighting to stay awake. 'Come on, you, let's climb those stairs and put you to bed.'

Sometimes at this point, Phoebe would realise what was happening, or at least that's what Celeste assumed. She'd wake up and start fussing and Celeste would think, *good for you, woman power, no means no.* But tonight, she snuggled into Celeste's chest as they climbed the stairs and Celeste took her over to the travel cot assembled with the brightly coloured alphabet quilt lying inside. She stayed a while, leaning over the cot as Phoebe stared back at her, turned her head to look at what was a different view to the one she usually got at bedtime. Although she'd had this one a few times before.

Celeste crept away and pulled the door to what was once Jade's bedroom almost closed. Was it possible to be jealous of a baby who'd been given a bath, warm milk and been tucked in nice and early? Pure heaven, that's what it was. She smiled as she reached the final few stairs on her descent back to the lounge and heard Phoebe gurgling like she was trying to get her second wind. She didn't put any music on or the television; she listened

out for her niece to settle and, sure enough, when she crept
upstairs half an hour later and peeked through the gap in the
door, the little girl was fast asleep.

In the kitchen, she poured herself a glass of wine, wondering
what it was like in the Star and Lantern right now. What was the
atmosphere like? Same as usual or noticeably different? If Quinn
hadn't come into the bakery today, she would've gone to the pub
tonight for sure. She really wanted to. She was going to visit
Barney in the hospital tomorrow and she wanted to assure him
that the pub was in very capable hands, that he had nothing to
worry about, that their local was still standing the way it always
had been and he should look forward to a pint of Guinness in
there when he came home.

Seeing Quinn had been a shock to the system in more ways
than one. The second she'd heard his voice, it was like someone
had poured a powerful liquid through her body and she couldn't
feel her limbs as she moved, her insides felt fluttery, she was
light-headed. But all of her senses came back when he wrapped
her in a hug, when she felt the vibration of his voice against her
cheek as he spoke.

But Quinn being here for a few days, a week, even two,
would've been exciting, exhilarating even. They could've picked
up where they left off.

Except he wasn't here for a holiday. He was here long term.
And that left her well and truly all over the place.

Jade did one better than sending a text to her sister when she
realised who owned the Star and Lantern – she came back to the
cottage far earlier than she'd said she would.

'I couldn't message you,' Jade said the second she came
through the door. 'This is too big for a text.' She hung her coat on
the coat stand in the corner and joined her sister on the sofa.

'We've got a good hour before Linc comes and we take Phoebe off your hands, so talk.'

Celeste shrugged. 'You know as much as I do now. You know he and his brother have taken on the pub.'

'I do know that.' Her sister bit down on her lip. 'I also know he came into the bakery yesterday. Something you neglected to inform me about. He asked whether you were coming along tonight.'

'What did you tell him?'

'Well, I wasn't about to tell him that you refused.' She gave an exasperated sigh. 'I knew something didn't add up that you just wanted a quiet night. In all the time you've known Terry and Nola were leaving, you've been obsessed as much as any of us about who the new owners of the pub might be.'

'So what did you say to Quinn?'

'I told him you had to wait for a late-night delivery so doubled it up with babysitting.'

'I bet he knows that was a lie.' She held up the bottle of wine but her sister shook her head at the offer. Celeste poured another measure into her own glass.

'Yeah, well, had to think of something.' Jade flopped back against the sofa. 'I couldn't wait to get back here and see you. I didn't mention it to Linc, kept it to myself, and nobody else seemed to recognise him and connect him to you.'

'I doubt anyone else would remember him. We kept ourselves pretty much to ourselves when he was here before.'

Jade grinned. 'Oh, I know you did. Bumping into him wearing next to nothing on the landing is something a girl doesn't forget easily. He still looks fit, by the way.'

'I know.' After a sip of wine, Celeste admitted, 'I was shocked when he showed up in the bakery but pleased to see him. I really didn't know how to feel when he said he'd bought the pub.'

'You guys left it as a no-strings-attached affair, didn't you?'

She nodded. 'I thought to myself, this guy's in the navy, I won't hear from him ever again. And I was all right with that. Do you know he left the navy?' At Jade's face she berated herself. 'Stupid question. Obviously, or he wouldn't have the pub.'

'People were very interested to know he'd once been in the navy. He got admiring glances from every single woman at that little bit of information.'

'I'll bet.' And his looks and muscles didn't hurt either.

'One girl, who I'm pretty sure is the older sister of one of Linc's students, touched him on the arm when she asked him why he left, as though he was going to spill everything to a stranger and would fall into bed with her afterwards.'

'You got all that from her touching his arm?'

'She was stroking it...'

Celeste laughed. 'How did he react?'

'He tactfully moved away to grab some empty glasses.'

'No, I mean what was his answer to the question about leaving; did he say it was the right time?'

'Yeah. Something like that, something about settling down from what I remember. I bet that got a few women stirred up, thinking a muscly ex-navy guy could be the perfect marriage and father material.'

Celeste didn't like where this conversation was going, so she steered it in another direction. 'What was it like, the first evening under new ownership and management?'

'It was pretty much a full house. There were a fair few murmurings about the tree but I think everyone was trying to be respectful when they've only just reopened. I can't imagine that will last. Once people have been in a couple of times, I'll bet it's mentioned again.'

'And again... and again. It's really bothering people.'

'I know. But for what it's worth, they do seem like a nice couple of guys, Quinn and Eddie.' She put a hand to her mouth. 'I haven't even asked how Phoebe is. Oh my goodness, does that make me a terrible mother?'

'Yes.' Celeste laughed when Jade lightly slapped the top of her knee. 'She was fine, went down easily. Why don't you leave her here with me tonight? I'm sure she'll sleep through. And I've got the formula for when she wakes first thing.'

'She might not sleep all night.'

'I'll take my chances. And if she wakes, I'll get up and go to her.' She doubted she'd be sleeping much herself anyway; she had way too much on her mind, like when Quinn was going to pop up out of nowhere again.

'You're the best sister.' She gave Celeste a hug. 'I'll creep up and see her.'

'Do not wake her, Jade,' Celeste warned. Linc told her the last time Etna looked after Phoebe, Jade had insisted on giving her baby girl an extra kiss goodnight, had managed to wake her and that was it; she wouldn't settle again.

When Jade came back down the stairs, Celeste repeated her offer. 'Honestly, wait for Linc and then you two go on home and leave Phoebe with me.'

'Okay. But I'll get started at the bakery in the morning, you have an extra hour or so in bed as long as Phoebe lets you.'

'Deal.'

'I'll get Linc to collect Phoebe just before seven with the pram and drop her at day care before he goes up to the school.'

'See, easy. Great plan.' She held up the wine bottle again.

'Oh, go on then, seeing as Phoebe is so happy here and settled.' Jade went to the cupboard and pulled out another large wine glass. 'I reckon we've got another hour or so of girl time, sister and sister. And you can spend that time telling me how you really feel about Quinn.'

* * *

Phoebe didn't wake at all during the night but she was Celeste's alarm clock the next morning and Celeste was happy for a cuddle first thing while she gave her her bottle.

There was no time to continue the chatter from last night with her sister when she saw her at the bakery after Linc collected Phoebe, and besides, Celeste had said as much as she was going to say about Quinn for now. Last night, she'd admitted more than once that yes, it was exciting to see him, yes, she was beyond stunned that he was becoming a local just like they were, and yes, she had thought about him in a non-pub-landlord type of way. Jade had been well into the wine by that point, asking all kinds of intimate questions, which Celeste refused to answer. Celeste had partly wondered whether any other women had made a pass at him last night, whether he'd spent the night with them, the way they once had. She couldn't blame him. She'd pretty much rejected him in the bakery, glad to see him one minute, panicking the next that he was here to stay.

Today it was back to business. The girls were both good at monitoring stock levels – what sold well, what they had left over at the end of the day. There was never wastage, though both girls took things home with them and they always packaged up surplus for Patricia from the tea rooms who did the same there and took everything to a homeless shelter where she volunteered. There was a delivery of supplies, and juggling those as well as getting products onto the shelves and into the display cabinet was a full-on workflow for the sisters. Celeste made more chia loaves, glazed doughnuts and doughnuts with jam in the centre, all of which were good sellers daily. Jade took charge of gingerbread men, this time icing them with little scarves around their necks for a bit of variety and red buttons on their fronts rather than white. They made turnovers, rosemary and garlic focaccia, sausage rolls, bread rolls in various shapes to different recipes, and eventually, the chaotic routine that was always the root of their day to provide customers with fresh products gave way to a steadier pace.

Early afternoon, Celeste saw Quinn approaching the bakery. He'd timed it well because she already had her keys in her hand and escaped out the back to drive off to the hospital to see Barney. She couldn't avoid him forever but for now, she was choosing the easy option.

Until now, Barney had only had a few close visitors – Lois, of course, Melissa and Harvey, and today Celeste was down to visit, Tilly in the early evening. As she parked up at the hospital, and paid the extortionate pay and display fee, she wondered how long it would be before Barney came home. Everyone in the Cove wanted to see him and they couldn't all turn up at the hospital. The poor nurses would be inundated if people in the village had their way. Instead, the local grapevine, courtesy of Etna, had made sure that visits were staggered and in a lot of cases, held off in the hope that he would return to Heritage Cove very soon.

Celeste was pleasantly surprised to find Barney with a smile on his face and chuckling away with a nurse before he spotted her.

'Come, sit down. This one's boring me anyway,' he joked to the nurse who was clearly taken by the old man who could charm even the coldest of subjects with his humour. And it was a good sign to see him that way. Although, when he started coughing again, it was a reminder of why he was still here.

Celeste poured a glass of water from the jug next to his bed and handed it to him. 'Better?'

'I keep thinking I am and then the cough reminds me that I'm not. I hate it.'

'I won't stay long; I'll let you get some more rest.'

'Oh goodness, please, no more sleep or rest. I need company. I'm improving every hour I'd say, but the blessed cough and the exhaustion catch me out when I least expect.' He coughed again but soon recovered. 'It looks cold out.' He indicated the layers she'd arrived in. She'd already peeled her scarf off, but it was warm in here with the big coat on and she removed it, putting it on the back of her chair.

'Definitely cold out there.' But warm in here. She pushed her emerald-green jumper up her forearms. 'It's dry today, though, at least. You'd have loved the frost this morning.'

He looked to the window. 'I can see the blue sky and that the sun's shining but I'm missing out on milling around the Cove on those beautiful crisp winter days we all love.'

'Won't be long, Barney,' she encouraged, even though she didn't really know for sure how long he'd be in here.

'Tell me what's new with you,' he asked, shifting his focus away from the window and back to Celeste. 'I need people to help me stay in the real world.'

'Stay in Heritage Cove, you mean.'

'The best world I know,' he grinned.

She filled him in on the bakery's most popular items as he was always interested in those and she made him laugh as she talked about the challenges of wet weather when she and Jade had to make deliveries. 'It's not easy carrying platters of sandwiches in the rain, no matter how much cling film they're covered with.'

'Soggy sandwiches... nobody wants those.'

'Quite,' she laughed.

He looked beyond her and out of the window again. 'No sign of snow yet. I suppose even the end of November is a bit early. I'm hoping for some soon.'

'It's harder to get around in the snow.'

'Not sure how many snowfalls I have left at my age.'

'Barney, you're so dramatic. You're only in your seventies; that's no age these days.' But his words were a reminder of the scene in the barn that day.

His face relaxed and a smile formed. 'There's nothing like the first snow in Heritage Cove.'

'It's pretty magical.'

'Good job this happened before Christmas then. I intend to be back in situ well before the big day.'

Celeste relaxed onto the chair near the bed after she'd pulled it a bit closer. 'We're all looking forward to you being back in the village.'

'You and me both. But it'll be a while yet. Nurses and doctors are keeping a close eye on me and for once, I'm not complaining. Well, not too much. I daren't or Lois would have me on a twenty-four-hour watch.'

'I bet she would.'

'So come on, tell me, I'm desperate to hear more about the Star and Lantern. I've only seen Lois this morning, Melissa doesn't reply very quickly to texts and so I'm relying on you. What's it like under new ownership? Do they know what they're doing? Is it the same?'

She reached out and patted his hand. 'All in good time; you haven't told me much about you yet.' And she needed a stalling technique, so as much as she knew he wouldn't want to focus on himself, she had to probe in order to buy her time to think of what to say.

'I'd rather talk about the pub.'

'And we will, when you've told me how you're doing.'

He recapped on his time in the hospital: the dehydration, the rounds of antibiotics and the nurses and doctors who'd been taking care of him. Some of them he liked, others he really liked. 'They're happy I'm heading in the right direction,' he told her. 'Despite the cough and the exhaustion that comes with it.'

And even though he'd taken his time and explained everything, she still had no idea what to say to him when he asked about the Star and Lantern again.

'I didn't make it to the pub last night, Barney.'

She might as well have said she'd run down The Street with no clothes on given the shock on his face. 'What do you mean, you didn't make it? It was the first night without Terry and Nola. In my absence, I need people like you to fill me in, give me all the details. I'm going to have to get out of here, see for myself. I've got a good feeling about those boys; they seem to have their heads screwed on right. I hope you're all making them feel welcome when you see them around.'

'Of course we are.'

A nurse came in to check on him and lingered when his verbal response was coupled with a cough. A concerned expression stayed with her until she was satisfied he was all right and she told him she'd be back again soon.

'They make a lot of fuss,' he said when she left him with Celeste. 'There must be other patients who need it more than I do.'

'It's their job and you're just as important as everyone else, Barney.'

'So tell me, why didn't you make it to the pub? What happened?'

'I was just really tired after a busy day in the bakery. I knew I was coming to see you and I was worried that I might be coming down with something so thought an early night away from everyone would be the best thing.'

'But you're not sick?'

She shook her head. 'Woke up right as rain today. I looked after Phoebe for Jade last night too.' And now she'd put her foot in it because you didn't look after someone's kid if you thought you were sick. 'I felt better, like right after work.'

Usually, Barney would've jumped on the discrepancies in her story but he didn't this time. Perhaps all this had taken it out of him and he didn't have the energy to think about too much else other than the basics of his beloved Cove.

'Perhaps you'll make the pub soon,' he said.

'I'm sure I will. And Jade said there was still the same great vibe and the warmth it's always had.'

'Was that from the fireplace or have they got a Christmas tree in yet?' Barney asked, although his eyelids were beginning to get heavy, his blinks lasting longer each time.

Celeste suspected visitors had intentionally kept the news about no tree this year to themselves and she wasn't about to drop that bomb either. Barney didn't need to hear it.

'No tree yet, but it's still very early, remember. The village tree will soon be up; I can't wait for that.'

'It's always spectacular. I remember Melissa seeing it as a young girl; she'd get so excited. Harvey too.'

'Nothing's changed; they still get that way like the rest of us.'

He tried to hoist himself up a bit in bed but couldn't do it without Celeste's help. 'I'm worried about Melissa; did you get a chance to talk to her?'

'I asked whether anything was bothering her but she didn't say anything.'

'She told me Harvey was working late this evening and perhaps he is, but I also know that she's hiding something.'

'Well, for now, don't you worry. Melissa and Harvey are just fine, the pub is still standing, the only thing wrong with Heritage Cove is that you're not there.'

Eyes closed, he patted her hand when she put hers on his. 'I'll be back before you know it.'

'We'll all be waiting for you.'

Celeste left Barney to rest and drove back to the Cove. He'd always been the same way: worrying about other people more than himself. It was his nature and she doubted he'd ever change. She'd do her best to let Melissa know she was here to talk to if Melissa needed it. That might take one worry away from Barney if she could reassure him that the girl who was like a daughter to him and her husband Harvey, who was like a son, were doing fine.

Back at the bakery, Celeste thought again about the Star and Lantern. She knew she'd have to go in there eventually. She couldn't avoid it forever. She had to see Quinn. He was living here in the village; there'd be no avoiding it.

But when Jade went out to deliver the sandwiches to Aubrey House and the doughnut delivery to a local charity hosting a fundraising event, Celeste packed up the mince pies ready to take over to the chapel for this afternoon's choir practice and was on high alert every time the bell in the bakery tinkled. Each time she heard the noise, she expected it to be Quinn and part of her was relieved it wasn't, the other part was disappointed.

And she had no idea what to say to him when they next crossed paths.

8

Last night had been a success at the Star and Lantern, much to Eddie and Quinn's surprise and relief. The brothers had turned the sign on the door to *Open* and when nobody showed in the first ten minutes, they'd thought perhaps the local boycott they'd feared was actually about to become real. But Benjamin soon arrived to get things going in the kitchen and he'd assured them they didn't have anything to worry about. Sure enough, the initial worry had soon been replaced by thoughts that the residents of Heritage Cove would never leave the confines of the Star and Lantern because nobody seemed willing to exchange their comfy chair or position at the bar for the cold weather outside come closing time.

Quinn was used to hard work. To get into the navy in the first place was no easy feat. He'd had to be physically ready before he even got accepted and then it was into the training. The navy was tough on rules and on discipline and if you didn't measure up, you were out. And Quinn had been determined he wouldn't be one of those recruits who didn't go the distance. He'd trained for ten weeks, most of it gruelling, but he'd buzzed on it, wanted nothing else out of life. The initial training was, as expected, physically and mentally challenging. He faced the notorious high ropes on the training course, not once wanting to give in even when he was terrified, he'd endured the survival trek across the harsh terrain of Dartmoor with a team who didn't have much of a clue. They'd argued, there'd almost been fists flying, but they'd all pulled through in the end. When he first went in the navy's sinking ship simulator, he'd thought perhaps this was it, the moment he bottled it and failed. The pressure of water filled where he and the others were in minutes. It was dark, threatening, the simulator recreating the conditions of a ship flooding after coming under attack. Quinn knew it had seen one of the other recruits leaving for good. But when he and others had emerged from the simulator, the reality of the gruelling conditions hit them all and it was exhilarating; he felt like he could do anything, take on whatever challenges were thrown his way.

In his thirteen years with the Royal Navy that followed, Quinn had been deployed to the Med, the Gulf, Afghanistan. He'd been to the Middle East where they were safeguarding merchant shipping, tackling criminal and terrorist activity. He'd had the navy in his sights since he was nine years old and he'd watched a navy ship dock in Portsmouth. He'd been there with his family at the end of a week's holiday and he'd watched the ship back in home waters, the sailors coming home to their families. He'd been in awe of the uniformed personnel, their pride, their elation. And it was that day he knew what he wanted to do with his life. He wanted to represent his country and he wanted to do it in the Royal Navy. And he hadn't known full-time civilian life until he left almost two years ago, just after he turned thirty-five.

Opening up a pub with his brother was hard work in a very different sense. There weren't the physical demands or the strict rules he had to follow in the navy but those had been replaced with financial commitments, responsibility and immersing himself in a trade he only had basic knowledge of. And he'd swapped his worries as a sailor for concern that this might not work, that they'd mess it up and he and Eddie would lose out financially. That he'd let his brother down. That he'd let himself down.

Perhaps somewhat naïvely, Quinn had thought that this new business, this massive commitment, was going to be such a focus for him that it would be the miracle cure he needed to get away from all his problems, from the memories that haunted him. But it hadn't managed to do that yet. And so, to cope, Quinn did the only thing he knew how: he handled the emotional fallout, turmoil, whatever way you referred to it with physically exerting himself, pushing himself to his limits. Discipline made sense to Quinn, order and routine were what he needed – not having those things threatened to undo him. And so he went to a spit-and-sawdust gym a short drive from the Cove and punched the living daylights out of a leather punchbag to get rid of his frustrations. And he'd got out of bed this morning, dropped to the floor for press-ups, sit-ups, then taken himself out on a run through the village, out into the surrounding countryside, his legs carrying him with the need to escape.

Once Quinn was showered, he was in a good headspace and ready for another day. He took the second delivery of the morning, this time wine and spirits, Eddie changed one of the kegs in the cellar, Quinn made sure the bar was stocked while his brother ensured the cleaners were paid on time. The brothers had tidied and done the basic clean last night but the cleaning team who were just finishing up had arrived bright and early today to do the bulk of it – the kitchen, toilets, mopping the hallway and the floor behind the bar, hoovering the main pub area. They weren't the cheapest of teams according to Eddie and the brothers had toyed with the idea of taking on the cleaning themselves to cut costs, but had agreed they had plenty to get their heads around as it was. And besides, Terry had assured them that he'd tried two other cleaning firms and nobody did such a good job as these guys did. And so Eddie and Quinn were going to swallow the extra cost for now.

The cleaning team had just finished and loaded all their gear into their van parked out front when there was a call at the door to the pub.

'Bit early for punters, isn't it?' Eddie had picked up a big bucket and was holding it beneath one of the beer pumps, having just changed the keg, pulling the pump to get the beer to flow through nicely.

'I'll get it. Might be the gas man with those extra cylinders we needed refilled.' Because to propel beer and lager out of the pumps, you needed the gas.

Quinn opened the door to the pub and was instantly reminded that just because he was wearing a T-shirt and jeans inside, it was still fast approaching winter. 'We're not open until 11 a.m., sorry, mate.' He was about to close the door when Benjamin joined the cheerful guy with grey hair who'd knocked on the door to the Star and Lantern.

Benjamin introduced the pair. 'This is my dad, Danny.' And it made sense now; no wonder Quinn had felt a flutter of familiarity because they had the same face shape, the same smile and upbeat demeanour.

'Come in out of the cold,' Quinn urged.

'We've got something for you.' Gloves on, Danny clasped his

hands together as he and Benjamin headed for the truck and out of the back pulled a Christmas tree.

Quinn hadn't thought the trees were arriving until tomorrow.

'It's on the house,' Danny insisted as they arrived once again at the door, him taking the base of the tree, Benjamin with the tip. 'It's one of our most beautiful Fraser firs, the same type as is here at the pub every year. We insist, Heather and I. Call it a *welcome to Heritage Cove* offering from the Doyle family and our Christmas tree farm.'

He wasn't sure why they'd brought it now and not with the others. 'Bring it round the back; it's a bit wide to come in this way. I'll go open the gate up for you. And... thank you, appreciated.'

Danny nodded and set off down the side of the pub while Quinn scooted back along the corridor, into the pub's main area and over to the back doors, doubling back to the bar to grab the big bunch of keys when he realised that obviously these doors were locked.

Eddie looked up from his laptop at the bar. 'What's going on?'

'Looks like we've got ourselves a tree.' Quinn fumbled through the bunch of keys to find the right one. Thankfully, a few had tags on them to help the process.

'The trees aren't due today.'

'Tree singular today, not sure why they did it early. I'll go and open the back gate.'

The back door successfully open, he found the next key required and let Benjamin and his dad in the side gate. He led them to the back entrance of the pub past the wrought-iron trellis that was bare except for some very sorry-for-themselves branches weaving through.

'It's a beauty,' Danny reiterated as Benjamin rested the tree's tip up against the outside wall.

Quinn put a hand to his jaw. 'I'll need to find a bucket.'

Danny smiled. 'He's on it.' Benjamin had already headed back down the side of the pub.

'Don't tell me we get that on the house too?'

'What can I say? Us locals like a tree in the pub – it doesn't feel right without one – so we're going all out to help you create the magic.'

'I'm assuming the others won't come with a bucket or a stand.' Quinn puffed out circles of cold air.

'Others?' Danny took the stand from Benjamin and positioned it inside the pub at Eddie's direction.

'A batch of twenty,' said Eddie after introducing himself to Danny.

'I'm not sure I follow.'

Eddie's brow furrowed. 'You're delivering to us tomorrow so we can sell trees out front.'

Judging by Benjamin's face, this was the first he'd heard and it soon dawned on Quinn that Danny had no idea about it either.

Eddie pulled out his phone and brought up the contact he'd added. But when he read out the name of the farm, Danny shook his head. 'Not us, we're Mistletoe Gate Farm.'

'Shit.' Eddie's face fell. 'I didn't realise. I had a visit from these people, they gave me a good deal, I assumed it was the local farm.'

'They're a few villages away,' said Benjamin.

'I'm sorry,' said Eddie, adding in another curse for good measure.

'Please, it's a genuine mistake,' Danny insisted, although Quinn wouldn't mind betting that the conversation back at the farm might go a little differently. 'I'll be off. Enjoy the tree.'

'Thank you.' Quinn and Eddie's words sounded pathetic now.

They'd gone and upset more of the locals. It had been bad enough announcing they weren't having a tree – Quinn had heard murmurings last night – but people hadn't brought it up. Perhaps they were trying to find their footing with new publicans too.

But this could well be a bad move on their behalf. A very bad move.

9

'We had no idea,' Eddie said yet again to Benjamin after Danny headed back to Mistletoe Gate Farm. He'd already tried to call the other farm and cancel the order but it had been processed and they wouldn't refund.

'No harm done,' said Benjamin after he watched Quinn and Eddie secure the tree into its special stand. If he was miffed, he was probably minding his language given he worked here and likely wanted to be sure to keep his job.

Eddie cursed yet again, scratched the back of his head. 'We'll know for next year.'

When Benjamin went into the kitchen to get organised for his own day, the brothers looked at each other. And neither needed to say what the other was thinking. They'd messed up big time.

Benjamin poked his head out of the door. 'We're almost out of milk.'

'I forgot,' said Quinn. Milk had been on the list of things to get this morning. 'How much do you need?'

Volunteering to duck out for the milk was a good way to escape the tension that was of their own making. But his escape was short-lived because it was swapped for a different tension when he bumped into Celeste in the convenience store.

It was clear that, had she spotted him first, she would've turned on her heel and left before he cornered her. But as it was, she appeared at the milk fridge from around the end of the aisle just as he did and there was no pretending not to see each other.

'You settling in all right?' she asked him as though they'd never seen one another naked. She smiled when he gestured for her to open the milk fridge first.

'Something like that.'

His tone had her interest. 'Everything okay?'

He pulled out the milk he needed. 'Looks like we've upset the locals.'

'Again?'

He puffed out his cheeks. 'This is worse than not having a tree – which incidentally we do now have, courtesy of Mistletoe Gate Farm. Problem is, Eddie ordered a batch to sell out front of the pub, thought it would draw in punters.'

'Doesn't sound like a terrible idea, although the farm isn't too far away, might have been better to point them in that direction.'

'The farm supplying the trees which arrive in the morning wasn't Mistletoe Gate Farm.'

Eyebrows raised, she looked about to tell him what she thought of that, so he leapt in first.

'Eddie was contacted by a tree farm, assumed it was the one around the corner, and thought he was doing the right thing placing an order.'

'Do the Doyles know?' They made their way towards Lottie at the till.

'They do and they were very polite, very professional but I can imagine they're annoyed. Can't blame them. The other farm won't refund us either. So we're stuck with twenty trees from a competing Christmas tree farm which will all stand out front of the pub just to taunt everyone – or maybe to taunt us – with our mistake.'

Etna came out from the end of the aisle nearest the till just as Quinn set down his milk, ready to pay. 'You ordered trees from someone other than Mistletoe Gate Farm?'

'He did what?' This time it was another woman who was with Etna.

Had everyone in Heritage Cove decided to go to the convenience store at the same time as him? This was getting worse.

'It was an honest mistake,' he told the ladies.

'Did you know about this, Celeste?' They bypassed him and addressed her instead.

'Only just heard.' She left cash for her milk and almost scarpered before he could use his card. He left Etna and the other woman gossiping at the till with dagger looks coming his way.

'Thanks for leaving me to fend for myself in there,' he said, catching Celeste up even though he had to go the other way.

'I'm in a rush but it was kind of fun watching you squirm.' She grinned. 'The question now is what are you going to do to rectify the mistake?'

'Told you, not much we can do.'

Her phone rang and she took the call but not before she said, 'Well, I'd think of something, and quickly, if I were you.'

Perhaps this was her way of dealing with what had once gone on between them. Pretend nothing was happening, focus on another drama and hope that it all blew over.

The thing was, that wasn't what he wanted. Not in the long term.

Back at the pub, he had another word with Eddie. 'We need to rectify this.'

Frowning, his brother shook his head. 'It's ridiculous. There's nothing I can do about it now. I'm not going to lose out on the money I've paid. Next year we'll know.'

'There must be something we can do.'

Eddie seemed reluctant to spend any more time talking about it but after Quinn took the milk to the kitchen and Eddie finished changing one of the optics, it was clear Quinn's concern had given him pause. 'Let me try calling them again.'

'It's worth a try.'

Eddie disappeared upstairs to make his call and came downstairs less than half an hour later. 'Sorted.'

'They've refunded?'

'No, they weren't having any of it. But I had a pub contact less than fifty miles away and I chatted with the landlord who is happy to take the trees, say they sell well every year out front. I called the other farm back and I've been charged an extra fee to sort the delivery given it's out of their way but at least we won't be stuck with our mistake like a noose around our necks.'

Benjamin was happy enough with the news when he came out of the kitchen with some details of today's menu options, although when Eddie suggested they sell some of the Doyle Christmas trees out front instead, he said it was better to point customers towards the farm itself.

'They'll get the full experience then,' said Benjamin, 'get to choose from a wider selection, and it means the tree will be freshly cut for them. I'll get Dad to drop in some flyers you can put on the bar. If that's okay?'

'Great idea,' Eddie nodded.

Benjamin looked across at the tree he and his dad had delivered on the house. 'It's not really fulfilling its Christmas destiny, you know.'

'How's that?' Quinn pondered.

'Where are the decorations?'

* * *

Quinn went to Mistletoe Gate Farm and bought up a few sets of fairy lights so at least the tree wasn't totally bereft of cheer. And it would have to do for now. They had neither the time nor the spare cash to go all out with decorations. And it was still a stunning tree, still had that beautiful smell. Surely that had to count for something.

'You should thank me for going out into the melee, you know,' he told Eddie the minute he returned to the pub with the boxes of lights, coloured at Danny's suggestion as that was what they tended to have in the pub every year.

'That bad?'

'It's been, what, a couple of hours since I opened my big mouth in the convenience store, and I swear I got dirty looks from every person I passed in the street and up at the farm.'

'You're being paranoid.'

'You didn't have to experience it. I set the record straight with Danny, though, shook hands, told him to please, please spread the word.'

Eddie laughed at that.

'I was thinking of something else we could do to keep the peace.'

'Buy some decorations?' Eddie began to unravel the first set of lights when he pulled them from the box.

'That wasn't quite what I had in mind.'

Quinn told him about his brainwave, buzzing that he had his head in this new business enough that he didn't feel he was a silent partner when it came to the management of the place as well as the day-to-day work.

Eddie took charge of the lights and left Quinn to deal with his idea that involved making up a dozen or so flyers, which he did quickly enough on the computer and using the coloured printer they'd bought between them. They weren't very fancy, but they'd do the job.

Before he did the rounds with the flyers, he accepted the coffee Benjamin had made from the new machine.

'I needed this, thank you.'

'Those machines are the boss,' Benjamin admitted. 'Bit big for just us, though.'

'Eddie thinks it might be an idea to offer coffees to punters, maybe a few pastries or baked goods too,' said Quinn after an approving sip from his own coffee.

Benjamin said nothing.

'What's that face for?' Eddie prompted. 'Come on, you've got the local knowledge; will people hate it? Is it not in keeping with pub tradition?'

'Let's just say you can offer coffee of the instant variety in here. But... you might be stepping on a few toes with the coffee machine – Etna's to be precise; she was pissed off when she thought the girls at the bakery were going to install a machine.' Quinn's ears pricked up at the thought of the *girls at the bakery*, or at least one girl in particular. 'And the Twist and Turn Bakery as well as the tea rooms are the pastry suppliers around here.' He shrugged. 'Look, it sounds a bit petty, I know, but Etna has had her tea rooms for a long time; she sees things a certain way. I don't want to overstep; I'm not here to tell you how to run your own business, but...'

'We've already pissed people off with the trees,' Eddie finished for him.

'It's just that if you make the coffees too good in here, it might take business away,' Benjamin pressed on, clearly still worried about overstepping. 'If it helps, Terry rarely made many coffees or teas when he was the owner. I think locals are used to going to the tea rooms instead.'

When Benjamin went back to the kitchen, Quinn took another appreciative sip of his coffee. 'Petty or not, we should probably listen to him, you know. Damn, this coffee is good.'

'Should be, the machine cost enough,' Eddie mumbled. 'It could've been another way to boost the pub's footfall.'

Eddie had a good business mind as well as experience with turning pubs around, although the local areas he'd previously been in hadn't had quite the infrastructure of Heritage Cove or quite the closeness between its residents. And while Eddie had the better business mind, Quinn was often the voice of reason. It had been that way when they were kids too. He remembered Eddie struggling with his exams, wanting to toss everything away when two exams in a row went so badly, he thought he'd failed. He did, he failed one, but it was Quinn's encouragement that had sent Eddie to evening school to retake, the thought of the long-term future rather than the here and now that Eddie could only see with that failed mark against him.

'The pub isn't doing badly, though; we need to be positive,' said Quinn.

'Positive is good but we took this place on knowing that we had a challenge to increase footfall and profits. It was part of the attraction for me.' Eddie looked at his brother, who was invested in running the pub but didn't have the same breadth of experience. 'It's not in dire straits, we know that, but the Star and Lantern is suffering like every other pub in England right now. I don't think the locals see that. Terry and Nola seem to have done a good job of pulling the wool over their eyes. But now we're the owners, we need to do something to keep people coming in.'

'Not upsetting them is likely a start,' Quinn shrugged.

'I hate it when you're right.'

'You love it when I'm right.' He pulled the plastic off the top of a carton of cans of Coke, ready to stack them in the fridge.

'I'll take that, you go deliver those flyers. The sooner we do it and get the residents of Heritage Cove on side, the better.'

Armed with the flyers that declared the Star and Lantern was having a bring-along-a-decoration drive as of now, Quinn set off to try and get the locals on board.

Even though it was daylight, the character of Heritage Cove shone through with its festive decorations strung across The Street, the shops with their window displays, the nativity scene that was being set up in a display cabinet out front of the little chapel.

He started at Tilly's Bits 'n' Pieces and asked her to pin up a flyer. She'd loved the idea and put one in her window right next to the door to capture the attention of arrivals. 'Who knows,' she said, 'maybe they won't want to part with anything from home and they'll come in here and buy something new.' It had made him think about his own collection – he didn't have one. He'd spent so many Christmases away and when he'd come home, he'd stayed with his parents or his brother, so there'd never been any need.

Quinn left Tilly's Bits 'n' Pieces feeling like he'd done his bit to help a local and vice versa. Next stop was Lottie in the convenience store, then it was on to Lucy at Lucy's Blacksmithing. He took a flyer to the chapel, the Little Waffle Shack, the inn, the ice-creamery. He braved the tea rooms after a few deep breaths and before Etna could get a word in, he told her the trees from the competing farm had been redirected. Then he thrust the flyer under her nose while he explained the tree at the pub and how it needed locals to help decorate it. He left the tea rooms feeling as though they'd achieved world peace getting her on side.

Quinn finished up the flyer drop at the Twist and Turn Bakery. Saving the best until last – or was it the one he was most apprehensive about? He honestly had no idea where he stood with Celeste. There was the initially good reaction the first day he saw her again, then there was the no-show at the pub opening, then the way she'd been when he bumped into her.

Quinn had almost reached the door to the bakery when he slipped on a patch of ice he hadn't seen. A patch of ice that somehow escaped being melted like all the other patches that had been around earlier when he looked out of the window in his room above the pub.

'You all right?' a woman on horseback asked when he righted himself before he went over onto his arse.

'Bum didn't hit the ground thankfully.' He looked up. 'It's Hazel, right?'

'It is. Good to see you again, Quinn.' She'd been in the pub briefly last night with her brother Arnold and her boyfriend Gus. 'I'd shake your hand but Weetabix here is a little nervous on the roads, so I need to keep a firm grip on the reins. He started when he saw you slip.'

'I won't pat him then.' The horse looked wary.

'I appreciate you not reaching out to him; he's new for us at the Heritage View Stables. He won't take long to feel like one of the locals, though, I'm sure.'

Stopping to chat to someone on the high street and being able to laugh off his near miss with hitting the ground made Quinn feel as though Weetabix might not be the only one who'd soon feel like he belonged in the Cove.

She dipped her head as if to say goodbye before riding off on the horse with eyes as deep brown as its coat. Weetabix. Cool name.

But now he'd recovered from an almost-fall and he had

nobody on horseback to talk to, it was time to go into the bakery. And he had no idea what to expect from Celeste this time. Perhaps their history was destined to stay just that: well and truly in its place.

It was Jade who saw him first. She waved over to him but didn't bother to ask what he wanted. She knew he wanted Celeste, who was laughing with a couple of kids sitting at the stools next to the little bit of counter against the wall. They were discussing the gingerbread men, talking about the coloured buttons on their coat, and he enjoyed the time she didn't spot him.

When she did, she changed demeanour and drew in her breath before smiling in his direction.

'Hey,' he opted for in the absence of knowing what else to say.

Jade swapped places with Celeste and talked with the kids while Celeste went behind the main counter with the glass-fronted display cabinets. He handed over the flyer.

She looked at it and smiled. 'This is a great idea.'

He explained how they'd redirected the other trees already. 'So you'll bring something in?'

'I expect this will be *very* popular.' She hadn't answered his question but he'd noted a brief flutter of thought process across her face before she spoke, as if realising that with only one local pub, it was either face him or stay home. And he figured in this sort of village, she was in the pub as much as the rest of them.

'Bring something along.' He did his best to keep his eyes on the flyer she was holding and not her or the way her jumper was just short enough to ride up and show her soft, pale skin at the top of the waistband of her jeans. He knew how that skin felt; he'd held her and run his fingers along it, kissed her enough times to remember the taste.

'I will.' She let her gaze fall from his. 'Now, let me put this on the door so customers see it as soon as they come in.' She went out back and returned with a piece of Blu-Tack to fix the flyer in place. 'If you give me another one, I'll pop it facing this way so if the customers miss it on their way in, they'll see it on their way out.'

'Genius idea, thank you.'

'Well, I do try my best.' And there she was: the Celeste he'd well and truly fallen for, the smile on porcelain skin so delicate, he'd sometimes run his fingertips down her cheeks and along her jaw softly, as though she might break beneath his touch. But he'd always had an inkling that she wasn't as fragile as he sometimes assumed. She looked at the flyer again and read: 'Bring-a-decoration... I really like it. I'll get in there quick before the branches are full.'

He almost said out loud how amazing that would be, how he couldn't wait to see her, but instead he thanked her again for helping and left her to it.

* * *

'All right, what's with you?' Eddie asked as Quinn came up from the cellar whistling, having changed one of the lager kegs. It was late afternoon and Quinn had been in a good mood ever since he'd come back from distributing the flyers.

'I'm allowed to whistle, aren't I? Call it Christmas joy, if you like.'

'It's unnerving.'

Quinn put his hands on Eddie's shoulders. 'It's all good. The pub is going well.'

'We've only just opened.' But his brother was smiling; perhaps his joy was infectious.

Quinn looked at the tree as Patricia, who worked at the tea

rooms, hung a snowman on one of the lowest branches. 'I can't believe how many people have already brought in ornaments.'

'Well, we all know how fast gossip moves in this village,' said Eddie quietly. 'Worked out well for us this time.'

Almost every person who'd come through the pub doors as of opening time had brought with them a decoration, sometimes more than one. The tree now had little elves with stripy stockings, reindeer, a fireplace decoration, china ornaments, sparkly ones, breakable ones – placed high up out of the way – and Etna had brought them an angel for the top. Having the tree and the crackling fire in the hearth not too far away as well as the dark beams in the room, the laughter on faces of locals who didn't look completely put out that the pub had changed hands, gave him a good feeling. They were settling into local life and it felt good.

It wasn't until almost 7 p.m. that Celeste came in. Quinn had done his best not to look at the clock, wondering when she'd turn up, but he'd be lying if he said it hadn't been in the back of his mind all day since he'd seen her. She'd changed out of her work clothes and into a short woollen dress that showed off long, endless legs he wasn't going to look at given he was seeing her in a professional capacity. And when the image of those legs across his on a lazy weekend morning the last time he'd been in the Cove popped into his head, he dampened it down by focusing instead on the spillage at the end of the bar before someone put their arm in it.

Celeste smiled in his direction after she hung a decoration on the tree, but the Star and Lantern was heaving so he didn't get much of a chance to try to get her attention after that. Or perhaps that was her intention.

Quinn had worked with the same guys in the navy for so long, it had been a while since he'd had to learn so many names

in a short space of time. He met Harvey again – he was with
Melissa and they ran a home renovations business and if he had
it right, they weren't Barney's kids but the man was like a dad to
both of them. He wasn't sure how that all worked, but he'd hear
about it some day, he was sure. Slowly, he and Eddie were
learning names of locals, relationships between them, what they
did for a living. It was a gradual process and he knew he'd fail a
quiz if they had one now, but he'd get there. Eddie was better at
it, he'd had more practice in the pub game, and more than once,
he had a quiet word in Quinn's ear when someone came up to
place an order, telling him who they were. Earlier, a man called
Kenneth had come to the bar and before he'd even opened his
mouth, Eddie had his fingertips on a pint glass and asked, 'Pint of
John Smith's today?' When Kenneth was settled with another
man on one of the tables to the middle of the room, Eddie had
told him that Kenneth had an allotment; he was close to Etna.
And then he'd reminded Quinn that Etna was Linc's auntie.
There were a lot of faces to remember, a lot of intricacies
between them.

'We're almost out of Prosecco.' Eddie stood up from peering
into the fridge behind the bar and opened the bottle he had. 'I
just had an order for three glasses. This isn't enough.'

'I'll go get it. Harvey is waiting for the Guinness on the
settling tray and I haven't taken payment yet.'

'Right you are.'

Quinn disappeared off to the cellar and grabbed another
couple of bottles of Prosecco from the bigger fridge there. And he
was soon back behind the bar, pouring the drink from the fresh
bottle into the third glass waiting.

When he looked up, it was Celeste who came to collect the
order. 'Which one's yours?' he asked.

'I don't think it matters, does it?'

He grinned. 'I meant which decoration on the tree.' He nodded in the direction of the Fraser fir. 'I saw you hang one.'

'I didn't want to miss out.' She stepped over to the tree and put her hand up to a tartan heart with a big red bow on top before she came back to her position at the bar. 'I have a set of three at home so thought why not put one in here. I hope we all get to see our decorations every year from now on.' She swallowed as if she'd just referenced the fact he was staying here when she hadn't meant to.

'Every year, we'll get them all out; we promise to look after them, although I heard Mrs Filligree brought in a furry cat decoration and she'd like it back after New Year for safe keeping.'

Celeste sniggered. 'That sounds like Mrs Filligree. Keep mine, I trust you with it.'

'Good to know.'

Her chest rose beneath the mulberry woollen dress. 'Peanuts.'

'Excuse me.'

'Dry roasted peanuts. Melissa wanted some.'

'Right.' He turned round and crouched down to get a packet for her and once she'd paid by card, she took two Proseccos before coming back for the other. 'Are you enjoying it? Here, I mean, working in the pub. Owning the pub.' He liked that she was stumbling over her words a bit; it meant she felt something for him.

'Yeah, it's different, something to get our teeth into.'

'I never realised this was what you wanted when you got out.'

'You make it sound like I was in prison.'

'Sorry.' She took a deep breath. 'I suppose we didn't talk much about the future.' And then she realised what they'd done rather than talking and a red flush promptly crept up her cheeks.

'We didn't know each other for long.' And they'd had better things to do than talk from what he remembered. 'Although…'

He leant across the bar to keep this between them. 'Long enough in some ways. I know, for instance, that you don't like stepping out of the shower unless there's a fluffy mat underfoot, that you think watermelon is too watery, and that you like having your arms and your neck tickled.'

A blush might have crept across his own face if he was that way inclined because as soon as he'd said it, they both realised Danny was standing right there and had heard every word.

'I'll get over to Melissa,' said Celeste. 'Hey, Danny. Thanks, Quinn.' And she scurried away.

He put a hand on his jaw. He couldn't pretend that hadn't just happened.

'Won't go any further, promise,' said Danny. 'Just came in to ask if you're happy with the tree.'

'Over the moon with it. And I'm glad we sorted the other misunderstanding; we felt terrible.'

'You've apologised too much already, no hard feelings,' he insisted.

The evening passed quickly and although he didn't get another chance to talk to Celeste, he was happy to at least have her in their pub at last.

And he fell into bed that night shattered but with a feeling that this was going to all work out.

10

Quinn might have been exhausted when he went to bed last night but for him, the problem when he went to sleep was that he had absolutely no control over what happened.

He was out of it.

But somebody was yelling at him.

Quinn's eyes flew open, he gasped for breath, he fought his brother's hold but got nowhere. He swore over and over again, his entire body tense, he had no idea where he was.

'Quinn, wake up, man!'

Where were they?

In a room somewhere – a different room.

It took a few more moments to realise it was his bedroom in the pub, in the village they'd moved to.

Eddie had his hands on his upper arms so that Quinn couldn't wrestle himself away.

And when Quinn's body finally slumped as he realised the safety of their home and Eddie let go, he swore.

Moments ago, in his nightmare, Quinn had been drowning in flood water. It was freezing cold, he couldn't see the shore. And then Celeste had been waving to him but he couldn't get to her. She was on a little island safe from the rising waters. She was smiling and calling out that she wasn't going to leave her bakery. He'd battled against the water but still couldn't get to her, he couldn't warn her that the water was coming, it was going to obliterate her bakery, take her with it. And so he kept swimming; he wouldn't give up, he couldn't. It had taken the power out of his arms and legs as he swam in vain, never getting closer, the water creeping up the sides of the island, spilling around the bakery. And as another wave crashed over him, he couldn't move; his arms wouldn't work.

And that's when he woke up to Eddie's hold.

It was a recurring nightmare. Although usually, it was a random stranger he needed to rescue. Never Celeste. Not until now.

Quinn sat on the edge of his bed, his breathing ragged, sweat across his chest.

Eddie came back in with a glass of water. 'Drink this.'

'Did I wake you up?'

'Dumb question. Drink.' He waited until Quinn did as he was told. 'And of course you did. Man, you're loud.' Eddie sat down next to him. 'You okay?'

'Yeah.' He glugged the rest of the water.

He wondered how much longer Eddie would tolerate it before he got annoyed with Quinn for not getting the help he likely needed. Stupid of him to assume that coming to a new place, doing a job that was entirely different, would erase everything he'd seen or done in over a decade. The night terrors like this one and sometimes nightmares that woke him up before he could disturb anyone else had taunted him at the end of his time in the navy, then when he'd been back on dry land full-time, and they'd never really gone away. Some nights, he got time off for good behaviour. But last night he hadn't.

Quinn was proud to serve his country; he'd buzzed on being in the navy and that buzz had seen him through things civilians could only imagine. He'd thought he'd seen the worst he ever would but without realising, those events had built up on top of one another as though, inside, his mind had been assembling a house of cards and all it took was one more on top to make it come tumbling down. It was a natural disaster that had been the final card to make it all fall apart around him. How was that even possible? It wasn't brutal, it wasn't in an unfamiliar country where threats were on a far bigger scale, it was mother nature unleashing, but it had been what finished Quinn and his navy career for good.

He'd never been the same after that.

But others had seen worse; they'd had worse happen to them. Some had lost limbs or their lives.

And here he was bleating about emotions and nightmares. Or rather he wasn't bleating, at least not to anyone other than Eddie. He'd resisted any suggestion to get more help because what kind of man needed that? He should be grateful he'd got out of the navy in one piece when others hadn't.

This was something he had to deal with. He had to get it together.

11

'Here you go, Lottie: three cranberry and brie focaccias.' At the bakery the day after she'd braved the pub and hung her decoration, Celeste handed the festive combos to Lottie.

Lottie put them all into the reusable bag she'd brought with her. 'Can you believe we're almost into December?'

'I know, Christmas is getting close.'

'The nativity outside the chapel is all set too. The Cove is almost ready. I assume I'll see you at the tree-lighting ceremony tonight?'

'I wouldn't miss it for the world. I haven't escaped from here all morning; is the tree in situ?'

Lottie laughed. 'You really have been busy. It's going up as we speak.' With a smile and a wave, she went on her way.

Celeste felt excitement mount. She must have missed the Mistletoe Gate Farm truck taking the tree along The Street to its final destination. On previous years, she'd had enough time to poke her head outside the door to the bakery and watch with great excitement either at the tree going past on the truck or as it was hoisted into position. The village Christmas tree, each year, was erected on the grass area behind the bus stop that ran from the roadside up to the Little Waffle Shack.

Jade had been feeding her Christmas cakes again and came out to the front of the bakery with a tray of mince pies to replenish what they'd sold already. 'I hope we'll see Quinn tonight.'

'Now why would you want to see him tonight?'

'Because he's a decent guy.'

'So is Eddie. And yet you didn't mention him.'

'Didn't I?' She smiled, trying to be innocent and failing miserably.

'Stop fishing,' Celeste scolded.

'I was doing nothing of the sort.' But one look from her sister and she admitted that of course that's what she was doing.

'We had a fling once. Neither of us planned on long term.'

'He wasn't living here then,' Jade said under her breath as she counted what rolls and loaves needed replenishing while Celeste turned her attention to a customer who had come in for three gingerbread men for her grandchildren.

When it was just the two of them again and Jade had pushed three more white bloomer loaves onto the appropriate shelf and stood up, she asked, 'Aren't you at least tempted? I mean any idiot can see the attraction between you two. I see the way you are when I ask about him, I clocked his reaction when he asked whether he'd be seeing you in the pub when I went in the first night without you.'

'Never going to happen,' she answered with an implied full stop.

'May I ask why not?' Jade followed her through to the kitchen as she rinsed out the cloth she'd used to wipe the counter and hung it on the hook behind the taps.

'You may ask… but I reserve the right not to answer. And right now, I'm going to take the mince pies up to the school.'

'Fine,' she sighed.

Celeste decided to walk and, after assuring Jade she wouldn't be too long, set off, catching a glimpse of the village tree being hauled into position. She smiled. Christmas really felt like it was on its way.

The forecast today had said sleet and possibly snow but as Celeste walked, there was no sign of either and so, wrapped up against the cold, she enjoyed the fresh air. On her way from the school back to the bakery, she spotted Melissa on the bend before the pub. She looked like she was heading in the direction of Barney's place.

Celeste called out Melissa's name but Melissa was in a world of her own and hadn't heard her, so Celeste crossed over to catch up with her friend.

'Hey,' Melissa smiled.

'Do we have an expected date for Barney's return home yet?'

'Not yet.' Melissa indicated the little cardboard box she was carrying. 'I need to get these to Lois.'

'I'll walk with you.'

Melissa led the way. It wasn't much further to the cottage Barney and Lois shared.

'So, what's in the box?' Melissa hadn't elaborated. She was usually up for a good chat but today, she seemed away with the fairies.

'It's a treat from the Little Waffle Shack. Daniel insisted on getting them to Barney if he isn't going to be at the tree-lighting ceremony tonight.'

'That's kind of him. What flavour?'

'Fresh waffles dusted with icing sugar and a small pot of

chocolate sauce plus another with strawberries. No ice-cream for obvious reasons but these will still be good cold. And at least he won't be missing out.'

'He won't get a mulled wine.'

'No, he was grumpy about that when I saw him this morning. But he loved hearing about the tree in the pub and the fact we've all been decorating it between us. And Lois will be with him this evening; she'll take the waffles and we'll do FaceTime for the ceremony.'

When they reached the cottage gate, they passed through and knocked on the front door. Lois, who was on the phone, made an apologetic face but Melissa assured her it was okay, passed over the waffles and the girls left her to it.

They walked back towards the village. 'Work busy for you and Harvey?' Celeste was keen to get her friend talking some more, no matter what it was about. Maybe then she might confide what was bothering her.

'Steady, which is great.' Harvey was the hands-on part of their home renovations business with his experience in loft conversions and Melissa was a whizz with interior design. 'January is shaping up to be really busy. You know what it's like – New Year means new projects for a lot of people.'

'You can work your magic for them,' she agreed, 'transform the drabbest of places into something colourful.'

'I guess I can.' But her smile barely reached a curve before it was gone, just like that.

'You still enjoying it?'

'Of course. And the bakery? You're busy too?' Melissa pulled her coat a bit tighter around herself as they approached the bend that would take them on to The Street. Dark clouds scudded overhead with the threat of wetter weather lurking.

It was such a staccato conversation that Celeste knew she should probably abandon it but she wasn't giving up that easily. 'Very. I escaped for a walk after delivering to the school. Need to make sure I do that, Jade too, otherwise we'd rarely see daylight.' She looked up at the sky with a silent prayer that dismal weather would hold off until they'd at least seen the tree on the green burst into glorious colour after the countdown this evening.

'I hope this weather holds off,' said Melissa.

'I was just thinking the same myself.'

'Actually, I might leave you here.' Melissa pointed down the road Celeste had come up earlier. 'I'll head that way. I need a bit more fresh air, you know.'

She did, she'd said as much moments ago. 'I do know, but...' She hooked her arm through Melissa's. 'I also know that you need a friend.'

And at Melissa's surprise, she ushered them both across the road when the coast was clear. 'We're going to the pub and you're going to talk. Because something tells me you need to.'

Cosied up in the Star and Lantern, Celeste couldn't help noticing Quinn as she placed the order at the bar with Eddie. In a deep green T-shirt hugging his biceps and with the smile that came her way when he looked up, she wished things could've been different.

Melissa was tasked with giving updates on Barney but once they were alone, she said, 'You're right; I do have something on my mind.'

Conversation paused when they received the swift delivery of chips in a basket from Benjamin, along with the little pot of ketchup on the side.

'So talk to me.'

Melissa bit into a chip and gasped as the steam burst out.

'Think I'll wait for them to cool,' Celeste laughed. 'And that was a drastic step to avoid talking to me.'

'These chips should come with a government warning, Benjamin!' Melissa called across to the table where he was piling up empty plates.

'Last customers I had complained they were cold,' he batted back, the pile of plates now in his arms. 'What would you rather?' He winked and went on his way.

When Eddie picked up on the conversation and came to check whether everything was okay with the food, the girls just laughed and told him they'd been teasing Benjamin. 'You get used to it,' Celeste said before he went back behind the bar to where his brother had been serving a customer but looked up and their way again.

Celeste turned her attention away from Quinn, back to Melissa and the chips. 'Let's leave them five minutes; it'll give you a chance to talk.'

Melissa seemed lost without something in her hands and instantly moved her glass in front of her to wrap both palms around it. 'This will take longer than five minutes. Don't you have to get back to the bakery?'

'I do but Jade and I do this regularly. We have to for our sanity so when one can cope on their own for an hour or two, the other gets some time out. Works both ways. And I've texted her; she knows to call or message if she's desperate, otherwise I'll head back in half an hour. That gives us plenty of time.'

Melissa's eyes misted over. 'Something happened to me the week before the party.' She looked down in her lap. 'I had a miscarriage.'

'Oh, Melissa—'

'And it wasn't my first. That's three, and counting.'

'I'm so sorry. I wish you'd told me, said something.'

'Nobody else knows other than me and Harvey.' She looked

around to ensure they were alone but there were only a few stragglers who'd been asking after Barney on the table right in the corner and by the back door, and another two men enjoying a pint near the Christmas tree that was quite the conversation starter now it had ornaments from the locals.

'That's an enormous burden to be carrying yourself, even with Harvey.'

Melissa shrugged. 'I think I thought if we just kept trying, it would happen, then I could share happy news and the bad news would pale into the background. I think it's making me even more desperate to conceive, having it go wrong three times already. It feels like I'm running out of time.'

'How does Harvey feel about it all?'

'Worried. About me.'

'I'll bet.' They were love's young dream. And despite a separation for a while when Melissa left the Cove, nothing could keep them apart these days.

'How long do you think we keep trying?'

'It's not something I've had experience with; I can't advise you. Have you talked with your doctor?'

'They're suggesting some tests to see what's going on.'

'It might be reassuring.'

Melissa put her head in her hands. 'I'm not sure I want to go through all that. Maybe this just isn't meant to be for us.'

'Does Harvey want to go through the investigations?'

'He says he'll do what I want to do.'

Celeste already knew the answer but still asked, 'Have you talked to Barney about it?'

She'd been about to pick up a chip and have another go. A healthy appetite was a good sign when she was so clearly stressed out. 'How can I? He's got enough going on and I don't want him to worry, to make him stressed.'

'He's worried anyway.'

Melissa's gaze locked with Celeste's. 'He told you that?'

'He knows you; he knows something's up.' She braved taking a chip, dipping it in sauce and putting it tentatively in her mouth.

On a sigh, Melissa admitted, 'You know, I thought we were hiding it well.'

'Not much gets past Barney.'

'Well, I can't talk to him about it when he's in hospital. So for now, business as usual; let's get him home and well first. It'll give me time to sort my own feelings too.'

'Perhaps talking to Barney when he's still in the hospital might be the best thing for the both of you.'

It was at least three chips later and, more than that, many surreptitious glances over from Quinn as the girls sat and chatted that Melissa asked, 'You ever think about it?'

'What?'

'A family, settling down, kids, the whole package.'

'I think there are many ways to have the whole package.' She dragged her chip through ketchup. 'Everyone's package is different.'

Melissa sniggered. 'Is that right?'

'Don't be rude.' But she was laughing too and glad Melissa could at least smile. What she was going through wasn't easy.

'So, have you?'

'I think everyone in the Cove knows me well. I'm married to my business; my business is my baby. For me, it's enough.'

'So no kids, but what about a man?' Melissa might be upset but she wasn't stupid. 'You've been checking out our new pub talent ever since you got here.'

'I have not!' But even to her ears, she was a little too defensive.

'I saw you, looking at Eddie.' She turned, saw the boys behind the bar, only Quinn looking this way. 'Ah, or is it Quinn?'

'Keep your voice down. There's nothing going on.' She looked at her friend. 'At least not any more.'

Melissa gasped. She was down, unhappy, with worries; Celeste thought she might as well brighten her day and so gave her the history in a nutshell.

'Well, I never. You and Quinn.' Eyebrows raised, before Benjamin came to collect their empty bowl, she added, 'Won't say a word, but I approve. He's gorgeous. I think round two is definitely in order.'

Celeste shook her head. 'No, round two will never happen.'

Melissa scrunched her nose. 'Pity, he looks like a bit of a catch.'

He was. If he'd visited like before, on leave from the navy, only here for a short time then Celeste was 99 per cent sure round two would have happened. But him moving here on a permanent basis changed everything.

Melissa excused herself to go to the bathroom and Celeste's eyes wandered over to Quinn, who'd come closer to wipe the tables. And it wasn't long before he came over to theirs.

She smiled, trying to rid her mind of the way his chest and arms looked in his T-shirt and the memories of round one that her conversation with Melissa had conjured up. There was no denying it; the guy was still physically fit, no matter that he'd left the navy and changed career.

'Good to see you in here again so soon.' He was hovering at her table and in the corner of her eye, Celeste saw Melissa pause on her way back from the bathrooms so she could talk to Danny and Heather from Mistletoe Gate Farm.

Eddie called over to Quinn. 'Any idea where we put this?' He had a bag of what looked like mistletoe poking out of the top.

Quinn reluctantly left Melissa's side and went over. And from where she sat, Celeste deduced that the bag was complimentary.

'You'll need it replacing after a few days,' Danny instructed, 'won't last long with the heat in here, but customers love it; we'll bring in more. We've got plenty to spare.' It seemed the locals weren't done with decorating the pub for Christmas. And Eddie didn't seem to have any clue where to put it.

Melissa pointed out the hooks at each side of the bar, up high. 'Terry usually puts some there.'

'Won't customers be kissing and in the way of punters getting more drinks?' Eddie asked.

Celeste began to laugh and called over to Eddie, 'It's not a full-on kissing fest; Heritage Cove can behave itself over Christmas, and this is a family pub, after all.' She felt her cheeks colour when Quinn looked her way and suggested he might well be thinking otherwise about the mistletoe.

Eddie put some on one of the hooks, Quinn stretched up to put more on the other. Benjamin pointed out the archway that led through to the bathrooms and suggested they have it there, then another piece could hang near the back door. 'But not too close to the dartboard,' Benjamin instructed before Quinn hung it on the closest hook there. 'We don't want potential lovers getting injured. And do not let Celeste play darts. Not unsupervised, anyway.'

Celeste lifted her coat from where it was folded on the seat next to her. 'Very funny, thank you, Benjamin.' She looked at Quinn, thinking of the way she'd thrown the pastry at him the first time they met, and told him, 'I'm a useless aim.'

Quinn said softly, 'I already know that but in my case, it worked in my favour.'

Before anyone could pry with awkward questions, Celeste announced it was time for her to get back to the bakery and Melissa grabbed her own bag and coat from where they'd been sitting.

'Are you working today?' Celeste asked her as the men left them to it.

'I am and I like keeping busy; keeps my mind off things. I'm meeting Harvey at a property in an hour. Don't start worrying about me because of what I told you.'

'Would I do that?'

'Yes, because you're a good friend. But I'm okay. And honestly, thank you for making me talk, I really appreciate you listening.'

'Any time.'

'I have a lot of thinking to do.' She began to grin before she leaned a bit closer. 'And so do you. The way Quinn keeps eyeing you up, I'm pretty sure he wouldn't mind catching you under the mistletoe as soon as he can.'

'I should never have told you,' she batted back, buttoning her coat.

'Yes, you should; I needed cheering up and that did it.'

Celeste pulled on her gloves and peeked out at the skies beyond the rear doors to the pub. 'Please, weather, hold off before you turn. Let us get the tree-lighting ceremony done before the sleet, rain or whatever the weather gods have in store.'

'I'll second that,' said Benjamin, coming up behind them to look outside for himself.

'Looking forward to a mulled wine already,' Celeste smiled at him. 'Who's doing the cart tonight?' Benjamin did the recipe for mulled wine – it was known locally as the best – but he didn't run the cart on the green space behind the bus stop. Instead, he was usually able to enjoy the evening and Terry and Nola had had someone else man the cart with the spicy beverage.

Benjamin called over to where Quinn was setting a freshly pulled pint on top of the bar. 'Who's doing the mulled wine cart tonight?'

Quinn came over to them once his customer was sorted.

'What mulled wine cart?' He had a beer towel and wiped manly hands on the material. Celeste knew what those hands felt like and it sent shivers right through her thinking about his touch.

'The mulled wine cart that the pub puts on for the tree lighting every year,' said Melissa, as if it should be obvious.

'Did you know about this?' Quinn asked Eddie who came over to join them.

'Know about what?'

Benjamin explained the mulled wine cart and Eddie cursed. 'Terry didn't mention it. At least I don't remember him saying. And we'd need a temporary events notice to do that. Which we don't have. And which we can only get with more time.'

'No mulled wine? It's a tradition. People like a hot drink, adds to the atmosphere.' Celeste felt for the new pub owners because locals weren't going to like this. It was another mark against them.

'All right, don't rub it in.' A muscle in Quinn's jaw clenched.

'Sorry, didn't mean to go on.'

Quinn put a hand on her arm and even through her coat, she wasn't prepared for the closeness. 'No, I'm sorry. I shouldn't bite your head off.' He was watching his brother, who was talking with Benjamin near the bar. 'I thought we were done with upsetting people, that's all, at least for a while.'

'The tree decorations in here have been a real hit; I'm sure people will understand.'

'Will they?'

She wasn't sure, despite her words of encouragement. 'I need to get back to the bakery. But I'll see you soon.'

And as Celeste and Melissa left the pub, Celeste caught one more glimpse of Quinn and realised that much as she'd wished this was a fleeting visit at the start so they could've had a repeat of last time, the more she saw him and thought about him here, the more she wanted everything to go right for him.

And that meant she cared. Maybe a little too much.

12

The fifty-foot Norway spruce from Mistletoe Gate Farm had the crowds on the green in the village mesmerised. Celeste had seen it earlier when she delivered the mince pies to the school, she'd seen it again on her way back to work, but that was nothing compared to what it looked like now in the dark, with the crowds and their excitement. She held her niece Phoebe tight in her arms while her sister took her turn to eat her waffles.

'Melissa.' Jade waved an arm over at Melissa making her way onto the green space, hand in hand with Harvey, and they turned in their direction.

Melissa fussed over Phoebe first and Celeste's heart went out to her for what she was going through. 'You okay?' Celeste asked discreetly.

Melissa nodded and leaned into Harvey.

'Don't get too comfortable,' Harvey warned, putting a kiss on his wife's lips. He held the iPad aloft. 'Time to connect with Barney; he hates that he isn't here.'

A collective sound of sympathy from the group accompanied Harvey connecting to Lois's iPad.

'I hope this is allowed,' Melissa wondered, 'I'm worried the nurses will ban the iPad.'

'Unlikely,' Harvey assured them all, 'I expect Barney has charmed his way into all of their hearts and could get away with anything.'

And then there he was, the man himself, smiling at them from his hospital bed. And if Celeste wasn't mistaken, with a tear in his eye as they all crowded together to say hello. Him in stripy pyjamas, them bundled up in coats, hats and scarves, their cheeks rosy red against the cold.

'Turn me round, I need to see the tree,' Barney begged after greeting Tilly, who'd just joined them. Lois was at his side, clutching his arm as she leaned in against him on the hospital bed.

Harvey flipped the camera around and slowly panned the green space to take in the crowds, the tree, the waffle shack at the top, Jade and Linc finishing their waffles, and then all the way back around to settle on the tree.

'Are you ready for this, Phoebe?' Celeste whispered to her niece. 'We get to count from ten down to zero and then the tree will have all the lights.'

Phoebe seemed awestruck, looking around to take it all in.

And then there was an ear-piercing squeal from the microphone that let the crowds know someone was about to talk and sure enough, it was Danny Doyle at the foot of the tree on the little makeshift stage, except this year his introduction was brief before he handed over to his daughter, Charlotte. It was well known that it was she who would eventually take over Mistletoe Gate Farm.

After introductions from Charlotte and wishes for a wonderful festive season in the village, the countdown began and as they reached the moment the lights powered up from the bottom to the top of the tree, a big cheer erupted. Everyone had a beaming smile on their face, the sheer joy of the season, and Celeste squeezed a giggling Phoebe a little tighter. She was already clapping her hands together with glee. She might not have been able to do the countdown but she knew the deal already. This was special.

Tilly asked Jade, 'Have you taken Phoebe to choose your tree yet?'

Phoebe, on hearing her name, smiled, her chubby hand against Celeste's cheek.

'That's a job for the weekend.'

'You don't need to shovel it in,' Celeste assured Jade, as she ate fast. 'You'll give yourself indigestion.'

But Jade was having none of it and popped the last of the waffles into her mouth.

Celeste's waffles were waiting, balanced on top of the sturdy changing bag in front of them. Phoebe had eaten before she came out but Linc gave her a little bite of waffle with icing sugar dusting, the last of his, and she seemed happy.

'Just need a wipe for my hands,' said Jade, 'and I'll take my daughter back.' Linc pulled a packet out from his back pocket. They were a well-versed duo when it came to parenting.

'The ice-cream on my waffles was sen-sa-tion-al.' Jade wiped at her fingers. 'Christmas cake crunch from Zara's ice-creamery. I'm totally going to buy a tub of it for home.' She gave her mouth a little wipe too.

'Who's this little one?' A voice Celeste recognised came from beside her shoulder.

She turned to come face to face with Quinn, who gave Phoebe a smile, and Phoebe responded by reaching out a hand to him. Quinn took it and made her giggle by giving it a little high-five action.

'Why aren't you at the pub?'

He looked around at the crowds. 'Funnily enough, we don't have many customers.' He greeted Jade as Jade took Phoebe from Celeste's arms.

'Phoebe is my niece,' Celeste explained and then, glad of something to distract herself, bent down to get her portion of waffles with cranberry and icing sugar topping. 'We were on shifts for eating. It's my turn now.'

He looked good with his coat collar turned up against the cold, skimming his jaw. He blew into his hands to warm them.

After her first bite of waffle and an involuntary shiver, she admitted, 'Phoebe is like a little portable radiator. Amazing how you feel the cold when you hand her back.'

Laughter rumbled up as he looked over at her niece again. 'She's a cute kid.'

Celeste was well aware of Jade and Linc's tactful – or was it tactless? – moving away from them both. She felt self-conscious eating the waffles now she had an audience, an attentive one at that. 'It's a good turnout,' she said, hoping he'd watch the crowds rather than her.

He obliged and looked at the tree, the lights, the people around them laughing and full of seasonal joy. 'It's a stunning tree; Mistletoe Gate Farm grows them well.' And then his lips twisted as though he was worrying. 'How many people have commented on the lack of mulled wine cart?'

She was glad her mouth was full so she could put it tactfully when she finally answered, 'A few, not too many.'

'It was an oversight – either by ourselves or Terry and Nola doing the handover. I suppose Christmas wasn't really the best time to take over but both parties wanted to move quickly on it and it was a case of getting on with it.'

'I'm sure people will understand.'

He beamed a smile her way, one that reminded her of the first day they met in her bakery. 'I hope they will and that's why I'm here. I'm here to spread the word.' And with that he cupped his hands around his mouth as he called out, 'Mulled wine is on special this evening at the Star and Lantern – buy one get one free!'

Celeste chuckled as more than one passer-by nudged whoever they were with, some thanked him, others upped their pace down the green, presumably to head in the direction of the pub quick smart.

Celeste was halfway through the waffles already. 'Got to hand it to you, that's a great idea.'

'We'll be prepared next year,' he said, holding her gaze. 'Promise.'

Next year. The thought had her catch her breath.

She shoved more waffle into her mouth and wished he wasn't watching her so intently. 'You really should get some of these,' she managed as soon as she was able.

'You seem to be enjoying them.' He was still watching her. 'I'll grab some another time, see what all the fuss is about.'

'You won't regret it.'

He turned to look up at the waffle shack. 'Help me out again – am I right that Daniel runs the waffle shack and he's dating Lucy, the blacksmith?'

'That's right.' She could see Lucy handing out portions of waffles. Before the countdown for the tree lighting, she'd seen Lucy up there with her apron on, roped in to help out on what was always a hectic night for Daniel and the waffle shack. He'd come out and stood with his arm around her shoulder as they embraced the evening with the rest of the villagers.

Quinn looked around at the delight on the faces of residents, some out-of-towners too, but not many. 'Eddie was all right with me ducking out to see this while I spread the word about mulled wine at the pub. I think he's calling it market research to see whether it's really worth having a cart next year. The village where he had a pub before had a tree-lighting ceremony one year and only a dozen or so people showed up.'

'Definitely not the case here.'

'I can see that and I will of course report back.' And now he was looking at her again as she licked her thumb to get rid of the stickiness that lingered from her waffles. She stopped when his gaze dropped from her eyes to her lips.

But within seconds, he looked up and extended a palm out into the air.

She was about to ask what he was doing when she realised the weather had decided it was time to change things up a little. And she had a hat on that would keep her dry from a light shower but not much else. 'Looks like this was timed well.'

'Yeah, and it could've been worse; the forecast was terrible.'

And then it was as though their conversation gave the skies up above permission to do whatever they wanted. The pitter-patter of delicate raindrops turned very quickly into a downpour that necessitated an umbrella rather than just a woolly hat and crowds began to disperse up to the waffle shack, down the green to home or to the pub.

They were all laughing as they gathered the rubbish, Phoebe's bags, Harvey shoved the iPad inside his jacket and they all made a run for it together.

A lot of them had headed for the pub and the reality of running alongside Quinn only really hit when they glanced sideways at one another and shared a look that said they were so much more than two locals who were on friendly terms.

They bundled inside the front door of the Star and Lantern and into the dry. They weren't the first and Quinn took off his coat. 'That's me back to work. Good to see you tonight.' He said it so softly into her ear that only Celeste heard and it sent a ripple through her insides before he left her with everyone else.

The mulled wine, made to Benjamin's recipe, was a dream. Celeste hadn't realised how cold you could get from a little bit of rain and she stood close to the fire, given Jade and Linc had managed to commandeer the table closest to there. They weren't going to stay long because they wanted to get Phoebe down but both Linc and Jade had wanted to finish off the evening in the Star and Lantern because Harvey suggested he might try to get Barney back on FaceTime.

'He making an appearance soon?' Linc asked Melissa when she came back from the ladies. Phoebe was getting fractious and wouldn't even go to Celeste; the variety usually worked but not tonight.

'He and Lois weren't picking up before.' Melissa frowned. 'Let me go and ask Harvey.' She went up to the bar but was soon back to tell them that neither Barney nor Lois were answering.

'I'm sure it's just a bit late or the nurses don't like it,' Celeste assured her because she could see Melissa was worrying. 'Don't stress, I'm sure he's fine.'

'I might send Lois a message.'

'Let's get this one home, Linc.' Jade zipped up the bag from which she'd taken a rattle and then a cuddly toy, neither of them helpful. 'The mulled wine was very good, but this young lady can't appreciate it yet and she is our boss.'

Phoebe didn't even want a hug from Celeste and turned into Linc's chest when Celeste tried to say goodbye. Celeste stroked her hair. 'See you soon, little one.'

Etna came over to say farewell too. As Linc's auntie, she was besotted by Phoebe but she got the same reception as Celeste.

'Grumpy,' said Jade, 'which is what I'll be if she doesn't sleep tonight.'

'That little girl has a very special place in my heart,' Etna said once they went on their way. She positioned her woolly hat on the ear of the chair nearest the fire in the hope it might dry. 'Would you like another mulled wine? I'm going for a second.' She looked full of mischief. 'I think it'll sleet by the end of the night; perhaps we'll have one of those lock-in things.'

Celeste laughed. 'Maybe. And thanks for the offer, but I'm good with just the one. Early start at the bakery for me.'

'You work too hard. Don't forget to have a life.'

'I could tell you the same; you work as hard as I do.'

'But I'm not in my prime; you are.'

'She has a life,' said Lucy, coming to her side and her defence.

'Lucy, you're here!' Celeste gave her friend a hug. 'You've left Daniel at the shack on his own?'

'Course not, Brianna and Troy are both working tonight and it's quietened down now the tree lighting is done. The weather is sending everyone home. Or in here. Are you off or staying for a while?'

She had been about to finish her mulled wine and get going herself but with Etna telling her to make sure she had a life, perhaps she should prove that she already had one. And besides, with Quinn looking over every now and then, it was all too tempting to stay. Because as much as she was resisting getting involved again, she couldn't deny the feelings slowly burning away inside of her.

And that meant one of them was going to get hurt.

13

It had been a busy few days at the pub since the tree lighting, and now they were into December, Christmas was fast approaching. The pub was looking festive with the tree and copious amounts of mistletoe and the boys both felt as though they were beginning to find their feet. They'd been talking strategy too, discussing the events they could hold come the start of the New Year, ways to draw in greater footfall. They were keen not to step on any more toes but at the same time, they didn't want to wait too long to implement changes.

As usual, Quinn had woken up early this morning, well before the sun had even contemplated coming up. If the night terrors or the nightmares came, he had a disturbed night which sometimes meant he was later to crawl out of bed, but last night, he'd been gifted with a long stretch of sleep, blessing him with more energy for a decent workout.

Fitness for the navy was full-on, both before he joined and again when he was a fully-fledged part of it. On board the ship, they'd done drills, circuits, weights, and when he'd left that world, he'd needed the mental escape physical exertion provided. He started off with a run around some of the undiscovered parts of the Cove. He went down The Street and noticed a low glow of the light in the bakery but didn't look in to see whether Celeste was there, even though he was tempted. He carried on around the bend, past the guesthouse and then ran around the back of the village along the bridleway surrounded by countryside with green as far as the eye could see. It was as though he was in the middle of nowhere and yet the Cove wasn't that far away at all. He dodged mud still lurking from the wet weather they'd had, the lamp fixed to his cap lighting the way just enough, although some of the ground had begun to harden given the plummeting temperatures. He wouldn't come this way if it got much colder or running on hard-packed dirt could risk rolling an ankle, and he might struggle to be discovered, especially at this hour of the day.

Quinn emerged from the bridleway and countryside, out of the wind for a while as he was sheltered by houses along the street. He passed the veterinary practice, waved at Gus who was starting work as the sun came up, but he wasn't ready to stop just yet and so rather than head back towards the pub, he kept going. He'd seen the cove itself once before with Celeste and thought he might remember how to get there. And after a wrong turn at the chapel, following the path to the cemetery behind, he remembered that it was the track next to that that he needed to take.

He ran all the way to the very end of the track and paused to take in the view. Spectacular.

He had a good feeling about this village. A very good feeling.

The spray from the sea didn't quite reach him all the way up here but he could smell it, the salty tang, the draw of its freshness that soon saw him heading carefully down the path and jumping off the steps at the end onto the sand with a sense of freedom. He ran towards the ocean's edge, onto the hard-packed sand all the way along, doing sprints every other minute. He leapt over the breakwaters in one direction and again on his way back and when he reached the cove, the wine-glass-shaped body of water that was a secret from hardy tourists who preferred the beach further around, he stood, hands on hips, facing out to the sea.

The sea had been a huge part of his life for years. He took in the rolling waves, their size governed by the wind, as they rose up before thundering into shore, the way the water fizzed and retreated back after it had shown off its menace. The sea was a volatile beast. Some days on board a ship had been calm, serene despite the job they were doing. The sun had come out, there'd been a camaraderie amongst the crew, laughter, joking at the same time as the seriousness as they pulled together in one team with no two days the same. On other days, the oceans had swelled and moaned with a mind of their own, their looming presence, coupled with impending threats in the waters they were trying to protect, a reminder of how real it all was.

Despite its volatility, Quinn had a sort of affinity with the sea. But it had the power to swallow you whole if you let it and he knew of men who'd never got themselves to a good place. They'd walked into the waves and never come out again. It would be a nice way to go, wouldn't it? Surrounded by nature, beauty, water where he felt so much peace when he let himself.

Then again, perhaps it wouldn't. And he wasn't in that place. He was one of the lucky ones, his thoughts had never gone so low and he recognised he still had a life to live. He just needed to keep putting one foot in front of the other. Order, rules, routines, running, pummelling the punch bag at the gym helped keep his mind as clear as it could be; it let him work off frustrations, anxiety that came out of nowhere, anger that sneaked up on him. He wasn't angry at anyone in particular either, only himself for not being in control when memories plagued him.

Some nights, even when he didn't have the nightmares or night terrors, he'd still find it hard to sleep and would get out of bed and do push-ups, as many as he could until he literally couldn't lift his body weight from the floor. Sit-ups worked too until his abs were screaming at him to stop, when he'd crawl back into bed and close his eyes, hoping it would work and the intrusive thoughts would stay the hell away.

This run today was one way to keep his head and his life in check.

And yet none of that had made him wobble, had ever made him want to walk away. Or perhaps it had; perhaps he hadn't seen it coming like an enemy managing to creep up on him and he hadn't realised until it was too late.

He moved so that his trainers were on the cusp of getting wet as the waves crept tantalisingly close. Standing here at the water's edge now, it was as though his brain dipped into his memory bank and plucked out the event he saw as his downfall, the one that had really finished him.

He closed his eyes, inhaled the salty air, let the spray carried on the wind whip against his face in the same way as thoughts of that day lashed against him and kept on doing so no matter how much he wanted them to stop. He was so close to the edge of the water, he wanted it to have one last go at him, finish it once and for all, then let him move on, let him be the man he wanted to be. He felt as though he was losing the fight, as though no matter how many days and nights passed, he'd never defeat the enemy.

And then something tugged his arm and he lurched from his thoughts, spinning round.

Celeste opened her mouth to say something but no words came. He'd almost hit out, his mind somewhere else, ready to defend, to protect, his body prepared for danger.

And he'd scared the living daylights out of her.

He stepped back from the water's edge. Swore. 'I'm sorry.'

Her eyes locked with his. 'You're shivering.'

He hadn't realised and tried his best to hold it together, pretend this was nothing out of the ordinary. 'Post-run shiver, cooled down too quick.' It was the only thing he could think of. Anything else sounded lame.

'It's freezing.'

She was right, it was damn cold. And out of his trance, he felt it. He needed another layer or to bolt for another mile or so, although his heart rate was already up there as though he had. 'What are you doing down here?'

'Early morning walk, needed the fresh air.'

'You come down here for fun?'

'It's beautiful no matter the season. Quinn—'

He kept the forced smile. 'Sure is. But it's cold so I'll run up to the top, that'll do me.'

'Quinn!' she called after him, but he'd already left. He didn't want to talk; he didn't want to try to explain the chaos whirling its way through his mind.

When Quinn got back to the Star and Lantern, he kept his head down. Eddie was busy taking a delivery so he called over an absent-minded 'hey' and headed straight for the shower.

As he stood in the shower, the water running over his hair and down his face so he couldn't see, he cursed loudly and whacked his hand against the tiles. One minute, he'd felt as though this fresh start was working, the next he felt as though he hadn't moved on at all.

He'd been okay this morning after a decent sleep but the mere act of looking out at the churning waves, the greying skies, had taken his head to a very different place, hypnotising him and taking his mind somewhere else entirely. His mind had shifted back to that day, the day he hadn't been able to save someone, the sheer devastation at the loss of life. He'd seen it time and time again; it was part of his job the way an accountant dealt with spreadsheets, the way a publican pulled pint after a pint. He'd always dealt with it until that day. Until he hadn't been able to handle it any more.

He rubbed his hair rigorously after the shower, his body quick enough. He often forgot he had the luxury of being able to take his time. It was the same with his bedroom. Standards on board were strict and he hadn't left those behind – in here, nothing was out of place, not a discarded sock or the corner of the duvet left upturned, everything pristine and orderly, the way he needed it to be.

'You were out a while this morning.' Eddie emerged from the cellar as Quinn came down from the top floor. He was cradling a cardboard tray of soft drinks to put in the chiller cabinet behind the bar.

'I went for a long run.' His brother didn't need to hear what had happened on the beach. 'I ran along the sand and finished at the cove itself.'

Eddie ripped open the plastic covering from the top of the tray and Quinn took over filling the chiller cabinet, seeing as Eddie was the one who dealt with most of the admin and paperwork. It was an arrangement that suited them both well.

Quinn took a stock delivery which Eddie checked and then he restocked crisps, popcorn, nuts and put the surplus in the huge cupboard down beside the cellar. There was a second delivery for the kitchens which Benjamin was on hand to deal with after Quinn had checked everything that had been ordered was there.

'We almost ready?' Eddie had finished inventory on the laptop.

'Almost.'

'Time for a coffee, don't you think?'

Benjamin emerged from the kitchen. 'I'll make it in two minutes, just got to take another delivery.' He headed to the front of the pub.

'He probably doesn't want us getting in his way,' Eddie laughed.

Quinn began taking the chairs off tables and turning them up the right way. He'd done three tables when Benjamin came through, followed by Celeste. That explained the delivery – her and the big box containing loaves.

Quinn managed a smile in her direction, uncomfortable at the way he'd run away from her on the beach earlier.

Eddie addressed Celeste. 'I might want to talk to you at some point about possible business apart from just the loaves as and when our chef needs them.'

'I'm not sure I follow,' said Celeste.

Eddie used one hand to flip a chair off the table closest to them and set it down for Celeste, another for him. 'We might consider doing baked goods and lighter snacks as well as some of the menu Benjamin offers. It's only a thought at the moment but if we do it, it might be easier to do a deal with your bakery direct rather than add to Benjamin's workload.'

Quinn wished he hadn't addressed this just yet and he was right to think that when Celeste said, 'It sounds good in theory, but you have to remember you're just one business in Heritage Cove.' She spoke pleasantly, clearly trying to be tactful. 'There's also the waffle shack, the tea rooms and both of those do your more casual snacks during the day. Villagers have always been quite clear on the distinctions. I know it sounds dramatic, but...'

'It's the way things are,' Eddie said for her.

She nodded. 'This is your business, but it might just be a good idea to run any new ideas by the locals. It might save ruffling any feathers.'

Eddie's reaction told Quinn his brother was thinking a few unchoice words about having to ask permission to make changes, but he shot his brother a look. They were the new ones here; the last thing they wanted to do was offend and drive customers away when their aim was to do the opposite.

'I'm sure we'll sort something out; we won't rush into anything.' Eddie had a definite charisma and a way of making people feel at ease, even though he'd just floated the idea that he was going to upset a community. 'We're finding our feet, as it were.' When someone else knocked at the front door to the pub, Eddie went off to see who it was.

Quinn went over to Celeste. 'We're just trying to find ways to make the pub work and work well. He knows he needs to tread carefully. We've already had the coffee machine warning.' She matched his smile, which was a relief. He felt awkward as it was. 'The machine is still here; we're not returning it, we'll use it ourselves. Fancy a coffee?' It was the least he wanted to do after running off like that this morning. 'I can make it look unappealing if that helps, you know, in case someone else was to come in and think we were stepping on the toes of local businesses.'

'Please don't, I've got time and I'll take a decent coffee if it's all the same with you. Just don't tell Etna.'

'Promise.' Eddie had come back with a couple more boxes and headed out back with them.

Quinn made for the kitchen but had a word with Eddie first. 'I offered Celeste a cup of coffee; you don't mind, do you?'

'I don't mind. But I wouldn't let anyone in the Cove know you're doing it; you'll be in trouble unless it's Nescafé.'

'We'll keep it quiet.'

'And I'm not your boss, Quinn.' He slapped a hand to his brother's shoulder after he set down the second box and pushed it inside the cupboard with his foot. 'This is a joint venture, brothers together. And when you take her a coffee, can you make it clear I didn't mean to offend with what I said?'

'I think she already knows that. But I'll put in a good word.'

He chuckled. 'I'm sure you will. You always were the most charming out of the pair of us, much as I hate to admit it.'

'I'd say it was the other way round.' And he headed off to make the coffee, glad his brother didn't realise that talking with Celeste had absolutely nothing to do with their pub or their future business strategies.

When Quinn came out of the kitchen with the coffees, he delivered one to Eddie who was at the farthest table at the back of the pub along with his laptop, away from where Quinn and Celeste were sitting, and the other two he set on their table.

'It's quite nice like this,' she said, looking around the pub. 'It's rare to see it so empty and quiet.'

'Let's hope it's not a frequent event – packed to the rafters is Eddie's aim. Every day, every night.'

'He does know this is Heritage Cove and not the centre of London, doesn't he?'

'He thinks big. But hopefully not all of our ideas will offend the people of the Cove.'

Her pixie cut had been covered in an ink-blue hat when she arrived but she'd put that on the table and left her coat on the hooks in the hallway that led to the entrance. At busy times, those hooks were so full, it was nigh on impossible to find your coat; he'd seen it several times since they took over. The other

night, after all that rain, Mrs Filligree had put on Etna's coat and
they'd argued about it for a good couple of minutes because they
did have the same coat, as it happened. Etna had finally pointed
out that should Mrs Filligree reach into the pockets, she'd find a
dummy in one of them from the last time Etna had looked after
Phoebe. Her great-niece had dropped the dummy in a puddle
outside the bakery and Etna had pocketed it for safe keeping.
Quinn sensed it was the only way she'd managed to get her coat
back from a woman who was convinced it was hers.

'How are you?' Celeste asked, just when Quinn thought she
was going to let him get away with this morning on the sand.

'You're talking about earlier on.'

'You did run away from me.'

'I was cold; I had to run to warm up.'

She wasn't buying it at all. 'Is that all it was? I mean, when I
went over to you, it seemed as though you were a million miles
away and you looked... well, I've never seen you look like that.'

'You haven't seen me look anything much other than happy.'
He quirked an eyebrow. 'Didn't have much time for that last time
I was in the Cove.' *In your bed*, he wanted to add. There hadn't
been time for anything other than happiness and it had been a
completely different time in his life: a time when he buzzed on
his career, on the life at sea and intermittently on land, a life full
of adventure and surprise.

She picked up her spoon and stirred the froth on her latte
from the edges of her cup so that it sank into the liquid. 'You can
talk to me, you know. We can be friends.'

'Friends?'

'Why not?'

Because he wanted so much more and had to wonder why
she didn't. He leaned forwards so that the hands around his cup
almost met the fingertips of hers around her own drink. 'What if

I want to be more than friends? I know we both said no strings when I was last here but that was different; I was away at sea more than I was on dry land.'

'Why did you leave the navy?'

He looked around. Eddie was still in the corner, concentrating on whatever was on his laptop. Benjamin was in the kitchen; he could hear clanging every now and then, chatter at a volume they might need in there with food prep and cooking happening.

'Quinn...'

Her voice and demeanour said she was ready to listen. She was close enough on the opposite side of the table that her knee brushed against his beneath. Even through denim, he could feel it. He wondered if she'd felt it too because she hadn't had much of a reaction, or perhaps she had, but the reaction was one that said she didn't mind at all, that it felt natural. Which again made him wonder why she kept fighting any attraction. Because it was still there, right? Or was he making it up to soothe his ego?

'It's a long story.' He looked at his watch and tried to make a joke out of it. 'Pub opens soon; no way can I get it all out before midday. You don't want customers dying of thirst.'

'Quinn...'

If he didn't like hearing his name on her lips so much, he'd make her stop it.

With a sigh, he leant back and moved one of his hands from his cup to one of the other cardboard beer mats awaiting customers at opening time. He turned it over and over, its corner tapping against the wood irritatingly for anyone else, like a metronome for him, keeping steady beats, helping him work his thoughts.

'I always said I'd leave when the time was right.' He didn't look at her. He couldn't. They'd lain in bed, her in his arms, his hand circling the skin at the top of her shoulder, her hand resting on his chest, her fingers flickering gently every now and then. They'd talked about her life, her business, his life, his job in the navy. And yet as personal as they'd got back then, getting this out felt impossible.

'You did say that. But I figured it wouldn't be the case for a long time.'

'I'm old.'

His remark made her laugh. 'You are not old. You're thirty-seven. And I saw you running this morning, remember; nobody takes the track up from the cove at that kind of speed unless they're insanely fit.'

'My brother would be a contender.'

'Did something happen? Were you hurt?' She rightly ignored the deflection.

'Do I look hurt?' He wasn't, not physically. Sometimes, he wished he was. It would be easier to justify, to understand.

'Well, no, but...'

'Maybe I wanted to settle down. Make a home.' It was what he'd told everyone since he arrived here in the village; it seemed an easy way to avoid too many questions, too much pity, the latter what he hated the most.

'Have a family?' she asked quietly.

'Life at sea isn't conducive to any of that...'

'Quinn...' Her chest rose as she took an impatient breath in and let it out slowly. The sort of breath his teachers might have taken when they asked him why his homework was late yet again and he'd simply shrug and say he didn't know. 'I don't get why you won't talk to me properly.'

Benjamin came through to tell them he had a supplier on the phone and with Eddie busy, Quinn held a hand up to Benjamin to acknowledge he was coming.

Before he left Celeste, he leaned in, spoke close to her ear and he knew he wasn't mistaken when he felt her shudder with what he hoped was pleasure. 'Talking wasn't what we did best, though, was it?'

And he left her to it without glancing back.

14

Celeste spent the rest of her day at the bakery operating on autopilot. It was obvious Quinn had feelings for her but he'd said it himself; he wanted to settle down. And that was a whole lot different to a no-strings-attached fling, the fun that allowed her to continue with her own business in the way she always had.

'Sorry, was that three iced buns and two Christmas cookies?' Celeste asked Mrs Filligree, who came in towards the end of the afternoon. She'd already forgotten the order in the time it took her to pick up the tongs and a paper bag.

'No, dear. A Victoria Sponge. Same as I always order and have done for years.'

'The buns and cookies were for me,' Lottie interrupted.

Was she so away with the fairies that she hadn't even acknowledged which customer was which?

With a shake of her head, she set down the tongs and bag and instead took the one remaining Victoria sponge and boxed it up for Mrs Filligree. Once Mrs Filligree paid and went on her way with an amused murmuring that she was twice Celeste's age and still had a better memory, Celeste saw to Lottie's order.

'Promise they're not all for me.' Lottie pulled on her gloves, took the bags from Celeste – one with cookies, the other with iced buns – and with a wave, bustled out of the door.

Jade was delivering two cakes this afternoon, both customers a good few miles away, but luckily today had been steady in the bakery for Celeste on her own. Celeste had been about to start the cleaning up when Melissa came in.

'We're out of mince pies, I'm afraid,' Celeste trilled but soon realised Melissa wasn't smiling. 'You look worried.'

'I am. They're still not letting Barney out of hospital. I thought he'd be on the mend a lot quicker than this, bounce back to his usual self.'

Celeste ushered Melissa out back and told her to sit down on the stool. She was clearly stressed. 'He seemed in good spirits for the tree lighting until the nurses had to do their checks.'

'That's the thing. Lois says it was Barney who'd had enough. It was Barney who put an end to the FaceTime. And that's so out of character, it's playing on my mind. Apparently, as soon as our call finished, he was coughing, he was lethargic, he didn't want to carry on talking about the tree or the Cove.'

'Pneumonia can knock anyone about, and at his age, it's a huge toll.' She hated to point out the obvious but Barney was in his seventies and neither he nor anyone else would last forever.

'What if he doesn't ever come home?'

'Is that what the doctors are saying?' Celeste was hovering between the kitchen and the bakery, Melissa out of sight, her in full view in case a customer needed her. There was still a good couple of hours until closing time and they often got a bit of a rush on right at the very end of the day when those who'd been out at work before returning to the Cove decided to make an impromptu visit.

'Well, no, but—'

'Then let's stay positive. It's what Barney would want. When are you next going up to the hospital?'

'I went this afternoon with Harvey; he's working tomorrow so I'll go back in the daytime, he'll go in the evening. All of us are well aware that while we don't want to inundate Barney with visitors, people are important to him. He's always been in amongst it, hasn't he?'

Celeste smiled. 'Ever since I've known him, yes.' He often came in the bakery just for a chat, the same as he did with all the businesses in the Cove. He usually bought something, but it wouldn't matter much if he didn't; it was his company they all loved so much. 'Do you remember at the Wedding Dress Ball last year when Dessie was too shy to dance?'

'I do; she ended up having a wonderful time.'

Dessie worked part time at Tilly's Bits 'n' Pieces and she was one of those girls who just needed a bit of encouragement to flourish.

'She wouldn't have danced if it hadn't been for Barney,' Celeste smiled.

'He's always been that way, it's why he's like a father to me and Harvey. We were friends because of him; he gave us the barn to play in when Harvey wanted to escape his family home and I was just looking for adventure. He always said we kept him young, stopped him turning into a grouch.'

'Not a description I'd *ever* give Barney. He's the total opposite of a grouch.' But as much as she tried to reassure Melissa, there was doubt in the back of her mind too. Going into hospital was always one of her dad's fears. His own father had spent the majority of the last two years of his life in and out of the hospital and it had been stressful for everyone, including him. Didn't everyone want the same? To be going as long as you could, living your life, in your own home surrounded by the people you love?

Celeste knew they all, including her, took it for granted that it would happen that way.

After Celeste served a woman who came in for a thickly sliced, wholemeal bloomer loaf, she told Melissa, 'I'll come and see Barney with you tomorrow. Jade went the day before yesterday; it's my turn and perhaps we'll take him some mince pies.'

'He does love your mince pies.'

The bell tinkled in the shop and she went out to serve a customer who bought up the last of the gingerbread men. Returning to Melissa, she brushed her hands on her apron. 'Is there anything else on your mind?'

'You're referring to what I told you the other day,' she deduced. 'To be honest, thinking about Barney ending our call at the tree lighting has been a distraction from my own problems.' But with a sigh, she admitted, 'Neither myself nor Harvey can face thinking about investigations and tests, not with Christmas around the corner and work busy, Barney in hospital.' She leant against the wall, eyes closed briefly. 'Some days, I think me and Harvey will be fine just the two of us, but I know he wants a family. We've talked about it for a long time; we did even way back when it wasn't anywhere near being on the agenda. I think, given the upbringing he had, he wants to be a father so badly, this must be hurting him almost more than me.'

'It's tough for both of you.' And hearing how much they both wanted it when Celeste really didn't made her feel like a bit of an anomaly.

In their twenties, Celeste and Jade had been to a school reunion. That night, Celeste had discovered that you were either judged on whether you were married, whether you had kids or whether you were a highflyer. And if you were really lucky, you'd been seen as having struck gold because you ticked all of those boxes. Like Harriet Hunt: blonde goddess from school. She looked almost the same as she had back then: still slim, still pretty, and she had four kids, a husband who was a director of something or other in finance, she had an equally impressive job title that Celeste couldn't remember and was on various committees. Celeste had got the head tilt from Harriet Hunt when she said she was single and had no kids; one girl had even told her, 'I'm sure it'll happen for you soon,' as if that was her dream. She and Jade had left the reunion laughing their heads off at the competitiveness and the ridiculousness of it all. But Jade hadn't only found it amusing and shared an eye roll with her sister more than once during the evening; she'd been bothered by it. Celeste had tried to tell her to take it all with a very big pinch of salt, but it had got to Jade when she was asked about children and had photos on devices thrust at her to approve, to admire, because it was what Jade wanted more than anything else. Celeste had tried to convince Jade that while these women, and men, might portray a perfect family image, the chances were it wasn't all rosy behind the camera lens. Celeste had been pissed off rather than anything else that people assumed you could only be happy if you had certain things in your life. And she'd been upset for Jade.

Neither of them had taken up the invite to another reunion three years later.

Melissa sighed. 'Maybe I should just be grateful for everything I already have in my life. I have Harvey, a lovely home, plenty of friends, perhaps that's enough.'

Celeste wasn't buying it. Because it was the same way Jade had been after that reunion. They'd laughed, taken the mickey, they'd joked about some of the women there and their claims on the perfect life, but after the laughter faded, Celeste had seen the look on Jade's face.

'I might not see kids in my own future, Melissa, but Jade

always did. So I really do understand. If it's what you want, you can't ignore that.'

'I didn't mean—'

'I know you didn't. But please don't push this aside thinking you're being spoilt and should be grateful; it's a big thing. Jade would've gone to whatever lengths she needed to to have a baby, you know that.' When the bell to the bakery tinkled again, she put a hand to Melissa's arm. 'Take a breather, time to think, talk to Harvey and decide what you both want to do. I know it can't be easy.'

'Thank you... for being here.'

'Always.'

As Melissa picked up her bag, ready to leave, she at least looked as though a small weight might have been lifted. 'I'll see you tomorrow for the hospital visit.'

'Great, see you then. Text me about times.'

Celeste saw to her customer and as closing time approached, packaged up anything that was left over.

Melissa was tying herself in knots about having a family. In some ways, it gave Celeste a sense of relief that she didn't have to worry about that. It wasn't in her future.

Patricia arrived like clockwork just after Celeste turned the sign to *Closed* and Celeste handed over a couple of bags and a cardboard box, all products heading for the homeless shelter. Jade appeared shortly afterwards to join in the clearing up and between them, they had it done quickly enough. Jade was focused, wanting to get home to her family at the end of another day. Celeste thought about Quinn the whole time she worked and it meant she wasn't up for idle chitchat either.

When Quinn had come into her life quite unexpectedly, way before the sisters had refurbished the bakery and given it an entirely new name, their no-strings relationship had been fun, crazy, exciting. If she closed her eyes, she could still smell the manly scent on his skin, feel the heavy rise and fall of his chest as they fell asleep beside each other. She could feel his breath in her hair as they talked, the vibration of murmurings against her temple. For those few days, it had been like they were a couple and yet neither of them had wanted it to be anything more than it was. A fling.

Back then, Quinn had talked a lot about Eddie, how close they were. She'd talked about Jade, their new business, how this was their future. Quinn had told her about his life in the navy too. He'd told her about a good friend of his who was struggling with leaving his family behind now that he had newborn twins. Quinn had told her he wasn't sure how anyone did it, how anyone said goodbye knowing that they would be away for long stretches of time, that they'd miss their kids growing up and changing so rapidly. And then he'd lain with her in bed, her in his arms with her cheek against his chest, and said he wouldn't want to raise a family and be in the navy. He'd said that having a family was surely a sign it was time to get out of the job.

And now he was out.

And to Celeste, the fact that Quinn wanted a family was something that kept screaming at her, loud and clear, time and time again.

And it was the opposite of what she wanted.

15

Eddie looked at the decoration Zara from the ice-creamery had brought in for the tree. 'I think that might be a bit too city-like for the folks in Heritage Cove.'

'Cheeky,' she admonished, with a bit of a flirty smile, Quinn noticed.

There was a definite undercurrent. Could Zara have a bit of a crush on Eddie? And vice versa? Eddie didn't seem to be batting away the attention. He was hooked on what she was saying, grinning at her as though his only job today was to trim a tree, never mind seeing to his pub.

Quinn closed the back doors to the pub, having opened them to air the place. The winter draught was powerful enough that the fresh air had swept into every single corner within minutes.

'I'm only teasing,' Eddie told Zara.

'Good. And just because we love the Cove, it doesn't mean we don't appreciate reminders of the big smoke once in a while.'

Eddie put a hand out to gesture for her to go over to the tree first to hang the nice festive red Beefeater decoration. 'Pick a place to hang it if you can still find one.'

With opening time fast approaching, Quinn saw to the fire, stacking the logs, breaking up the firelighters, adding kindling. He could hear Zara and Eddie talking weird and wacky ice-cream flavours and he didn't mind his brother's temporary distraction – he'd be the same if Celeste was here, preferring to give her his attention rather than anything else.

'May I get you a drink, Zara?' Eddie offered as Quinn put a match to the firelighters.

'Can't stop, got to get back to the shop.'

'Does business tail off in the winter months?' Quinn asked her as he waited for the flames to take hold.

'You'd think so, wouldn't you, but I was just telling your brother that it's as busy as ever. It seems if you have a hankering for ice-cream, a little bit of cold won't scare you away. You should stop by... both of you. Try some of the Christmas flavours.'

'I will as soon as I get a chance,' said Eddie.

Quinn almost started laughing but managed to turn his attention back to the fireplace while his brother walked their visitor down the corridor and out of the pub. The flames licked the kindling and the logs, gradually taking hold. The feature added a real ambience to the pub but he wasn't sure he'd be too sorry when it was summer and he didn't have to clean the grate again for a while.

When Eddie returned, Quinn couldn't help the smile creeping onto his face.

'What's that look for?'

'Oh, you know,' Quinn laughed. 'You're keen on her; I can spot it a mile off.'

Eddie didn't deny it. 'None of your business.'

'Definitely not.' He slapped his brother on the back as he passed. 'But for what it's worth, she seems a good sort.' He wanted to add that she was way better than his cheating ex-wife, but nobody needed reminding about her, least of all Eddie. 'Ask her out. What's the worst that can happen?'

'She could hear me.'

Quinn grunted. 'Don't be such a wimp.'

'She's local; what if it upsets someone?'

'Now you're being paranoid.'

'Well, as you've pointed out, we don't want to go stepping on any toes, do we?'

'Have it your way. But she seems nice, that's all I'm saying.'

'And she is. But women and I do not mix well.'

'Rubbish.'

Customers slowly began to drift in the moment the sign on the door was turned to say they were open, the first two making a beeline for the seating in front of the fire. The two older gentlemen looked perfectly in place in the maroon leather armchairs as though they were part of the furniture as well.

'Imagine this place in summer,' floated Quinn when he joined his brother behind the bar. 'I bet the beer garden will be packed.' There were things about the winter that he loved, but right now he wanted to see the Star and Lantern in all its guises – the cosiness of winter, the doors flung open in the summer and the smell and sounds of the season drifting in from the generous space with its picnic-style tables. It could house double or even triple the number of customers they could fit inside, perhaps even quadruple if they crammed in for some of the events they had in mind.

Eddie set a second pint of bitter onto the drip tray. 'Let's get through Christmas and New Year first. And we've got the pub quiz night coming up, remember.' He indicated the poster on the wall detailing the day and time of the festive pub quiz. Locals had been buzzing about it for days.

After Eddie took the pints over to his customers, he was keen

to discuss more of their ideas for increasing profits and Quinn
wanted to make sure he wasn't holding any details about their
financials back.

Eddie shook his head. 'Of course not, all out in the open, best
way. We're in this together.'

'Good.'

'You know the way my mind thinks, it comes from having
turned a few pubs around in my time and being with Mum and
Dad to look after theirs for so long. They always ran their pub
with a decent safety net in case of the unexpected. Don't you
remember?'

'I think once I had my mind set on joining the navy, I didn't
give the pub business much thought apart from when I was
enjoying a pint or two.'

'Well, that's what I'm here for, with all my expertise.'

'Careful or we'll have to expand the bar for your big head.'
But the joking passed for a more serious acknowledgement.
'Mum and Dad did well with their pub and you learnt from the
best.'

'The only reason you didn't was because you were focused on
playing action man.' Eddie knew he could get away with the
ribbing, the sibling teasing. 'What I will tell you is that Mum and
Dad always made sure they met their targets which were what
they needed plus a good 10 or 20 per cent. That way, they didn't
worry too much. You must remember the quizzes, the bands, the
karaoke night, the time they hosted a comedy festival.'

'All very successful events, that's what I remember.'

'And all generating extra profit. If they felt they needed
another boost, they'd plan an event before they *really* needed it.
I'd hear them debating what to do, strategizing on what would
increase revenue and as soon as they finished an event, they'd
evaluate it and future decisions would take it into account.'

'You know, sometimes I just saw them running the pub, pulling pints, clearing up, talking to customers. Easy to forget the business side of it.' Quinn had to hand it to his parents; they'd made the whole operation appear relatively seamless to everyone else who wasn't looking too closely.

'It kept them ahead of the game. And if we can do that here at the Star and Lantern over the next twelve to eighteen months, then maybe I'll start to relax a bit.'

Quinn's attentions were taken by an older lady who came up to the bar for three packets of peanuts and three glasses of Prosecco – never too early to celebrate reaching eighty with her pals, she'd told him.

'Better steer clear of them once that Prosecco is gone,' warned Eddie quietly.

'Why?'

'Heard them talking about the hunky barman and how a kiss under the mistletoe might be on the cards.'

'She might have been talking about you.'

'Fifty-fifty chance. Don't think I'll risk it. I'm sure the cellar needs another hose down.'

'Yeah, nice try. I'll block your way.'

Eddie wiped down the counter. 'We could have a karaoke night in here,' he suggested.

'Think the locals of Heritage Cove could handle it?'

'Maybe ask around, but don't see why not. And they always went down well in the past from my experience – well, mine and Claire's.'

'She was a good singer from what I remember.'

'She was. Lousy wife, though.'

Eddie went to the other end of the bar to serve someone else. Quinn hoped the mention of Claire was just the way it sounded, a joke with a hint of seriousness, and that Eddie wouldn't give her much more thought at all. His brother was a good man with a kind heart, he worked hard, he deserved so much more. Quinn was just thankful Claire hadn't finished him off. He'd picked himself up again and most people would have never known the mess he'd been in. The McLeod brothers were both quite adept at hiding their true feelings when they needed to.

Evidently, Eddie was still strategizing in his own head while he served behind the bar because once he was done, he suggested to Quinn, 'We could get a television in here, show football games, tennis, whatever we liked.'

'Nice idea. I mean, I've watched more than my fair share of games in pubs, but that's with a rowdier crew.' Usually when their ship docked and they had a few days to go blow off some steam. They tended to go a bit wild during that time, given they'd been confined on a ship with each other and its rules and regulations.

'Doesn't have to be rowdy; people might like it.'

'Or they might hate it. It seems the sort of village pub where people come to socialise rather than watch TV. Just putting it out there.' He held up his hands in surrender when Eddie gave him a look. 'I think if it was wanted, Terry and Nola would've already done it.'

Eddie shook his head but spoke low enough that nobody else would hear. 'Sometimes I wonder whether this village is a bit behind the times.'

'Agree. But that's kind of what I like.' The unspoiled cove, the little businesses on the high street, it was a little yesteryear. There weren't many places like it left any more.

'What about a twenty-four-hour event? Like a sponsored darts match? Or a pool tournament?'

'Both good ideas. Just don't leap in with both of your size elevens until we've thought about it.'

'Why are you the sensible one all of a sudden?'

'I'm not,' Quinn laughed, 'although it's nice to be described that way. Kind of the opposite to when we were growing up.' It had been Quinn who usually got into scrapes, came home late and got in trouble, a little bit all over the place until he found his vocation and couldn't be that way any more.

'Do you remember Mum hosted a knit and natter group at the old pub?'

'Can't say that I do.'

Eddie took out his phone and put in the idea. Apparently, he'd made notes in there whenever anything came into his head. 'We could do something like that – advertise it in local businesses around here. There must be plenty of groups who meet at each other's houses; we could offer a high tea-type arrangement at a great rate. We have the space; they could take over the entire room outside of our business hours.'

'We could, but again, I really think it's best if we let things settle for a bit.'

Quinn didn't know how else to try to put the brakes on his brother. Perhaps they were a good match – Eddie chomping at the bit to push the boundaries, him more wary.

Quinn flipped the top from a bottle of lager for Linc and pulled a pint of Tetley's for Linc's father, who was visiting his son. 'I'll head downstairs and grab another box of Budweiser.'

'Cheers, Quinn.' Because Eddie had muttered something about needing to restock and Quinn saw his chance when he noticed the older ladies heading towards the bar either for more Prosecco or to find out whether those mistletoe kisses were a possibility. 'Can you change the John Smith's while you're at it?'

'Will do.'

Changing the keg wasn't such a bad job, although the confines of the cellar were a daily challenge for the brothers and indeed any other publican running a traditional pub. He supposed that's how establishments like the Star and Lantern kept their character, because the bare bones of the place were left alone, but it would still be nice if the cellar was a bit bigger given it was the engine room of a pub.

The look Eddie gave him when he went back behind the bar left Quinn in no doubt as to what those women had wanted.

'I take it you got a mistletoe kiss?' Quinn could barely keep the smirk off his face.

'I did. Three of them.'

Quinn laughed so loudly, heads turned. But the women had gone.

'Laugh all you want; they're coming back next week and have you in their sights.' When Quinn's smile faded, it was Eddie's turn to laugh out loud. 'Kidding – they're visiting from London and go back tomorrow on the coach.'

Customers came and went over lunch time and when they were quiet again – empty apart from Harvey and Melissa, who looked deep in thought at the table closest to the fire – Eddie cleaned the maroon chairs using a dustpan and brush. They were nice additions to the standard wooden chairs and tables but crumbs had a habit of getting down the sides and at the back – not what you wanted as a customer.

Quinn tended the fire, which, after the addition of a couple more logs, crackled away nicely. Rain was forecast this evening yet again and he knew he wasn't the only one wishing for snow instead. It would make for an even cosier ambience and draw more people in here, he was sure of it. He'd seen photographs of the Copper Plough, as it was known as originally, and the rest of Heritage Cove covered in white and it was picture-postcard perfect. He knew the realities of course – the grey slush that came when the snow began to melt, the harshness of a wind with snow that stung your face, the slippery pavements. But that first snow-fall of the season? There was something magical about it, especially in a village as quaint as this one.

'So what do you think to the idea of hosting groups here?' Eddie asked him, still intent on deciding how they could best boost the pub's takings.

'You wrote it down with your other ideas, didn't you?'

'Had another one too,' said Eddie. 'How about a barbecue competition? They're huge in some countries, fast-growing in the UK. We've got a big enough beer garden to host the event. It'll be a huge drawcard for tourists.'

'Another great idea.'

'I'll make some enquiries. Summer would be the perfect time.' He finished brushing the second armchair and went to dispose of the debris before returning with a cloth to give the leather chairs a good wipe.

When the phone rang, Eddie went to answer it and Quinn saw to the drip trays – amazing how quickly they could collect liquid after only an hour or so of the pub being open. He wiped around them once they were sorted, polished the pumps and served more customers. Eddie was used to running a pub with high standards and at the same time, Quinn was used to keeping orderly quarters onboard a ship. Neither of them let standards slip and it worked well now without either of them having to nag the other to pull their weight when it came to being organised and tidy. A couple of the spirits on the optics needed changing and he saw to those, although thoughts of Celeste weren't far away when one of the punters waiting at the bar for a vodka and Coke was telling whoever he was with how good the doughnuts were at the Twist and Turn Bakery.

'I can vouch for the turnovers,' Quinn told them as he pushed the bottle of vodka into position and measured out the shot. 'Can't go wrong with anything at the bakery in my opinion.'

'We're heading there after this,' one of the men told him. They were clearly in the Christmas spirit as they told Quinn they'd just been to their work Christmas party and this was the after party.

As the men talked about what they'd grab from the bakery for their bus ride home, Quinn wondered how long it would be before Celeste made another appearance in the pub. Their last conversation had been odd. He'd been as open as he was prepared to be, which was a lot more than he was used to, but there was something different about the way she acted around him by the time she left and he couldn't put his finger on what had changed. One minute, she told him she was listening to him, that he could confide in her, the next, she couldn't get away fast enough.

As he closed the till, he wondered whether she had had a relationship in the time between when they'd first got it together and now. And whether that relationship had been a bad one. Perhaps she'd been hurt and that was why she was wary around him all of a sudden. Could that be it?

His fists clenched at the thought of someone hurting her emotionally, never mind physically.

Or maybe that hadn't happened at all. Maybe his head was so far up his own arse that he couldn't just admit she wasn't interested...

Or perhaps he was thinking too much about it full stop. Perhaps she wasn't interested in him now he wasn't a novelty: a man in the navy who was in town on leave before he'd return to sea.

And if that was it, he'd just have to accept it.

16

Celeste was at the hospital the following day with Melissa and they were half an hour early for visiting time, Melissa impatient to see Barney again.

'Well, you've got some colour in your cheeks,' Melissa gushed as she went straight to his bedside and leaned in to give him a hug. The nurses had taken pity on them and Lois, who arrived shortly after the girls, and they'd let them all in early as long as they were quiet.

'You really do,' Celeste assured him. 'You're looking much better.' On the other hand, Lois looked drained, her paleness illustrating the dark circles beneath her eyes all the more.

Celeste gave Barney a hug before they relaxed into conversation, but after they'd been there almost an hour, she went to Lois's side and asked softly, 'Have you been here every day and night?' The woman was tiny but felt even tinier when you touched her.

'It's where I want to be,' she replied softly.

'I know, but you need time out.'

'She's right.' Melissa shifted her attention from Barney to

Lois. 'We've got it for a little while longer this morning. Go home, take a long bubble bath, spoil yourself with those candles we've heard about.'

'It's broad daylight.' Lois laughed at the preposterous idea of a relaxing bubble bath so early in the day.

'Close the blinds,' Barney suggested. 'Please, love, you deserve it.'

'Honestly,' Celeste went on. 'Barney has us now, Etna is coming later on.'

Barney reached for his wife's hand. Lois was perched on the side of his bed, every now and then reaching over to stroke his brow. 'We don't want you collapsing with exhaustion. Who will wait on me hand and foot when I come home if you're incapacitated?'

Lois burst out laughing before cupping her hand to Barney's cheek and leaning in to kiss him on the lips. 'I can see I'm outnumbered. I could do with a trip to the supermarket and then I'll head back to the cottage for that bath. But I'm coming back late evening, don't argue. Harvey will drive me.'

'Harvey should be with Melissa.'

Melissa dismissed the notion with her hand. 'We see plenty of each other, don't you worry.'

Lois finally left them to it, happy to get the bus again even though Celeste offered to drive her. The bus gave her thinking time, she said; she got to daydream and didn't have to chat. Perhaps part of her exhaustion was the talking because Barney was a talker. And it seemed the colour in his cheeks had brought with it more of a voice.

'What have we here?' He gestured to the box Celeste had put down at the back of the cabinet beside his bed when they first arrived.

'Oh, no, I should've given Lois one before she left. I feel terrible that I didn't.'

'She can wander into the bakery any time,' Barney assured her, 'now, come on, my mouth is watering.'

'I was going to bring mince pies, but I thought I'd mix it up a bit...' Celeste grinned, opened the lid of the box and held it out.

'Cinnamon swirls?'

'Nothing wrong with your appetite,' said Melissa.

Unfortunately, Barney's cough returned halfway through his pastry, so much so that he had to abandon it in favour of water and help sitting up better.

'This blasted cough, I can't shake it. It just won't go.'

'Were you putting on a brave face for Lois?' Celeste suddenly realised maybe that was what he'd done, why they'd thought he was so much better.

'Busted,' he said. 'I do feel better than I did, Lois hears me cough as I do it often enough, but I haven't told her how tired I still am. She thinks I annoy the nurses with my talking all afternoon when she goes home between the visiting hours.'

'You don't?' Melissa asked.

Sheepishly, as though he might have said too much already, he admitted, 'I sleep almost the whole time unless they're taking me for more tests or poking and prodding me.'

And he was still pretending a bit, Celeste could tell by the way he sniffed, turned away.

'I might have a word with the nurse,' said Melissa.

'No need to make a fuss.'

Melissa ignored him. 'I just want to hear it from them, that's all.'

Celeste knew when she left the room that his lack of insistence Melissa do nothing of the sort was probably because he didn't have the energy to put up a fight.

'I hate this, you know.' His voice came out weak. He wasn't even looking at her.

'Well, now I'm offended. I worked hard on those cinnamon swirls.'

There was a bit of Barney-sparkle in his eyes as he turned back to face her. 'You know full well I didn't mean those.'

'I'll leave the box here; you can eat all of them or hand them around.'

'Much appreciated.' He looked past her as if to check who else was nearby and, in true Barney fashion, was onto worrying about someone other than himself. 'I need some answers. Melissa, what is going on with her? She's good at putting on an act – I should know, I've done it myself enough times. I asked her yesterday and she changed the subject. It reminds me of when she was little and she and Harvey would be pretending nothing was up and yet they were hiding something. Usually, they were up to mischief. And now, whenever I see either of them, they make out I'm imagining things.' He looked at Celeste and she didn't want to meet his gaze but it was hard to ignore the man. 'I'm right, aren't I? There's something going on.'

'Barney, please don't ask me.' She hated being put on the spot.

'See, the difference with those two is that I ask and they would never say, "please don't ask me," it's an out-and-out denial. Which tells me there very much is something. Are they rowing? In financial trouble?'

'Barney—'

'They're like children to me; I have to know.'

'Barney... what I will say is that they are both in good health, both love each other very much. Please don't ask me to break a confidence.'

He closed his eyes briefly speaking of the exhaustion he was still feeling. 'You're a good girl, Celeste.'

On a sigh, she suggested, 'Why don't we talk about the Cove instead?'

'Good idea.' He gave a small smile. 'I miss it. They're nice to me, the nurses, but it's not the same as having you lot around. And the food isn't bad but...' he nodded over to the box of cinnamon swirls, 'obviously it's not a patch on what I can get in Heritage Cove. Good news is my ticker seems healthy. I was dreading them telling me I had problems with high blood pressure or something else and I'd have to cut back on my visits to all my favourite places in the village.'

'Your heart has always been good, Barney. In more ways than one.'

'As is yours. Come on, give me some updates on the Cove. I know all there is to know about Tilly's Bits 'n' Pieces, Lois has already told me about the stock, about Tilly and Benjamin's romantic dinner for two at Mistletoe Gate Farm amongst the Christmas trees—'

'Now I haven't heard that. I might have to ask Tilly about it.'

'Oh, no, she'll think Lois is gossiping. Which she was, but with good intentions to lift my spirits.'

'That your excuse, is it?' she teased. 'Well, you saw the tree-lighting ceremony for yourself. Got to love modern technology; it meant you didn't miss out.'

'The tree is magnificent and I loved being a part of it, even from a distance. Lois brought in photographs for me too seeing as I wasn't on FaceTime for long.' He pointed to the little stand beside his bed beneath which, on the top shelf, was a paperback and what looked like a small photo album. 'She went old-fashioned and printed some out for me.'

Celeste had a flip through. 'Always good to have these. I should print out more pictures; it's easy to forget.'

'Danny and Heather came to see me and told me they've delivered a perfect tree to the cottage, ready for my homecoming. I swear the pair of them smell of Christmas tree. I almost asked them to leave their coats to act as a room scenter in here. I could close my eyes then and imagine I was at Mistletoe Gate Farm myself.'

The nurse chose that moment to come in. 'Not overdoing it, are you, Barney?'

Melissa had obviously had a word, got the story and then ducked off to use the ladies' or grab a drink. Or perhaps she'd wanted Barney to believe the nurse had come in of her own accord.

'How can I be overdoing it when I'm lying down in bed?' he asked.

'You have a steady stream of visitors, but any time it's too much, I'm sure they'd understand.'

'They most certainly do, but they also know I'd go crazy if I didn't see a soul other than you and your team for days on end. No offence.'

'None taken.' She answered seriously but cast a sneaky smile in Celeste's direction before she left them to it.

'How's the Star and Lantern?' he asked when it was just him and Celeste again. 'It still doesn't feel right not calling it the Copper Plough, especially as I haven't even seen the finished sign or been in there yet.'

'The pub is fine. Still serving a good Guinness by the looks of things, so don't you worry.'

'And the boys are settling in?'

'They are.' Celeste smiled when Melissa came back in to join them, bringing with her a hot chocolate for them both and asking whether Barney wanted a hot drink, but he didn't.

'I want to talk about you,' said Barney to Melissa.

'Oh, there are plenty more interesting things to think about,' Melissa dismissed. Barney didn't appear to have the energy to interject and so she carried on. 'You know, I heard the boys talking when I was in the pub with Harvey.' She blew across the top of her hot chocolate now she'd taken the lid off.

'Talking about what?' Celeste really hoped this wasn't the moment Melissa lumped her right in it and said she'd heard about Celeste and Quinn's torrid affair many moons ago.

'They were talking about the pub's turnover, how the pub is struggling like any other. They want to increase profits and get some sort of safety net financially.'

'They sound wise,' said Barney.

Celeste agreed. 'All businesses need a safety net.' She and Jade were always aware that they had busy times like around Christmas and Easter but they also had quieter times like right after the summer when the tourists dropped away and it was back to school, or in the New Year when the weather was so dark and miserable that they only got people who specifically ventured out for something rather than by-chance drop ins which made up a lot of their sales. It meant that they were well aware they couldn't get too excited by the busier times but rather they needed to squirrel away the extra income to tide them over when there was a lull.

Melissa hesitated before she explained what else she'd heard and if getting Barney's attention on something other than herself was her intention, she'd won by a mile. He didn't look at all sleepy now.

'I heard them talking about hosting a barbecue competition. Apparently, they're big in other countries; they think it might be great for the pub and the Cove. They're suggesting it'll draw people in, put the village on the map.'

'We're already on the map.' Barney's brow furrowed. 'Oh dear, I'm not sure something like that is the best thing for Heritage Cove.'

'I suppose it would bring people in,' Celeste said. 'We can't fight their ideas when they have a pub to run. It's in all of our interests to see it survive.'

Celeste made a joke about the coffee machine, although she wasn't sure Barney saw it as funny. Perhaps he saw it as a small thing but a possible catalyst for more change coming their way and altering life in the village. And he didn't even know about the kerfuffle with the tree farm competitor, although to be fair, the boys had rectified that promptly.

'It worries me,' Barney went on. 'I tried to draw in more crowds to the Wedding Dress Ball one summer and we ended up with louts from a few villages away; they caused a lot of trouble. And mess.'

'I'm sure that was a one-off, Barney.' Melissa did her best to reassure him, although Celeste could tell by the look on her face, she might be regretting mentioning any of this.

Barney's concerns and worry turned into a cough that attracted the nurses' attention and it wasn't long before the girls left him to rest. Celeste got the impression that if they hadn't, the nurse would have ordered them out of the hospital anyway.

* * *

'You've hardly said a word since we visited Barney.' Celeste pulled the car in at the back of the bakery and next to her cottage. 'He's in the right place, you know.'

Melissa leaned her head back against the head rest. 'I should never have brought up the topic of the pub.'

'Hard not to when it's such a big thing for the village. And he wanted to know.'

'I could've just talked about the atmosphere, the tree and the ornaments.'

'Well, yeah, that might have been better,' Celeste smiled.

'To be honest, I was going to brave talking to him today, about what's going on with me.'

'You were?'

'I thought it might even be good for him if he thinks he's helping. Is that really selfish when he's laid up in a hospital bed?'

The car's engine had only just gone off along with the heat but already, Celeste could feel the cold seeping through the glass. 'Not selfish at all.'

'But then I opened my mouth about the pub to avoid telling him what was on my mind.'

'He asked me, you know – asked me what was going on.'

'I was afraid of that.'

'I didn't say anything, I told him it had to come from you.'

'It will, it's just finding the right time, not when he's coughing and suffering.'

'Once he knows, you'll feel a lot better and so will he; he'll stop worrying and he'll be so focused on your well-being he'll probably scare the cough away with his determination.' She caught Melissa's smile. 'That's better. Don't stress about it. And actually, I've got a bit of an idea in mind when it comes to Barney. Want to help me?'

'Always.'

'It comes with a treat from the bakery too – perhaps a ginger-bread man, or two. I've already asked if Jade wanted to organise it instead and I'll take over in the bakery but she's happy in there for an hour or so while we do this.'

'I'm intrigued.'

Celeste shared her idea and, armed with a box of gingerbread men, they made their way along The Street, around the bend past the pub and on to Barney's cottage.

'Hello, girls,' Lois smiled as she opened the door.

Celeste immediately gave an enthusiastic greeting so Lois wouldn't suddenly think there was anything wrong. 'Call us your Christmas elves,' she said as they were invited inside and into the warm. 'Now how was the bubble bath?'

'Heavenly. I'm not one to laze in a bath in the daylight but I did what Barney told me, closed the blinds, I lit my candles and even put some music on.'

They went into the lounge room that had been widened to incorporate the kitchen and the dining area, given how much Barney loved to entertain and have everyone around him. Celeste admired a tree that must have been delivered from Heather and Danny at Mistletoe Gate Farm. 'It's beautiful.'

'It would be more beautiful with decorations on it, but I've been waiting for Barney to come home.' Lois offered them a cup of tea and popped the kettle on to boil. 'He hasn't mentioned much about the tree. Other than checking it arrived, he hasn't said a thing and that's not like him. Oh, maybe I'm being ridiculous; the man isn't here, why would he care about the tree?'

Melissa put her arm around Lois. 'Because he's Barney. And Barney is a sucker for all things Christmas.'

Celeste opened up the box of gingerbread men and offered one to Lois, if only to put a smile on her face again.

'These look so naughty, they have to be nice.' Lois picked the one with red coat buttons and a winning smile as Melissa made them all a cup of tea. 'Now what did I do to deserve a visit from two beautiful young women who have lives of their own to attend to?'

'We thought we'd offer to do your tree for you,' said Melissa. 'Now hear us out.' They'd talked about this on the way over, how Barney obviously loved to decorate every year. 'We know that Barney likes to do the tree with you, but time is marching towards Christmas. He'll be home if he behaves himself and rests but when he gets here, we don't want him overdoing it.'

'You know, I never thought of that.' Lois contemplated what they were offering.

'He'll be up a ladder doing the lights if we're not careful,' Celeste went on, 'putting the star or the angel on top—'

'He *always* wants to be the one to do that,' Lois laughed.

'Exactly,' said Melissa, 'but, if we trim the tree for you, he'll come home to a surprise. He'll likely be relieved even though he won't say. And what about other decorations? Doesn't Barney usually put up lights on the tile surround above the cooker? And add sprigs of ivy here and there inside?'

'I don't expect you to do all of that. The tree is enough, I can do the rest if you leave the boxes out.' Lois still had her gingerbread man in her hand. 'Oh, are you sure, you two? It's a lot of work.'

At that moment, the back door opened and Harvey's voice floated towards them. 'Knock knock. May I come in?'

'No need to ask,' Lois called out. He always used the back door, a habit from long ago and one Lois didn't seem to mind at all.

He went to Melissa's side and planted a kiss on the side of her head. 'What's cooking in here? You lot look like you're planning something.'

They filled him in. 'So while you take Lois to the hospital later on, we will be working hard to do the tree,' said Melissa.

Lois checked her watch. 'Harvey, are you early or am I late?' She took another bite of her gingerbread man in case it was the latter.

'Take your time with that,' he urged. 'And tonight, Lucy would like to go and see Barney so I've said she could take my place. She'll pick you up from here in twenty minutes, that all right?'

'You're a good man,' smiled Lois, finishing up her gingerbread man.

'I try,' he shrugged. 'Now where are the boxes of decorations? I'll get those and we can all get started.'

'You'll help?' asked Celeste.

'Try and stop me,' he grinned.

Lois showed them where everything was stored upstairs in a bedroom and between the three of them, Celeste, Melissa and Harvey brought the boxes downstairs. There was an entire box dedicated to lights which shouldn't be surprising given how many Barney added to the cottage and the barn in the winter months.

'Any particular way you want us to do this?' Melissa asked Lois, who was getting her coat and bag ready.

'You're doing the job for us; any way you think is fine. I trust you.'

'White lights or coloured?' Harvey asked. 'It's important.'

'Let's go for coloured,' smiled Lois. 'We usually have white throughout the barn so in here I don't see anything wrong with a flair of colour.'

'Right you are.' He stepped over the pile that Celeste was attempting to unravel.

'I'll leave you all to it,' said Lois when she heard Lucy call out a hello at the back door. 'And thank you.'

'Happy to help,' Celeste assured her.

Not long after Lois left, they had the lights wound from top to the bottom of the beautiful Fraser fir and it was time to start adding baubles.

'What do you think: red and gold or red and silver?' Melissa asked.

'Does Barney usually stick to a theme?' Celeste wasn't sure that sounded like Barney.

'Actually, I don't think he does. I'll put the reds on, Harvey, you do green, Celeste, do the silver. That'll probably be enough.'

Once the tree had enough baubles, it was on to the individual decorations – nutcrackers, woodland creatures, drummer boys, ornaments that sparkled, ornaments that glittered, modern decorations or those that spoke of age-old traditions.

Celeste made the next round of tea and as she waited for the kettle to boil, she watched Harvey and Melissa. The love between them could fill any room without them even trying. They'd make great parents too and Celeste couldn't wait to see it happen, however they managed to make it work.

Harvey was first to move to the back door when he spotted that it wasn't rain landing against the glass but rather an effort of snowfall.

'Quick, turn the lights off!' Celeste jumped over the half-open box of decorations they'd already waded through and Melissa flipped the light switch.

All three of them stood at the back of the cottage, looking out across the gravelled courtyard that separated Barney's home from the barn and the fields beyond. There were enough white flakes to say it was snowing and a few of the pretty-shaped lacy flakes even hung around on the concrete step below the door, just for a second, but long enough to sigh and know that Christmas was almost here in Heritage Cove.

Harvey and Melissa decided they'd wait at the cottage for Lois while Celeste returned to the bakery to take over the last hour or so and do the final clear-up so Jade could finish for the day.

Celeste rounded the bend and looked across at the Star and Lantern. She hadn't been able to make out who the figure was at a distance but now as she got closer, she realised it was Quinn standing on the path, scattering grit from an enormous bag.

'I see you've got the good job,' she called over, her face emerging from where it was buried in the warmth of a thick scarf.

'Yup. Eddie is in the nice, heated pub and I'm out here,' he called across to her. 'Come inside for a drink? Enjoy the fire.' He set the bag down beside him.

Hearing his voice sent a trickle of pleasure right through her. 'I can't tonight – got to close up at the bakery.'

'Another time, then.'

'Sure.' She waved goodbye and he returned the gesture. She wondered whether she had the same effect on him whenever they crossed paths and if she did, was that what she really wanted?

At the bakery, Jade already had Phoebe with her.

'Did you see the snow?' Celeste asked her niece with excitement.

'You did, didn't you?' Jade smiled at her daughter. 'She was out with her daddy when it started.'

Celeste groaned. 'I'm sorry, I took so long and you've been waiting.'

'Don't worry, it was for a good cause, and the only reason she's here already is because Linc has a late staff meeting. She's been fine. How's the tree at Barney's place looking?' She took off her apron now she had her reprieve.

'It looks wonderful. I think Lois will be relieved we've done it when she sees it. All we need now is for Barney to come home.'

'Fingers crossed that happens soon.' Jade shrugged on her coat. 'I'd better get this one home, give her a proper meal and a bath.'

Celeste had a bit of an end-of-the-day rush the second Jade left, as though the customers had been waiting in the wings, although the bus had gone past shortly before so it was more likely these were people who'd come to the end of their working day and couldn't resist a treat for themselves or to take home to their family.

When Celeste had finished up, cleaned everything that still needed to be done, reordered a couple of products they were low on already, she locked up and set the alarm and went home. There'd not been leftovers for Patricia today; the only things left were two wholemeal loaves and she'd taken those back to her cottage for the freezer as she hadn't any left.

Without taking her coat off or turning on the lights in her cottage, she sank down in the dark on the sofa and picked up one of the velvet cushions, gazing out beyond the windows, longing for more snow again, the magic of the season.

Maybe she should've said she'd go in the pub later. She could get ready, go now if she really wanted. But sometimes it was worse to be in close proximity with someone you knew you had no future with.

Christmas was such a wonderful time of the year and if you were in a relationship, it could be hopelessly romantic. Celeste didn't usually mind being on her own – sole possession of the remote control for Christmas movies was a big bonus – but this year, knowing Quinn was around had her feeling a bit sad. She could imagine both of them curled up together on the sofa with nothing but the tree lights to illuminate the room, indulging in each other.

For years, Celeste had thrown herself into the bakery and,

come Christmas, her biggest concern was that she could keep variety for customers as well as delivering their festive favourites. And for a long time that had been all that mattered. She'd been content.

But as she gave up on the hope of seeing any snowflakes soar past the window and she drew the curtains on the world outside, she had to ask herself, was it still enough?

17

Quinn sat up. He was yelling, or at least he thought he was. His whole body was sweating, his heart thumping hard. And he could hear a voice, his brother's voice, as Eddie squeezed his arms around him in an effort to calm him down enough to bring him back to reality. He was fighting the hold using all the strength he had left.

Quinn had been bobbing about in the ocean, at least in his dreams, his alternative reality. The serene water had supported his body at first, let his muscles relax, it had taken away every bit of pain that he'd ever felt. But then it had changed; the sky had grown dark, a bolt of lightning struck and the waves began coming at him as though the game had changed and they were the enemy. One after the other, the waves crashed over him, again and again until he could barely breathe. And then he was washed into a house, there was a woman there in the corner holding on to a door frame and the water level was rising, faster and faster. She couldn't hear him; she didn't hear him yell at her to leave now before it was too late. And then another wave, as though the sea was inside, well away from its rightful place,

crashed over her and she was gone. He turned and another
wave came for him. This was it, the one that would finish
him off.

And that was what he remembered, what was still in his head
as he finally gave in to the struggle with Eddie, lay down again in
the safety of his bedroom at the top of the pub and went back to
sleep.

The next morning, Quinn woke up to daylight peeking
through the curtains. It took him a while to realise that shouldn't
be happening, not in the winter. He swore and leapt out of bed,
pulled on jogging pants and an old sweatshirt and hurried
downstairs.

'He's awake.' It was one of the cleaners, who didn't stop
moving as she talked to him.

'I was knackered.' Pathetic explanation and one he didn't
have to give but she was nice; he didn't want to be miserable
with her.

'This place will do that to you,' she said in the process of
taking her mop and bucket towards the kitchen.

He found Eddie out at one of the tables, the only one with a
chair turned over and set down on the carpet.

'Why didn't you wake me?' Quinn picked up the other chair
and turned it the right way up for himself.

'Figured you could use the catch-up on sleep.'

'You probably could too.' He scratched at his jaw, in need of a
shave. He bet he looked a right mess with bags under his eyes
that could rival those kegs in the cellar.

His brother put down his pen. 'Mate, this has to stop.'

'It will.' When he yawned, he put a hand against his chest
and circled his arm back and forth, his shoulder sore either from
a fitful night or Eddie's powerful grip last night. It was cold in
here; he should've put on an extra layer despite the winter

sunshine that had tricked him into thinking it was warmer than it was.

'Just saying it isn't going to make it stop.' Eddie looked him in the eye. 'You know that as well as I do.'

'I apologise. I don't want to ruin your beauty sleep.' His joke fell flat.

'This isn't me thinking about myself and you know it.' Eddie closed up the ledger he'd been writing in. 'This is a new start for us.'

'I know, and I think eventually, I'll move past the nightmares. I honestly do.'

'Then you're stupid.'

He was about to bite back but his brother had a point. And some days, like today, his brother looked like he'd had enough of it all.

'I can make some enquiries, Quinn.'

'Don't.' He hadn't intended it to be quite so snappish. But it was enough to make the other cleaner who was wiping down the glass at the back door turn and look at the brothers before she carried on. 'I appreciate it, Eddie, but it's my battle.'

'And drinking and gambling were mine... didn't stop you interfering.' Eddie gently tapped Quinn's knuckles with the ledger in his hands. 'Now go get dressed and make yourself presentable. It's the quiz tonight, remember, and once we open late morning, that's it till closing.'

He'd forgotten that as well. Sometimes the pub closed late afternoon for a few hours but in the run-up to Christmas, Terry and Nola advised they extend those hours and take advantage of people in the festive spirit and willing to spend more money. Eddie and Quinn had decided to act on that advice and monitor it for next season, make adjustments if they needed to.

As he stood in the shower, Quinn knew Eddie was right on

both counts. Quinn had interfered in his brother's life for good reason and although he'd never pat himself on the back and give himself credit for Eddie pulling himself together, he knew he'd played a part. Eddie was also right that Quinn needed to do something for himself. Just coming here to Heritage Cove wasn't enough, that much was obvious. And perhaps if Celeste and he had fallen back into bed with each other, it might have gone some way to helping him feel better, but even that would never have worked long term. He needed to accept that neither the Cove nor Celeste were plasters on a wound that was too big and too raw to heal without a lot more help.

He turned the water off and vigorously dried his hair first, across his chest, his legs and hurried himself up. His brother was going to lose sympathy if he started slacking off.

Working in a pub, it was easy to get carried along on a wave of friendliness, of banter, of other people's lives, and he let it do exactly that for now. Gus came in with Arnold for a late lunch and their talk was about horses mainly. Then came Daniel, who led a conversation with Harvey about the various merits of having their Christmas dinner at the waffle shack this year. Etna came in with Patricia and their talks centred around family, in particular those members of Patricia's who didn't appreciate everything she did. Quinn had chimed in with that one, encouraged her to put her foot down when she worked at the tea rooms so much. It wasn't right she had to do everything at home. She'd asked if he had a free room going and they'd had a laugh about it, especially when Carol, Harvey and Daniel's mum, overheard them and asked Etna and Patricia whether they'd sneaked a shot of something naughty into their seemingly innocent apple juices.

Quinn went back behind the bar late afternoon and when he saw Celeste come in just as he'd begun to stack freshly washed and still-warm glasses, he was glad she made a beeline for him at the bar rather than joining anyone else.

'You're early.' He stacked the final glass on top of another.

She looked up at the clock on one of the beams. 'I told Lucy, Melissa and Jade I'd make sure we had a decent table so I thought I'd better get here as soon as I could. Melissa is usually on a team with Harvey for the quiz but we're doing the classic girls versus boys tonight.'

'Be warned, the questions aren't easy.'

'I'm sure they're not. Did you dream them up?'

'Some of them,' he grinned.

'It's already getting busy in here,' she said, looking around.

'Yup. And we were worried we'd face boycotts because we're new.'

She took off her hat and her coat. 'We're not that petty. You'll have the full backing of people in the village if you do the right thing.'

He tensed. 'What's that supposed to mean?'

'Nothing, it was just a joke.'

Since when was he so paranoid and on edge that he couldn't pick up teasing a mile off? Maybe it was another gift from the interrupted nights – moodiness.

'You've got a little something...' He put his finger to his own ear to show where he meant. Now she'd taken off her coat, bereft of a collar he could see a spot of white dusting above her collar bone and below her neck. 'Either it's snowing or it's flour.'

She gave it a good brush. 'No snow today, so I'd say the latter. It happens all too often – hazard of the job. Gone?'

He spun his finger in the air and she turned her head on his cue. 'All gone.' He wished he hadn't told her and instead had leaned forwards to brush it away himself. 'I've heard murmurings that it might snow properly soon.'

'Fingers crossed – it's stunning here in the Cove.'

'I'm sure it is.'

'It's cold enough for it tonight.' She held his gaze. 'Did you make it this cold to drive people inside the pub? A bit like the rain at the tree-lighting ceremony.'

He grinned. 'Yes, I have a divine power... it lets me get whatever I want.'

She didn't respond to that. Probably a good job because he was finding it hard not to tell her exactly what he wanted. He wanted her. And ever since he'd come to the Cove, he'd done his best to hide the hurt he had inside, to keep his weaknesses from her. And so far, it wasn't helping at all.

'Listen, I was thinking...' he began.

'Sounds dangerous.'

'Sometimes it is.' And he suspected by the way her body tensed, she was thinking about their history, how together they'd been the last time he was in the village. 'I was thinking some time maybe we could go for waffles.'

'You want to go for waffles?'

Not particularly, he'd rather have her to himself, but it would be a start. 'Sure, what do you say?'

'Quinn, I—'

'Is it because I didn't stay in touch?'

'What?' She stood a bit closer so nobody would overhear. 'You know that definitely isn't the case. We both wanted no strings attached and that's what we had.'

'You never wanted more?' As soon as Quinn asked the question, he wondered if it was his availability that made him unappealing now. Perhaps Celeste, like so many girls that he or any of the crew had met when they docked, were caught up in the rapture of dating a guy in the navy. Maybe now his consideration and sensitivity might well be the least attractive qualities to

Celeste. But even as he thought it, the other part of his brain was denying it. Celeste wasn't shallow; he'd seen that the last time they were together. She was strong, together, genuine, no-nonsense. Those were the qualities that had drawn him to her in the first place.

Lucy chose that moment to come in and Quinn had to admit he was disappointed but did his best not to let it show. He switched into jolly publican mode. 'What can I get you, ladies?'

After conferring, they decided to go for soft drinks and a plate of nachos to share.

He took two bottles of the festive Glitterberry J2O from the chiller, flipped off the tops and set them down along with a couple of glasses he'd filled with ice. He'd scribbled down the food order on a slip of paper and passed it to Eddie, who was about to head into the kitchen.

'Thanks, Quinn.' As if they hadn't been talking about some-thing so personal, Celeste picked up her drink and her glass while Lucy took her own, and they went off to find a table.

He wanted to call after her, *Any time... any time you like, please*, but he didn't. Instead, he turned to serve his next customer.

And so it continued until they were well into the quiz night and the pub was its busiest yet. Word had got around that it was a festive quiz tonight, all questions relating to Christmas, and there was some healthy competition, particularly between Harvey's team – Harvey, Daniel and Gus, and Melissa's team – Melissa, Lucy, Jade and Celeste.

Once the quiz was over, Melissa's team being declared the winners by two points, the crowds thinned out and continued to do so as the evening wore on, but Celeste and her friends stayed put – something Quinn wasn't sorry about.

As Quinn went back for the remaining dirty plates on the

table nearest the back doors, he heard excitement from the girls'
table as they all leaned over a screen.

He went over to see what they were up to and nudged Lucy.
'Who's that?'

Celeste answered before Lucy could. 'It's Barney.'

'*The* Barney?'

Barney must have heard him because suddenly the iPad they
had on the table became exposed when they all sat back and
Melissa prompted Quinn. 'He'd like to say hello to you.'

Quinn set down the dirty crockery. He'd met the man once,
but he looked different on a device than in the flesh.

'Squeeze in,' urged Lucy, moving right over so he could sit
between her and Celeste, one arse cheek on each chair by the
feel of it. The proximity to Celeste was something he didn't mind
at all because he could remember exactly what it felt like when
she hadn't been resisting him but rather treating him as though
he couldn't get enough.

'Good to see you,' said Quinn to the screen. He noticed the
bed, the sterility that had to be a hospital. 'You're not at home.'

'Still stuck here,' Barney bemoaned, adding in a sarcastic
comment about the starkness of the bed sheets and the plain
walls with no personality.

It was then that Quinn wished he hadn't got pulled into this
little FaceTime session because Barney didn't beat around the
bush; he got straight on with telling Quinn that he'd heard about
the boys' ideas for the pub. He wanted to help in whatever way
possible so the brothers could be sure to make whatever they had
planned work for the entire village. Quinn assured him that they
would give everything careful thought but really, he wanted to
run and hide.

Quinn caught a glint of amusement in Celeste's expression.
She was enjoying watching him get a grilling and for some

reason, it made it easier to deal with. But it was time he escaped and so he picked up the dirty plates he'd collected. 'I'd better get on, Barney; lots to do before we get into bed tonight.'

'What was all that about?' Eddie asked when Quinn emerged from dumping the plates in the kitchen. Eddie had dirty glasses between his fingers. Quinn thought they'd got most of them, but they had the ability to hide – sometimes in the toilets, or on a windowsill quite conspicuously, even in plain sight sometimes.

'That was Barney, FaceTiming. I was sweating a bit by the end of the inquisition; I walked right into it.'

Eddie set the glasses down on top of the bar while Quinn filled him in on the exchange and what was said about any plans for the Star and Lantern.

'Jeez. The man is in a hospital bed and he's sticking his oar in,' said Eddie.

'I think we're going to have to get used to that.' Quinn took the glasses out to stack them in the glasswasher and left his brother to process the fact that this was a very different village they'd come to, one that was refusing to lose its personality and wanted to guard it in any way it saw fit.

When Quinn returned to the bar, Eddie was frowning. 'How did Barney get wind of our ideas? I haven't mentioned them to anyone.'

'Me neither...' Quinn picked a couple of beer mats off the floor the other side of the bar and had just turned around to put them in the bin when Melissa and Celeste came up to see him.

'What can I get you both?' He headed around the right side of the bar.

Celeste nudged Melissa to give her the cue.

'I'm afraid it's my fault Barney knew all about the ideas you and Eddie have for the pub. I overheard you guys talking one day when I was in here. I'm really sorry; it's just I wanted to get him

talking about the Cove, stop him asking me personal questions I
didn't want to answer. And I wanted to get his mind off being in
hospital and wondering if he'd ever get out. He asked about the
pub, you know, seeing as you're new to the village, and everything I said was complimentary. But I did let it slip about the
ideas.'

'Interesting.' Quinn finished mopping up a spill he'd spotted
on the bar and clasped the beer towel between his hands. 'To
save yourself, you sacrificed us?' His obvious teasing had Celeste
smile his way.

Uncomfortable and guilt-ridden, Melissa admitted, 'When
you put it like that…'

'Don't worry about it,' said Eddie. 'I'm sure you didn't mean
any harm.'

'I promise you I didn't.'

Quinn smiled. 'Perhaps it's better that we're aware of any
objections to what we have planned. We need to know local
opinions; they're important to us. We want to make this work as
much as you want it to. But at the same time, we do need to
increase profits.'

'Is the pub in trouble?' Celeste asked.

Eddie bellowed out that it was last orders at the bar. 'Can I get
you ladies anything else?' His question made it plain that the
conversation was over and neither brother was going to answer
Celeste's question.

'No, thanks – we're still working on the ones we've got.' And
with a nod, Melissa led the way back to where they were seated,
Celeste following close behind.

'I'm all for being a local,' Eddie had waited for the girls to be
out of the way before he spoke to his brother, 'but they don't need
to know everything.'

'No, I don't suppose they do.' He'd felt bad Eddie had cut off

Celeste's question with the call for last orders, but his brother had a point.

'Barney or someone else will be asking to see our financial statements next. And Terry didn't tell me that was a requirement.'

Eddie was being good natured about it but Quinn knew his brother; this wouldn't and couldn't put him off doing something to increase the profits at the pub. Both of them knew that turnover would be up and down – it was up right now with the festive season – but they also knew that the bank wouldn't understand the downs; either the repayments were made on time or they weren't.

Melissa seemed to be hanging on to her guilt because she came back over to the bar again before she left. She pushed one arm into the sleeve of her coat before wrestling in the other one. 'I swear Barney means well; we all do.' And when Quinn nodded, she added, 'We're not trying to make trouble for you, promise.'

'Appreciate that,' Eddie called over, adding, 'I'm just glad Quinn got it in the neck rather than me.'

Celeste, who was pulling on her woollen hat, came up behind Melissa. 'I've just thought of something, Melissa.'

'What's that?'

'For Barney to do the FaceTime call for so long tonight, for him to leap on one of the boys as soon as he knew Quinn was in the vicinity, he's not only taking an interest; it means he must be getting better.'

Melissa was a pretty girl and Quinn wasn't sure he'd ever seen anyone's face light up quite the way hers did at Celeste's remark. 'You might be right. Do you think this means he'll be home for Christmas?'

They both waved their goodbyes to the boys and Quinn heard Celeste's reply as they walked away, down the corridor towards the front door. 'Let's hope so.'

'I hope the man is in his own home for Christmas too,' said Eddie, 'but I'm slightly worried that whatever ideas we come up with, he's going to knock back.'

'You think so?' Quinn got a cloth to wipe one of the chairs that had what looked like a smear of ketchup on it and once it was clean, turned the chair upside down and set it onto the table.

With a few customers still lingering, Eddie kept his voice quiet. 'I understand tradition and that Heritage Cove has worked well for everyone, but what I'm worried about is that people like Barney will forget that this is a business. It's lovely that the pub is a community hub and I understand that other businesses have been here longer than the pair of us, but sentimentality won't necessarily pay the bills; it won't keep the Star and Lantern open long term. That's down to us.'

And with those words ringing in his ears, as well as Celeste's obvious disinterest in anything more than friendship now he was back, Quinn wondered whether coming here and taking on the pub had been the right thing to do at all.

18

Quinn tried the Little Waffle Shack out a couple of days after the pub quiz on a day when they closed the Star and Lantern from late afternoon for a few hours and wouldn't reopen until early evening. He'd rather have come here with Celeste, but life went on, right?

'You escaping the rigours of work?' Daniel brought over golden waffles topped with cranberries and chopped nuts and set them down in front of Quinn along with cutlery wrapped in a serviette.

'Something like that. I usually run to escape or head to the gym but I did both of those this morning; this is my reward.' And his taste buds were dancing ten to the dozen already.

Daniel whistled. 'You're brave running in this; it's freezing today.'

'Makes me run faster,' Quinn laughed.

There were days where it was bracing cold and good to wrap up and get out, but this morning had not been one of those days. It was the sort of morning where, if you could sleep, you stayed in bed as long as possible and then drank copious amounts of coffee or tea or whatever your drink of choice was to stay warm. But Quinn had faced worse conditions and wasn't one to be deterred by the weather and so he'd run all the way along The Street, headed out of the village, turned and taken the almost-deserted bridle path before heading back past the veterinary practice and the florist. He'd ended the run by heading along the track that ran parallel to the chapel, a route which was becoming more familiar to him these days, and headed down to the cove itself again. The waves had been wild this morning, the spray refreshing after he'd worked up a sweat. Part of him had hoped he'd see Celeste again but there wasn't even a dog walker in sight. And as he'd run as fast as he could back across the sands and up to street level, he told himself to let the idea of him and Celeste go, for his own sanity.

The waffles were as delicious as expected and Quinn liked it in here. There was a brilliant festive atmosphere with the lights and the tree and he almost felt like he was on holiday in a little shack set at the top of the green space. If he didn't know better, he could easily be fooled into thinking this was a log cabin in the alps in the middle of nowhere.

The Star and Lantern had helped with getting to know the residents of the village and when he saw Tilly and Benjamin come in, he suggested they sit at his table when they looked around and couldn't find another one.

'We don't want to chase you away,' said Tilly.

'Honestly, no bother, sit down.'

'Cheers, boss.' Benjamin took his coat off.

'Don't call me that,' he laughed. 'Quinn will do just fine.'

Tilly headed up to the counter to place her order.

'Well, thanks, Quinn,' said Benjamin. 'I haven't got long before I've got to be back in the kitchen.'

'Like I said, no worries at all. And besides, I should go; we don't want Barney to get wind of me taking up a table when a local needs it more than I do.'

Benjamin didn't seem sure of whether to smile and Quinn instantly regretted his so-called joke. 'Sorry, that was rude, not sure why I said it.' They got on well in the workplace but having Barney quiz him about plans, the awareness both brothers now had that they could very easily step on plenty of toes if they weren't careful, had created a bit of tension. 'It was honestly just a joke.'

'Don't worry about it.' Benjamin pulled out a chair.

Tilly came over still in her coat and even though Benjamin fussed that she'd soon get too hot, she refused to take it off yet. She must have overheard the conversation because she said, 'Barney means well, Quinn, he honestly does, but when everyone else is on side, it can feel intimidating. I bet we all seem like a big gang and I know I wouldn't have liked it if people had pushed against any of my plans for the shop. Fortunately, I'm the only gift shop in the village so I didn't have to worry about competing against anyone.'

Quinn wished he'd just left without whingeing but found himself sitting down with the pair of them and he didn't want to be rude by walking away just yet, not when Tilly was at least seeing it from their point of view.

'Eddie gets a lot of good ideas. And he's conscious, we both are, of making this work for us.'

'We all want to see the pub do well,' said Tilly.

Benjamin agreed. 'I bet your brother thinks we just say no to everything at the moment, doesn't he?'

'He leased a couple of pubs previously, turned them around successfully when they were in dire straits. Which the Star and Lantern isn't,' he added hastily, 'but all pubs are struggling and the one in this village is no exception.'

'It's not an easy business to be in when the cost of living keeps going up,' said Benjamin. 'I'm on board for changes in the kitchen, to the menu, if needed.'

'The way I hear it, you turned that around yourself already and we're impressed with everything we've seen so far.'

'Good to know.' Benjamin leaned to the side when Brianna, who worked in the waffle shack, brought over gingerbread waffles topped with a maple glaze and vanilla bean ice-cream.

'You two enjoy those.' Quinn picked up his jacket. 'I'd better get back myself.'

'Will do.' Tilly had already cut into the side of the waffles they were sharing. But she didn't pop the waffle and ice-cream into her mouth straight away. 'You guys are here in the Cove for good, aren't you?'

Quinn smiled. 'We bought the pub, didn't we?'

He left it at that and with a smile, wove through the gaps between tables and out into the cold.

The village tree, all lit up, was impressive from up here and he took a picture of it on his phone and messaged it to his dad. It was important to Quinn that their parents thought that he and Eddie were settling in no problem at all, finding their way without too many obstacles. As far as they knew, Quinn had left the navy because it was the right time for him to do something different. Eddie had kept his problems away from their parents and Quinn had continued to do that when he got home. They had enough stress and the boys could handle themselves at their age. Neither of them wanted to be a burden, although he guessed part of parenting was always being there for your kids, no matter how old they got. Perhaps he was doing them a disservice by not sharing everything but for now, it wasn't a lie; they were both doing okay with this new pub of theirs and he hoped that would continue.

He wasn't sure how long he stood there after he sent the picture to his dad. It was as though his feet were rooted to the spot; he was mesmerised by the tree and its lights. And as he gazed at the lights, the memories came unexpectedly at him. He'd managed to push them away, or out of his head this morning when he and Eddie talked about Christmas Day itself, and yet now when he didn't have his guard up, there they were again. He had such a clear picture in his mind of the scene on the ship the first Christmas he'd ever been away at sea.

That day, they'd had carols, the big dinner, games, merriment. But it had also been the first time Quinn had pined for home. Up until then, it had all been a job wrapped up with a big slice of adventure – tough, unbelievably demanding, but he'd often got by on adrenaline and determination. And then, out of nowhere, it was as though Christmas Day was a little injection of reality, a reminder that they were far removed from normal civilian life. They were here with purpose, doing their duty for their country. He'd seen a couple of crew mates devastated by the separation from their families, particularly those with kids. He hadn't admitted to his parents in their phone call that day, nor to Eddie when they spoke, how nauseous he'd felt about being at sea and so far from them all. And he wasn't sure he'd ever felt it quite as bad since. It was never great when those moments came but he'd learnt to manage them. He'd never thought anything would break him; he'd been in control, moving forwards with every day, with every step. Until he wasn't.

The following Christmas, he'd not been homesick but had instead faced his worst bout of sea sickness ever. The ship had jerked and rocked on the water and his stomach had done much the same beneath a stormy granite sky and on the murky waters in the midst of a storm. Brutal weather and brutal stomach flu came at him and with every vomit, he'd felt as though his insides were burning. It had been the lowest he'd ever felt. He'd woken in the night drenched in sweat and only just been able to pick up the bowl beside his bed before his stomach cramped over and over to get rid of its contents, which wasn't much by that point. And then he'd been so overcome that when he tried to stand up, he'd passed out with exhaustion, his body hitting the floor before he could do anything to stop it.

Standing on the green now, in front of the giant tree, his fists clenched at the memory, knowing it was a bad recollection that was bound to pave the way for the one that featured in his nightmares. He knew he had to take a hold of himself. Breathe. Before the worst of his memories came to the fore.

He closed his eyes, trying to do what he thought he needed to. It sounded ridiculous. Focus on breathing? Didn't each and every one of them do that every day without needing to think about it?

And yet he had to try. He'd been okay at the waffle shack. How had looking at a tree, mesmerised by its beauty, given way to memories of his time away, the worst Christmas he'd spent at sea? And the knowledge his head was on its way to a place he didn't want to go instilled panic.

A body slammed into his and on instinct he spun around and grabbed a hold of the defender to protect himself, to ward off any harm.

It took him seconds to realise it wasn't an enemy; it was a kid. He didn't need to protect himself from two boys larking about.

'Justin!' A woman he thought he recognised came charging over from the direction of the waffle shack.

Quinn let the boy's arm drop and he ran to the woman's side. 'I didn't mean to run into him.'

'You okay?' the woman asked the boy and when he nodded, she looked at Quinn.

Quinn held up his hands. He knew it didn't look good that he might have hurt him. Had he? Had he been violent with his grip? 'I'm sorry, he took me by surprise, I—'

'What have I told you?' the woman asked the boy. 'You and your friends can charge around out here all you like, but for goodness' sake have some consideration for others. Are *you* okay?' She directed the question at Quinn this time.

'Me? Yeah. I'm sorry, again.'

'I'm Carly, remember?' Her son had already charged off to be with his mate.

He put a hand to his head. She'd introduced herself to him and Eddie in the pub a week or so ago. 'I apologise. I didn't recognise you for a minute.' His head had been elsewhere, in a battle zone, at a natural disaster rescue, ready to protect, to defend. It wasn't the environment where you exchanged smiles and small talk. This woman was Terry and Nola's daughter, which meant the boy he'd just grabbed hold of was Terry and Nola's grandson.

'That's my son, Justin. He's running off steam – I mean, I told him to, but I didn't tell him to run into anyone.'

'I think I scared him when I grabbed hold of him.'

'No harm done.' Smiling, she tilted her head over to where the boys were playing another game, running in circles whatever it was, laughing at the top of their lungs. 'Does it look like it's affected him?'

'It doesn't.' Thank God for that. He was pretty sure Barney wouldn't approve of what he'd just done, regardless of whether the kid had been messing about and run into him.

'Well, it's good to see you, Quinn. I've been telling Mum and Dad that you and your brother seem to be settling in well.'

'How are they? Regretting letting their pub go yet?' He wanted to bring the conversation back to normal. Talk about anything other than why he'd overreacted just then.

Her laughter came out on a cold breath that misted against the air. 'I haven't heard a single mutter of regret. I thought I might, but they seem to be enjoying themselves so far. It's done them good. And I think they picked you guys because they got a good feeling about the both of you and how you'd fit in.'

'Let's hope they're right.' He explained that Barney had already had a word.

'He's bored in that hospital. But it's a good sign, I'd say.' She'd echoed Celeste's sentiments. 'Anyway, I'd better get these boys to their climbing party.'

'That'll work off some energy.'

'One can only hope.' Carly rolled her eyes before rounding up the two boys with a firm voice.

The boys both avoided looking at Quinn when they walked past and he hoped he hadn't traumatised Justin for life with his reaction. Or rather *over*reaction. Being jumpy was something he knew he had to work on, something he thought he was in control of but clearly wasn't.

He was still shaken when he crossed the road, head down against the cold as he passed the bakery. Celeste was holding the door open for her customer, who had a big cake box in her arms.

When he smiled at her in greeting, she urged, 'Come in, it's freezing out here.' She stood back and he was about to tell her he had to get to the pub but before he could open his mouth, his feet had other ideas and took him inside. 'What can I get you?'

So she hadn't been inviting him inside to talk; she'd thought he was heading for the bakery rather than just passing by.

'I'll take a couple of your jam doughnuts. Eddie will do two easy, they're his favourite.'

'Coming right up.'

As she busied herself at the other side of the counter, he watched her, taking the paper bag, picking up the tongs, lifting out the sugary treats and slotting them into the bag. Content in her work. The way he wanted to be eventually rather than terrorising the local kids.

'These are both for Eddie?' she asked as she handed him the bag and he waved his card in front of the little machine when he was prompted.

'I had waffles up at the waffle shack.'

There was a flicker of hesitation and he wondered if she remembered him inviting her there. 'It's good, isn't it?'

'You have way too many food places in Heritage Cove.'

'That we do, and locals love it.'

'Good to know.'

The bell behind him tinkled and a young woman with dark-brown hair tied back in a no-fuss ponytail came inside with a kid in her arms.

'Hey, Valerie,' Celeste greeted. 'What can I get you?'

Quinn was about to say goodbye when the little boy who Valerie had put down came toddling towards him. Obviously, he hadn't got the memo about his reaction with Jacob. He wasn't yet a pariah for locals to avoid.

'I'm sorry,' said Valerie.

'No need to be,' Quinn smiled, his hands steadying the kid, who looked like he'd only just learnt the art of walking. 'What's your name, buddy?' Or perhaps it was ridiculous to expect an answer; he had no idea how old the boy even was.

The boy just grinned and Valerie said, 'It's Thomas.'

'Thomas,' Quinn repeated. 'That's a cool name. I knew three men called Thomas when I was at sea on a big boat.'

Now *boat* was a word the boy could say.

'You just picked his favourite thing of all,' Valerie laughed.

The kid was now saying the word over and over again and although she laughed, Celeste had a peculiar look on her face.

Perhaps he was being way too familiar with a stranger's kid and she didn't approve.

He stood tall and picked up the bag with the doughnuts. 'I'd better leave you to it.'

He closed the door behind him and didn't miss Celeste glancing at him through the latticed window as he passed by the bakery and along The Street. Although she turned away quick enough.

For a woman who said she wasn't interested, she certainly seemed to be.

And that was why he couldn't work out why she was holding back.

With less than a fortnight to go until Christmas, the bakery was non-stop. Celeste and Jade worked all day every day with early mornings, late nights, and not much respite in between. The elf had been moved to peeking out from behind the till yesterday and today Celeste had put him inside the glass-fronted cabinet in charge of a tray of mince pies.

At lunchtime, Celeste went to Mistletoe Gate Farm to choose herself a tree for the cottage and she arranged for it to be delivered in the afternoon. Jade had had yesterday to choose hers in the middle of the day when Linc could get away from school and then she'd left early, before closing, to make it home in time to decorate it before Phoebe went to bed. Not that the little girl could help, but Jade had been desperate for her to be involved even if it was only by watching.

Today, it was Celeste's turn and after the early-evening rush in the bakery subsided, she headed to her cottage, leaving Jade to finish up. If she needed her help, she was less than a minute's walk away, but Celeste really hoped she didn't because she was knackered. And part of her was tempted to leave the tree for another day but she wanted to be able to sit and admire it, to have it in the background while she watched something Christmassy on television. And so, after a full day at the bakery, she went home, pulled out all of the boxes of decorations from their various hiding places and got going with it.

It took a bit of manoeuvring to get the tree into its stand but once it was secure, she pulled the lights from their box. She only hoped they weren't too tangled.

A knock at the door interrupted her and she opened it up to see Melissa. 'Come in,' she urged.

'I will, as long as you promise I'm not getting in the way.'

She reached out and pulled Melissa inside by the arm. 'I can sort my tree with you here.'

'I was hoping you'd say that.' She held a cloth bag up in the air. 'In here are mocktail supplies. I thought I'd make us some and help you decorate your tree.'

'Mocktails sound great but I'm not going to make you help.' She realised why Melissa might be suggesting it. 'Did Harvey guilt you into it?' She'd seen Melissa's other half in the bakery earlier and she remembered now making an offhand remark about it being lonely doing a tree on your own.

'Of course he didn't. But he mentioned you were doing yours tonight and seeing as I love decorating for Christmas...'

'Well, I won't say no; it'll be nice and quick with the both of us.' She took Melissa's coat for her and laid it over the back of the sofa.

It transpired that while Melissa had been so intent on getting pregnant, she'd had little to no alcohol and had tried mocktails but she'd enjoyed them so much, the habit had stuck – at least part of the time. 'Honestly, you wait until you try them,' she said.

They made a passionfruit martini mocktail with passionfruit, cloudy apple juice and lime. 'This is good,' Celeste approved.

'Really tropical – total contrast to the wintry weather; I could be lazing around on an island somewhere drinking this.'

'Now that would be lovely. Although don't let Barney hear you talk like that; you know how he's all about the seasons, especially Christmas in Heritage Cove.'

Celeste stood on the step stool so she could begin winding the lights from the top of the tree. 'How is Barney doing?'

Melissa had the pile of lights in her arms so she could walk around the tree as Celeste arranged the lights in the branches. 'Well, either he's still putting on an act or he's much better.'

'Any idea when he'll be home?'

'I didn't get a chance to ask the nurse but Lois seemed to think it would be soon. And like I said, he's definitely in fine spirits; that's got to mean something.'

'Certainly does.' She didn't need the step stool for long given her height and soon moved it out of the way to progress around the tree, working her way down over the branches with the lights.

'While I was there, we talked.'

'Talked?' She'd got to a much fatter part of the tree and stood back to make sure she was spreading the lights evenly before recommencing the job.

'About everything going on with me.'

'Everything?' Celeste took the pile of lights from Melissa, given she could manage to finish the lower branches on her own.

'He was talking about the Star and Lantern and wanted to know more about what the boys are planning. He kept asking what else I knew and it made me think of that night when Quinn said I'd sacrificed him to save myself. So this time I sacrificed myself.'

Celeste grinned. 'Good for you – not sacrificing yourself, but for being brave. How did it go?'

'I should've done it before.'

'Well... I hate to say I told you so.' She finished the very base of the tree and then plugged the lights in. 'I knew you'd feel better talking to him.'

'I really did. It was a relief to get it out in the open. I'm not good at keeping up a pretence when something is bothering me.'

'Well, if I know Barney, he'll be glad you confided in him.'

Celeste flipped the switch.

'Beautiful.' Melissa did a bit of rearranging of the lights in the middle of the tree where they weren't quite evenly spaced.

Celeste handed Melissa her mocktail and grabbed her own before they clinked glasses. 'To you, for being brave. Any decisions made as to what you want to do in the New Year?' But she grimaced. 'Sorry, you probably don't want to talk about it right now.'

'It's fine, talking is good as it turns out, so I'll do my best to keep on doing it.'

Celeste undid a box of baubles and between them, they began to adorn the tree with reds and golds.

'Barney turned back the clock and talked about my childhood and Harvey's. We reminisced, which was nice, and I wondered where he was going with it but he took hold of my hand and told me that the both of us were like children to him and it had never mattered whether we were biologically his or even legally. He loved us then and still does now.'

'Anyone can see that.'

'I can't imagine a life without Barney, not ever. He told me that me and Harvey have a lot of love in our hearts to give, the same way he did.'

Celeste paused as she positioned another bauble on one of the neglected lower branches. 'That's a lovely thing to say. And so true.'

'It got me thinking… in the New Year, we could do the investigations if the both of us want that.' Her tone implied there was an alternative.

'Or…'

'I need to talk to Harvey but the conversation with Barney has got me thinking. There are other ways to have a family.'

It wasn't something Celeste had spent too much time thinking about, but she knew Jade had over the years, her sister eager to have children in whatever way that was possible.

'There must be kids out there in desperate need of a home.' Melissa had a delicate robin she'd unwrapped sitting on her palm. 'Kids of all ages. Look at Harvey's childhood. A lot of kids could be in a similar situation or worse – and at least Harvey and Daniel had their mum on their side, despite the problems with their dad. Not all kids are that lucky.'

They carried on taking ornaments out from the safety of their boxes and hung them on the branches. 'Any kid, no matter what age, would be lucky to have you and Harvey as parents, whether permanent or temporary.'

'We have a lot of thinking to do.' Melissa hung a miniature wooden train carriage from its brown string onto one of the branches.

'You do, but even I can tell how much happier and more relaxed you are already.' A smile confirmed her impression. 'Maybe you'll enjoy your Christmas without as much stress.'

'Between you and me, I'm hoping Harvey wants to forget about all the tests to see what's going on, that I can forget about ovulation kits, the worry that I won't carry a baby to term if I get pregnant again.'

'For Christmas or for good?'

'Maybe the latter. Maybe we look at fostering, adoption, I'm not sure.'

Celeste climbed off the step stool after hooking a silver angel with transparent wings to one of the upper branches. 'I know you guys will find a way eventually. You both have a lot of love to give; don't give up hope.'

'I promise, we won't. And it's far better with Barney on our side. We all know he loves to talk but I forget how much I need to confide in someone like him.'

'He's like the oracle of the village.'

Melissa laughed. 'That he is. Now, let's get this tree finished.' She'd come across the star for the top and handed it to Celeste to do the honours.

Celeste might not get the deep desire to be a parent, but she understood wanting something badly. It wasn't the same, but the bakery had been something she'd desperately longed for, the business growth and success, and now there was something else she wanted – Quinn. But that was well and truly out of reach and in the never-going-to-happen category.

By the time they'd had a second mocktail each and admired the tree in the dark with only its fairy lights twinkling, there was another knock at the door.

Celeste opened it to her sister. 'Do you need me?'

Not dressed for the outside given the short distance from the back door to the bakery, Jade rubbed her upper arms to keep warm. 'I'm just about cleared up but it totally slipped my mind that Hazel and Arnold are hosting a gathering at Heritage View House tonight and wanted three dozen mince pies and a box of Christmas pudding cookies delivered.'

'They sound like something I need to try,' Melissa grinned.

'I've got some spares with your name on them,' Jade smiled back before her attention returned to Celeste. 'Could you pop everything down to them?' She jumped up and down on the spot a few times.

'Of course I can. I'll go now. And for goodness' sake, get yourself inside before you get hypothermia.'

Melissa had already picked up her coat. 'I need to go and see my husband – might take him one of those Christmas pudding cookies.'

'I'm sorry to rush you out after you helped with the tree.' Celeste rummaged in her bag for her car keys. She really should get in the habit of putting them in the drawer or on a hook when she came home rather than having to find them every time.

Melissa kissed her friend on the cheek. 'No need to apologise, I'll go with Jade.' She followed Celeste's sister back down the path to the bakery and they went in the rear entrance.

Once Celeste was wrapped up in her coat and a hastily grabbed scarf, given the winter chill outside, she picked up the delivery items from the kitchen of the bakery and set off for Heritage View House, which was in the same grounds as Heritage View Stables.

She had lights dipped at first when she first drove away from her cottage but once she'd turned onto the country lane that led down and towards the stables and the paddocks beyond, she flipped to full beam. These roads were difficult to navigate and she was worried about meeting someone coming the other way, although with it being dark, she only passed the odd car rather than the sometimes very wide farm vehicles that had you breathing in to squeeze past as though it would make a difference.

Was that a horse and rider up ahead? Or a walker?

Whoever it was had no lights or fluorescent clothing to help either of them out. She slowed down so she didn't hit them. She couldn't swing out yet as she was approaching a bend, so it wasn't safe.

'What the—'

It was a man, dressed in jeans and a dark coat and it wasn't until he turned and his hand shot up over his eyes that she realised she still had her full beam on.

And not only that, the stranger in the road in the dark was Quinn.

Celeste opened her window and called out to him because he'd turned back and carried on walking. And she couldn't pull up on this kind of road. They'd both be killed if someone came flying around the corner.

'Quinn!' she yelled again.

She crawled slowly behind him in the car. At least that way, nobody could drive up behind him and run him over. But he didn't turn around again and with the driveway to Heritage View up ahead now, she didn't want to overtake.

As soon as she reached the entrance to the lane which doubled as an extra-long driveway for Heritage View House and Heritage View Stables, she pulled up and this time, she got out of the car. 'Quinn, would you stop!' He was ignoring her and walking on further. 'Stop!' She ran after him and reached for his arm.

And when he turned, it was as though he looked right through her.

She went from bewildered to scared and worried for him. But finally, he seemed to register who she was. 'What are you doing down here?'

'I'm delivering to Heritage View House.' She pointed over at the grand residence which overlooked paddocks opposite and was surrounded by countryside views. 'For Hazel and Arnold.' She wasn't sure he was understanding much at all, so she may as well spell everything out. 'Where are you going?'

'I'm walking.'

'I can see that. Did you get lost?' She wrapped her arms

around herself, shivering despite the coat and scarf. He didn't look like he felt the cold at all.

'I'm exploring.'

'It's dark.' When he said nothing, she urged him to get in the car. He wasn't right. 'I can drive you back once I've made my delivery. These roads are nasty in the day, let alone at night.'

'They need a few pavements around here.' As he got into the passenger side, he sounded more like himself, as though coming out of a peculiar trance. 'Smells good in here.'

She drove slowly up towards the car park area near the house. 'That'll be mince pies and Christmas pudding cookies.'

Quinn cleared his throat and after a pause, as she slowed to pull into the car park area, he said, 'Hazel and Arnold are in for a treat.'

'They're hosting a party this evening.' Perhaps normal conversation rather than asking him again what on earth he was doing was the way to go. 'From memory, it's for their employees, otherwise I'd be asking where's my invite.'

Her joke fell flat. He said nothing.

It felt odd to have him sitting next to her in such a confined space, so she got out and collected the plastic containers from the footwell behind the driver's seat.

'I'll wait here.' Quinn looked over at the paddocks, next to which was the outdoor riding school. There was a horse and rider in the school, the whole area floodlit. 'Or maybe over there, see what's going on.'

'I shouldn't be too long; I'll come and get you.'

He merely lifted a hand in farewell as he walked away and Celeste made her way over to the main house.

Hazel answered the door, hair wrapped in a towel and wearing a robe. 'Come in out of the cold. I'm running behind, but at least the workers will all understand.' She led the way through to the kitchen. 'Did you see Gus outside?'

Celeste set down the plastic containers onto the kitchen table. 'So that's Abigail having a lesson on Denby in the school?' Abigail was Gus's daughter from a previous marriage and they kept her horse Denby here.

'You know what Abigail is like; she rides Denby as often as she can. Doesn't matter if it's early or late.' Hazel took off the lids of the plastic containers and put a hand to her chest each time. 'These smell so good, I almost want to smuggle one upstairs while I dry my hair.'

'I'd say go for it,' Celeste laughed, 'but flaky pastry crumbs or bits of biscuit in a hairdo isn't a very good look.' She looked across at the kitchen benchtop to the platters all lined up. 'It looks like you'll have some feast this evening.'

'We were going to do a proper sit-down dinner but given our long hours, we thought we'd make it a cocktail party so more casual. Etna and Patricia made most of the spread at the tea rooms, we've got some vanilla bean ice-cream from the ice-creamery to go with the mince pies, so we're all set.'

'I'll leave you to it then.'

'Was that Quinn I saw outside when you got here?' Hazel led the way back to the front door.

'I think he got a bit lost in the back roads of Heritage Cove.' She thought nothing of the sort, but she wasn't about to speculate as to what was going on with him.

'Easily done,' Hazel smiled.

'You go get yourself ready and have a wonderful time.'

'Will do. I need to be ready to greet everyone because Arnold is going to be a latecomer; he's promised to finish up tonight.'

'He's a good man, your brother,' she smiled.

'Thanks again for the sweets; say hi and thanks to Jade for me.'

Celeste made her way from Heritage View House over to the paddock, floodlights illuminating enough that she could see Gus and Quinn waiting. They'd moved away from the school while Abigail continued her lesson with Arnold.

Celeste hung back, not wanting to intrude, but she could just about hear what they were saying.

'She's a great kid.' Quinn looked over to the school where Abigail was making a good job of guiding Denby around and over poles spaced at various intervals on the ground. 'She was in the Star and Lantern the other day with Sandy. They each wanted to hang a decoration on the tree for us, do their bit, they said. She's very polite; you must be really proud of her.'

'She's pretty special.' Gus must have seen Celeste in the corner of his eye and turned a bit more to smile and welcome her into their conversation. 'She's had a tough time along the way.'

Celeste walked towards them as though she hadn't been hanging back at all.

'How are you, Celeste?' Gus rubbed his hands together and blew into them. Looked like he'd forgotten his gloves.

'Can't complain,' she smiled.

'You say Abigail had a tough time,' Quinn prompted.

'Yeah, long story,' sighed Gus, 'but she's in a good place now and Denby is a big part of that.'

'A girl's best friend?'

'Something like that. The magical powers of animals for company – never underestimate it.'

'I wouldn't dare,' said Quinn. 'You ready?' he asked Celeste. It was as though he hadn't been that lost man, both physically, as he claimed, or in his own head, and everything was totally normal now.

'I'm ready. Have a wonderful time tonight, Gus. I assume you get to go to the party?'

'Well, I am the emergency vet if they can't get hold of their usual one and I do have Sandy lined up to look after Abigail,' he said, 'so I get to enjoy some of that wonderful food. I hear we've got your bakery's mince pies.'

'You most certainly have. And Christmas pudding biscuits.'

Gus patted his stomach. 'I won't tell Abigail or I'll never get her home.'

Quinn and Celeste walked back over to her car, the quiet between them hovering awkwardly. The way Quinn had complimented Gus on his daughter tonight had tugged at Celeste's heartstrings because what it said to her was that this man was ready for a family, that this was the reason he'd left the navy for good. And she would never be able to give him his wish.

When Quinn climbed into the car, he said, 'I wonder what Gus meant when he said Denby has helped Abigail through a tough time.'

Celeste shrugged, even though she doubted he'd see the gesture when it was so dark inside the car as they left Heritage View House and stables behind. 'Animals have a wonderful healing power; I read an article about it once. I always thought it was dogs, though.'

'Yeah, me too.' The depth of his voice sent a flicker of excitement through her. It always had.

They barely said another word as she drove back along the lane where she'd picked him up earlier. But when she pulled out of the lane and onto The Street, she felt him watching her.

'Mind if I park at mine and you walk to the pub from there?' she asked.

'I think I can manage.' His chuckle was deep and throaty and it reminded her of the times they'd lain side by side in her bed and laughed about something or other. She wished now that she could remember what it was they'd laughed about.

'You have a tree yet?' Quinn asked when they got out of the car.

'I got it delivered today. Do you want to see it?' Part of her wanted him to say yes, the other part wanted him to say no to make this easier.

He came around the front of the car to meet her where she was standing toying with the car keys. And now there was no trace of that man she'd seen in the lane, the one who had looked through her at first, whose eyes seemed hollow, whose soul seemed troubled.

But before he could answer the question either way, Jade came out from the back of the bakery. She looked from Quinn to Celeste.

'I found him walking in the dark, brought him home,' Celeste explained.

Jade smiled and if she thought there was anything odd, she didn't let on. 'Can you come help me? I'm not sure which one of us suggested these late hours but whether it was you or me, that person needs talking too. I got busy after you left and I just need help in the kitchen; promise it'll only take half an hour between the pair of us.'

'Of course.' As Jade rushed back inside the bakery, Celeste wondered whether Quinn been about to agree to her suggestion of coming inside.

She guessed she'd never know now.

'I'd better go anyway,' he said. 'I know what being in business with a sibling is like; we watch each other's backs so each gets a break but that's not always possible.'

'Good job I didn't venture far away,' she smiled.

'I'll see you then.'

Celeste headed for the back door of the bakery but turned around before she opened up to follow her sister inside. Quinn was still lingering. 'I'll see you again soon.'

'I hope so, Celeste.' And with one look between them that held a lot more than a platonic friendship, he left her to it.

Accepting she and Quinn had to find their own way ahead, separately, was getting harder by the day. And with him living in the village, she wondered how impossible it was really going to get.

Or would she eventually give in to temptation?

20

It seemed fitting that the last time Quinn had spoken to Celeste, she'd been summoned into the bakery at the end of the day because here he was, a week later, and neither he nor Eddie had had much of a break today unless you counted his dash to get more milk for Benjamin in the kitchen and the run he'd done before the rest of the Cove had even opened their curtains this morning.

Tonight, it was no less busy than it had been all day.

'How are you going to keep it hidden?' Quinn, standing behind the bar at the Star and Lantern, had just pulled a pint for a local who'd bought their daughter a puppy for Christmas. 'You can hardly put it in a box, wrap it and tie it with a bow.'

'That's where I come in,' laughed Gus, who had returned for his pint of Guinness now that it had settled. He was here having dinner with Abigail this evening and she looked busy drawing a picture at the table they were sharing with Hazel. 'Abigail and I will look after the puppy until the early hours of Christmas morning.'

Quinn moved on to serve Kenneth and Etna, then Harvey,

then a couple of other locals who introduced themselves. Talk about a full house. But there was a reason for it tonight because a lot of these customers had apparently got the same letter Eddie and Quinn had received: a letter that said a community meeting would be held in the pub at eight o'clock.

It was Eddie who'd opened the letter that had been slid beneath the front door of the pub either this morning or very late last night. Quinn had spotted it on his way out for his run but had merely set it on the bar to deal with when he returned, and Eddie had got there first.

Both Eddie and Quinn had thought the letter wildly presumptuous until Quinn pointed out that one of their business ideas was to host more groups here in the pub.

'Whoever this is from should've asked permission,' Eddie had said, jabbing a finger at the piece of paper. 'Never mind that it's a so-called community meeting.' That was what the title of the letter said in big, bold letters, its content merely giving a time, the place – here – and that their attendance was required.

'Or look at it a different way,' Quinn suggested to him while he was still spent and sweaty from his run and desperate to hit the shower. 'Whatever the meeting is, it doesn't matter, does it? It's a good example to show everyone who comes that they could hold similar groups here should they want to.'

'Hadn't thought of that,' Eddie had conceded and since then had come around to the idea.

Quinn and Eddie were still none the wiser now as to what the meeting was about despite asking next to every punter when they came to the bar or in from the cold.

Quinn flipped a top from a bottle, then did the same with the other before setting the pair onto a tray along with a couple of glasses he'd already filled with ice. Benjamin came through with two meals and Eddie whizzed the drinks over to Mrs Filligree and her friend who'd just arrived.

Almost an hour later, still before the scheduled meeting time, Quinn pointed out to Eddie that business tonight had exceeded any evening they'd had so far. And he'd just taken another card payment for three more meals as well as drinks. 'I'm not sure we even used to do this well on New Year's Eve at the old pub.'

'It's busy for sure,' Eddie replied before moving on to serve Daniel, who was expecting Lucy at any second.

Daniel was as inquisitive as everyone else. 'Anyone work out what the meeting is about?'

Eddie shook his head. 'Nope. Did you have to close up the waffle shack for this?'

'No, it's not one of my late nights so it worked out well. And I wasn't going to miss this.' He frowned. 'I really am puzzled as to what this is all about.'

'You sound worried. Have you been up to no good?' Eddie joked.

'Not for years,' said Daniel before taking his drinks over to the couple of chairs his friends had saved. His comment had Quinn wondering about Daniel's history with the Cove. Maybe he'd find out what it was eventually – everyone seemed to have their own story.

Celeste and Jade showed up when the pub was almost bursting at the seams.

'You closed the bakery?' Quinn asked.

'Yes, an hour before it was scheduled, so this had better be good,' Jade grumbled and muttered something about being a busy working mum before she dashed off to the bathrooms in case she didn't get another chance.

'She okay?' He pulled out two glasses and filled them both with ice and then sparkling mineral water on Celeste's request.

'She's annoyed at having to close early, that's all.' She unwound her scarf.

'Why not send just one of you?'

She grinned. 'Neither of us wanted to miss out. And to be honest, it's not a bad thing. We've had a lot of late-night openings and with everyone in here, it's likely to mean the bakery is quiet anyhow. You're taking everyone else's business.'

'Oops.' But he returned her smile and couldn't help wondering what might have happened between them had he gone inside with her that night she picked him up from wandering in the middle of the road in the dark like a loony.

'Jade's tired and we'll be up early again in the morning so if this meeting goes on and then Phoebe has her up in the night, which happens sometimes, she won't get any downtime.'

'Parenting is hard work.'

'Yeah, it is.' She didn't look at him but rather at everyone gathering. 'I see it's standing room only.'

'Shame it's not summer; we could have had the meeting outside.'

'I'm dreaming of summer,' she admitted, turning back to face him. She bought a couple of packets of peanuts. 'About the other day—'

'You mean you inviting me in to see the Christmas tree?'

'Well... yes, but no.'

He'd hoped she wasn't going to bring up him walking in the dark so he'd deliberately misunderstood, and lucky for him, they couldn't continue the conversation because there was an undercurrent in the atmosphere, a murmuring around the pub, and all of a sudden, it got a lot rowdier.

And Quinn was elevated slightly behind the bar and tall enough to see why.

A great cheer went up and a collective call of, 'Barney!' rang out.

Melissa ran over to hug Barney, plenty of handshakes came his way and Lois did her best to get the man safely seated at the middle table.

'Did *you* call this meeting?' Lottie called out.

'I did. And thank you to Eddie and Quinn for hosting.'

'Didn't have much choice,' Eddie muttered behind Quinn.

'Don't lose it on him,' Quinn whispered back to his brother as Barney fielded questions from all directions about his health, when he'd got home, was he resting enough, was he taking care of himself?

Barney answered a few and then, palms outstretched, motioned for everyone to quieten down.

When he had his audience, his voice carried well but he still remained seated. 'Eddie and Quinn, I called this meeting for you both. Well, and for myself, as I haven't been around and I'm sorry about that. I wanted to be, to help you feel welcome and settle in.'

'We appreciate you thinking of us.' Eddie had been drying a glass but set it down and, with a tilt of his head, suggested he and Quinn go around to the customer side of the bar. It wasn't like they had any new customers; most of Heritage Cove's residents were sitting in here with food and drinks already in front of them. Couldn't complain about that.

Quinn found himself standing next to Celeste – not something he'd aimed for but something he wasn't at all sorry about. 'I never knew an old man could be so mischievous,' he whispered almost into her hair and got an appreciative giggle in return.

'That's one word for it.'

'Did you have any idea?' He got a bit closer so they weren't overheard and when someone else squeezed in on his other side, their bodies were almost pressed against each other. This was nice, or at least it was until he saw Carly, who nodded over to him. His discomfort wasn't that she might have seen how close he got to Celeste; it was the reminder of how he'd flipped at Justin when he took him by surprise on the village green that day. But he stood up straighter and nodded over to her all the same as Barney began to speak again and tell everyone why he'd called this meeting.

'Like I said,' Barney went on, 'the reason I called everyone here is because of these boys, Eddie and Quinn.'

'Shit...' Quinn said under his breath.

'No need to panic,' Barney said in his direction. 'We are happy you boys have taken ownership of our beloved pub. And we want to help.'

Quinn raised his eyebrows in Eddie's direction. Eddie might be around this side of the bar too but he was leaning against the wood, arms crossed in front of his chest.

'I've heard on the grapevine that you both have ideas of changes you want to make.' He held up a hand when Eddie tried to leap in. 'Hear me out; we want this to work as much as you do.'

But Eddie wasn't going to be pushed around and interrupted anyway. 'I don't think any of you know that the pub isn't doing quite as well as Terry and Nola always had you believe. They ran a seamless operation here, hats off to them, but they couldn't and didn't want to keep up with the pace. Because it's hard.'

'Nobody is disputing that,' came a voice of encouragement from somewhere. Quinn thought it might have been Kenneth from the allotments.

Eddie addressed the crowd, his voice carrying all the way to the back. 'The financial details are our business really, but I understand the vested interest. Both Quinn and I have pub experience; we don't pluck our ideas out of thin air and just hope for the best. You all might need to trust us for a while.'

There were murmurs of agreement until Barney chimed in again, although he asked Eddie's permission to speak first. It was clear he didn't want to upset anyone tonight. 'I called this meeting not because I want to put a stop to every idea you come up with, but because I want us, all of us in the Cove, to work with you and help.'

'All good in theory,' said Eddie.

'Terry and Nola always made a point of not stepping on the toes of existing businesses in Heritage Cove. In fact, everyone does that in their own way. That's all we're asking for, or I'm asking for, but assume I'm speaking on behalf of the village. Maybe it's me being big-headed—'

There were plenty of denials that that was the case.

'We don't want to step on toes either,' said Quinn. He couldn't let Eddie take all the flack; they were in this together. This was his future too.

'You're right about something,' Barney frowned, looking at Quinn and then Eddie, 'Terry and Nola never ever complained they needed a boost to business. I think they'd been here so long that they were just a part of the pub and the pub a part of them. They trusted ownership to go to you boys because they saw something in the both of you – they could've taken more money from someone else but didn't want to because they knew if they did, the pub might change so much, we barely recognised it any more.'

'The thought of losing our pub is frightening,' another voice called out.

'I don't know where I'd go for my Sunday lunch if you closed,' came another.

Voices all around were chorusing agreement, adding reasons to keep the Star and Lantern.

'The pub is still standing,' Eddie assured the crowd. 'You're all panicking, and I get why. We're new, you don't know us. But given half a chance, we'll show you that we are here to stay.'

Quinn felt Celeste stand a bit taller beside him and he lost the comfort of her arm brushing against his. A couple of late-comers caught his eye from the bar and he left Eddie talking to Barney and everyone else while he went over to sort the round of drinks. From his position behind the bar, he could hear ideas being called out, being batted back and forth. The fancy coffee machine idea was rejected straight away, there were objections to high teas because Etna did a lot of those for knitting groups and a new mother's group.

'What about getting in another good real ale?' Eddie suggested. 'We could attract people from far and wide for that if we have something we do really well.'

'Great idea,' someone called out.

'I'll be your first customer,' came another yell.

'I'm not sure outsiders are the way forward,' Barney frowned. 'We tried that for the charity Wedding Dress Ball and ended up with a lot of trouble on our doorstep.'

'No offence, but I think we can handle it,' said Eddie and Barney didn't add anything else because Eddie looked capable enough. 'We'll manage whoever comes to the pub; you let that be our worry. One bad experience shouldn't crush future plans.' There was a murmur of agreement. 'I'd also suggest a gin festival.'

A few of the ladies cheered and Quinn heard someone say, 'Now we're talking.'

'A gin festival...' Barney floated the idea in his head by saying it out loud. 'I think I'll be coming to that. Lois?'

She nodded her approval. 'Just try to keep me away.'

Zara proposed that she set up an ice-cream cart in the beer garden over the summer months. 'It's all business for me whether the ice-cream is consumed at the ice-creamery or here,' she said. 'And who knows, customers might try it here and pop in to buy a tub of something they like to take home with them.'

'Great idea,' Eddie agreed. 'Cheers, Zara.' He winked in her direction, leaving Quinn in little doubt that his brother wanted to spend more time with the owner of Heritage Cove's ice-creamery.

'We could do music events – get in live bands now and again,' Linc suggested to cries of how much people loved him and his guitar already. 'There's only one of me, you lot might enjoy a change, and it will bring in people from outside the Cove. There aren't that many pubs even in neighbouring villages, certainly not many that have live music, so that would appeal.'

The ideas went on with people chiming in – some suggestions were laughingly rejected, others were readily accepted and then Barney mentioned the barbecue competition idea.

'It would really bring people in,' said Eddie, 'and you never know, people in this village might love it.' There were a few murmurs, whether agreement or discord, Quinn wasn't sure. 'But I'm all ears if you have an equivalent suggestion.'

The barbecue event was one of Eddie's favourites, the one he saw as being a huge boost to their custom.

'What about a community barbecue?' Etna called out.

'It won't bring in much more custom than usual,' said Quinn.

'You could have a big event, publicise it: the barbecue to end all barbecues,' Lois suggested. 'You have the enormous beer garden; what about a bouncy castle at the far end for kids, face painting, then barbecue food?'

'It could be a ticketed event,' Barney put in.

'We could have a band too,' came another voice from somewhere.

'A day event,' Eddie pondered. 'It might work. But it'll take a lot of thought and planning.'

'A summer fair,' came another voice.

Quinn looked at Eddie. It wasn't a bad idea; market it as that and they might see great footfall, especially if they timed it with a gloriously sunny day.

'We could have ice-creams as well as barbecue,' came someone else's suggestion.

'I'm up for that,' said Zara, her hand in the air.

Suggestions continued and Eddie was taking them all down on a hastily grabbed notepad from behind the bar as Quinn went over to clear away some of the dirty plates from the tables.

When the meeting was at last adjourned with all parties still buzzing with ideas, Barney commandeered the brothers when they were near his table.

'I apologise if I over-stepped by calling the meeting here.'

'Hey,' said Eddie, 'no need to apologise. There's no rule about meeting a group of friends and I get the impression it's more what this was than an official meeting.'

'You're right there.' Barney smiled, although Quinn noted he didn't stand up again. 'I'm glad it's the both of you who've taken over, and the name change took a bit of getting used to, but it really suits this place.'

'I'm glad you like it.'

'I do. And the Christmas tree is just wonderful. All those decorations that mean something to the folks around here. You've done a very special thing.'

Eddie's brows raised in surprise. 'You approve?' He put a hand onto Barney's shoulder. 'Well, that's a relief.'

Later on, when they were both back behind the bar and the pub got back to normal, Quinn checked in with Eddie. 'Are you really all right with what went down tonight?'

'I am. I admit I was a bit blindsided but only for a second. This village is something else, you know.'

'You're not wrong there.' His eyes were on Celeste as he said it.

'And we can't complain about takings. They're through the roof tonight.'

'Even better.'

'I really like the guy.' Eddie grinned, nodding in Barney's direction as he wiped down the bar surface and the top of the drip tray.

'He's a character.'

'I don't mind when people object to our plans if they come up with alternatives. Believe me, I've been in places where people just complain but don't offer any reason other than they don't like something and there's no way they'd suggest alternatives.'

Quinn made up a glass of Pernod and black for a customer and a vodka and tonic for another. It seemed that nobody was in a hurry to leave the unofficial meeting and Barney was still centre stage.

They were well into the evening by the time Quinn was alerted to the conditions outside when a punter came in claiming he thought they might all be stuck here for the night given the snowstorm coming their way.

'What's he talking about?' Quinn would've squeezed through the crowds looking out of the back doors to the pub, but it was easier to go down the corridor and peek out of the front entrance instead. He whistled between his teeth.

When he turned, Celeste almost walked into him and her proximity was something he wanted to cling onto.

'Is it bad?' she asked.

He stood back so she could see. And when she turned

around, smiling, it lit up her entire face as she declared, 'It's snowing!'

'You could say that.' He couldn't take his eyes off her but pulled himself together enough to ask if she was heading home.

'Yeah, early start for us, remember. Jade left a good hour ago.'

'It's so busy in there, I didn't notice.'

'It was a great turnout.'

'When the man calls, you all come running.' He closed the door against the cold. 'Barney is a great guy. And I can see he wants what's best for everyone.'

Celeste smiled. 'Including the both of you.'

'Good to know.'

She looked at the front door to the pub. 'I can't walk through it if it's closed.' She slipped a hand into a glove and then pulled on the other one.

'Right.' He stood aside and pulled the door open for her. 'Well, I'll see you again soon.' Hadn't he said that last time? He'd wondered since that night whether he should've gone in to see her at the bakery or whether she'd pop into the pub but neither had happened.

She squeezed past him. 'See you.'

And it might be freezing but he stood watching her at the open door until the snow reminded him he only had a shirt on by sending flakes and an icy wind in his direction.

Last orders were called not long after Celeste left and the clearing up got underway. It had been one of the longest days since they'd taken on the pub, but it gave Quinn had a good feeling about their place here in the Cove, a sense of solidarity and togetherness he hadn't felt since he'd been in the navy and part of a team.

'Who does this belong to?' Eddie picked up a single key with a keyring up from the floor.

Valerie, who ran the local florist, spotted what Eddie was holding. 'That belongs to Celeste, at least I think so; the cupcake keyring is distinctive. I might be wrong,' she shrugged.

'Want to run it to her?' Eddie suggested to Quinn.

Quinn had to wonder whether his brother had picked up on something between them but right now, it didn't matter. If Celeste had got all the way home without her key, she'd be freezing by now and he didn't want her to have to come all the way back again.

He grabbed the key and his coat which he was still zipping up as he ran down the gritted path outside. He ran all the way from the pub along The Street, careful not to slip with snow continuing to fall, and to just past the bakery where he could turn right and go around the back. And sure enough, there was Celeste. And she'd emptied the contents of her bag onto the white-dusted concrete beneath her.

'Looking for this?' He pulled the key from his pocket and held it up.

She groaned. 'Yes.' She piled everything back into her bag and as she did so, something else fell to the ground. Holding the bag up high, she realised it had a hole in the bottom. 'Great.'

'You got everything else?'

She had a quick rummage whilst covering the offending hole with her hand. 'Looks like it. Thank you, Quinn.' She took the key, pushed it into the lock. 'Come inside, I'll make you a hot chocolate to say thank you.'

He was about to leap at the chance when both of them froze and not just from the temperature.

The key she'd pushed into the lock and turned had just snapped off.

'You have got to be kidding me.' She looked at the lock, at

him, back at the lock. And then she swore. 'What am I supposed to do now?'

'Go around the front?' he suggested, blinking away a flake of snow that landed on his eyelash.

'I only brought the back door key. Shit. I'll have to call Jade and she's already sleep deprived; this is the last thing she needs.'

'You're shivering. Where are your gloves?'

'In my pockets. I couldn't feel anything through them when I was rooting through my bag for my key.'

He stepped closer and pushed both his hands into her pockets, bringing both of them exceptionally close, before he pulled out her gloves. He put them on for her and the intimacy of the gesture had them both silenced.

'Thank you,' she murmured, brushing a flake of snow from her upper lip. 'I'll have to call a locksmith.'

'Not at this time of night. And not with snow already starting to fall.' He hadn't been forceful or firm since coming back to Heritage Cove, since she'd made it clear she wasn't interested in picking up where they'd left off. But now he couldn't help it. 'Come back to the pub with me. It's warm, you can take the bed, there's a sofa in the lounge fit for one.'

'You'd do that for me?'

He put a hand against the side of her face and she jolted either at the coldness of it or the mere touch, he wasn't sure. 'I would.'

And without another word, Celeste followed him away from her cottage, down past the bakery and onto The Street.

On their way to his place.

21

Quinn got Celeste settled upstairs and went back down to finish the clean-up in the pub. Celeste had offered to help but he'd insisted she didn't and so instead, she'd stayed up here in his room, tucked beneath the duvet with the hot chocolate he'd made her before he'd gone to help his brother.

'You warmed up?' he asked softly when he poked his head in a short while later.

'I have, thank you.'

He went to close the curtains.

'Leave them; I want to watch the snow fall.'

'You could see more from over here.' He looked down to The Street.

She'd seen it on the walk here, the Cove getting a decent coating, although the so-called snowstorm someone had predicted wasn't likely. It was expected to stop in the next couple of hours. Perfect – it was just enough to give it a festive feel, not enough to upset day-to-day routines. She wouldn't mind that happening at Christmas, though – a White Christmas was on everyone's wish list, wasn't it?

'I'm too cosy under the duvet,' she smiled, setting down her mug. She'd finished the hot chocolate but for some reason, clutching the still-warm mug had been comforting. 'I'm glad I didn't call Jade. I'd have felt terrible getting her out in this weather.'

'Your sister sounds busy.'

'She has a kid.'

'Mums are amazing. Dads too.' He perched on the end of the bed as though he didn't belong.

'Family, it's important.' And she could never take that away from him. Her heart thumped faster. 'Do you see yourself as a parent some day?'

'Er… sure,' he answered, sounding bewildered. 'You? Are you going to give Phoebe a cousin to play with?'

She pulled her knees up to her chest, wrapping her arms around them. When he'd been in the Cove the first time and they'd had their whirlwind few days together, she felt she knew enough about him to know the sort of man he was, but with him living in the village, the more she saw of him, the more she realised how little each of them really knew about the other.

'I have my business,' she told him honestly.

'So does Jade.'

'Jade has always wanted children. You know, she wanted them so badly, she was willing to go ahead without another half.'

'How does that work?' She liked the way his brow laced with confusion.

'She was going to go to a clinic, choose a sperm donor.'

His eyes widened. 'Wow. So I suppose then she met Linc and it happened without the intervention, am I right?'

'Linc came into her life at the perfect time – well, she didn't see it that way at first, because she had it all planned out. This *is*

Jade we're talking about. But now...' She shrugged. 'Now she couldn't imagine it any other way.'

'Some people are born to be parents. There was a guy I was in the navy with, Aaron, a great hulk of a man whose kids brought out another side to him. Most grown men would run a mile if they saw Aaron coming for them but seeing him hoist his kids up into his arms when we docked was something pretty special.'

She hugged her knees a little tighter. 'Did you ever miss having a family to welcome you home?'

'Eddie came to meet me off the ship a few times; so did our parents. But yeah, I suppose I did when other men and women fell into the arms of a special someone.' His eyes dipped to her lips. 'Wouldn't have minded seeing you there.'

'We had those few days and left it at that.'

He moved closer to her on the bed but hadn't quite reached the head where she was sitting. 'Neither of us wanted anything more. At the time. We both said as much.'

'We did.' And she might not want what he wanted, but she couldn't deny she wanted Quinn. She swung her legs off the bed so that she was sitting next to him. 'I should go. I shouldn't be here.'

'I invited you. And I can sleep on the sofa, remember.' He waited. 'Unless you really don't want to be near me.'

'It isn't that.' She stumbled over the words, looking down into her lap.

He reached a hand below her chin and tilted her face upwards. 'Then what is it?'

'I don't want to hurt you.'

'What makes you think you will?' He took his hand away. 'We had a great time when I was here in the village before but this time around, it's as though you want to keep a distance between us. Is there someone else?'

She smiled. 'Have you seen me with anyone else?'

'Well, no, but—'

'There's nobody else.'

'Then I don't understand why you avoid getting too close to me. Like now, you're here but you're not here, if you see what I mean.' He shook his head. 'I don't want to sound up myself but I'm pretty sure there's still something between us. Am I imagining it? If you tell me I am, I'll back off and I won't ask again.'

She knew he'd be good to his word too. And the thought that this was the last chance, the final time he'd push and try to have more than friendship and a civil conversation had her reaching for his hand.

He clutched onto hers and side by side, they sat in silence as though the charge between them, all those feelings, were shared by a simple touch.

When he turned his head, she knew he was about to kiss her. His face drew closer to hers, she felt his soft breath against her face, could almost taste the softness of his lips even though they hadn't yet touched.

It was one of the hardest things she'd ever done to pull away. 'We can't, Quinn. Or at least... *I* can't. It wouldn't be fair. On you, I mean.'

'Oh, I think it would be very fair.'

She stood up. She had to put some distance between them. 'I wish you wouldn't joke.'

'And I wish you'd admit your true feelings for me.'

She had to make him understand. 'Tell me again: why did you leave the navy? You always said you'd leave when the time was right – you left, so what was it that did it?'

It was his turn to stand up now. 'It's late, I don't really want to argue.' He went over to the wardrobe at the side of the room and took out a shirt that he passed to her. 'Here, sleep in this;

it's not that warm but once you're under the duvet, you'll be fine.'

She took the shirt while he went back and pulled down a blanket from the section at the very top of the wardrobe.

'Don't go, Quinn.' She almost wished, no matter whether it was the right thing to do, that she'd let him kiss her, let him stay with her. Why hadn't she done that? It would've made it easier; he wouldn't be annoyed at her right now, even though she knew it was for his own good.

'I'll see you in the morning. I can wake you if you need me to. Don't want you to be late for work.' He'd completely ignored her request that he didn't leave.

'I have an alarm on my phone.'

He nodded. 'Sleep well.' And he didn't even turn to look at her again before he pulled the door closed behind him with a gentle click.

* * *

Celeste couldn't sleep. More than once, she'd tiptoed over to the bedroom door, her hand on the handle, ready to go out to Quinn in the lounge. But she hadn't. She'd watched the snow fall beyond the window for a while until it stopped and finally, she'd climbed into bed.

She had no idea when she fell asleep; all she knew was the time on the clock beside the bed said 1 a.m. when she woke as she heard a knock on her door.

Bleary-eyed, she sat up in bed. 'Come in.'

The door opened slowly and Quinn poked his head around the wood. He was hovering, unsure whether to come in.

She turned back the duvet. 'You can stay in here if you like.'

'You sure?'

'I'm sure.'

He closed the door quietly behind him and when he climbed in next to her, the mattress moved and dipped with his weight. He reached up and put a hand against her cheek.

'You okay?' She could tell he wasn't. There was plenty on his mind, lots he wasn't telling her. She'd seen it that day on the beach, the night in the lane.

He didn't say anything, only nodded. He didn't take his gaze away but he edged closer, tentatively, until their lips were almost touching.

The kiss, when it came, was every bit as smooth and intoxicating as she remembered from their days together before. Her body pressed against the firmness of his chest as he manoeuvred the duvet so it was no longer between them but covering them both.

'I need the body heat,' he laughed when the kiss came to an end. 'That lounge room is freezing.'

She giggled quietly, aware that Eddie's bedroom was the other side of the wall. 'So you're just using me for heat?'

'Seemed like a good idea.'

'It's a bit cold in here if you let any of your limbs come uncovered.' She'd found that out when she couldn't sleep and she'd got out of bed to tiptoe to the door each time.

'Then I suggest we don't do that.' He kissed her again, taking his time, and pulled her body close.

Cold or not, both of them were sleepy, and the way he was kissing her, Celeste sensed this man was different to the Quinn from years gone by. That Quinn would've never left the bedroom in the first place; he would've had her clothes off by now, he would've saved cuddles and conversation for afterwards. Back then, it was as though each of them knew they had a limited time and they didn't want to waste any of it.

She buried her head against his chest and breathed in the scent of a man she never wanted to let go.

'Celeste...?'

'Hmm...' Her fingers stroked the hair on his chest, dark, thick, sexy.

'Mind if we just sleep?'

She propped herself up on one elbow. 'I don't mind.'

He was running his fingers along her collarbone until it reached the buttons of the shirt of his that she was wearing. 'You look good in my clothes.'

'As long as you don't try to borrow mine, we're all good.'

A low laugh rumbled up his chest and she felt the vibrations when she reached a hand out to make contact with his body and laid her head against his skin again. 'Aren't you cold with no top on?'

'Not with you here,' he said sleepily.

Her fingers still tracing the hair on his chest, she closed her eyes and it wasn't long before she felt herself falling asleep.

Falling asleep in his arms.

* * *

Celeste had never been woken up quite so brutally before. But the duvet was yanked away from her by the body in the bed next to her yelling, thrashing about.

For a minute, she had no idea what to say or what to do.

'Quinn...' Her voice came out small.

He'd sat up on the edge of the bed, facing away from her, and was mumbling loudly, incoherently.

She cautiously walked around the bed but stopped before she got to his side. 'Quinn... it's me, Celeste.'

It was as though he was awake but not fully and he yelled

something else, although again she couldn't decipher the meaning. His fists were clenched around the duvet, as though he was
trying to turn it to dust by squeezing the life out of it.

She stepped a little bit closer but the terror in his eyes
stopped her again. It was a look she never wanted to see again.
She backed away.

She hadn't realised but the fear of what was happening had
tears streaming down her cheeks and she only knew when she
tasted the salty tang on her lips.

She wasn't sure how long she stood there before the low light
of the middle of the night changed when the bedroom door
opened and a brighter light from the landing spilled inside.

She turned. 'Eddie, I—'

'How long has he been like this?'

'What's happening?'

If Eddie was surprised to see her there, he didn't show it. 'He
has night terrors.' He too was wary of his own brother and stayed
back at first.

'Help him,' she urged.

'He's still asleep. I don't always step in.'

They were talking like there wasn't something out of the ordinary going on in the room with them right now.

Eddie eventually went to his brother's side. He gripped
Quinn's shoulders firmly, and slowly, Quinn began to quieten
down. His body gradually gave up the fight and he fell back onto
the bed, curled into a ball.

Celeste picked her clothes up from beside the bed. 'I should
go.' She looked back at Quinn before she left the room, clothes
cradled in her arms.

Eddie had followed her out and before she could go down
the stairs, asked her to join him in the lounge. 'Quinn told me
you're locked out of your place. You can't go anywhere else.

Come on, I'm harmless, I promise. And I'll put the heater on for us.'

He was right. She didn't have many options at this point in time. And it was still only 4.30 a.m.

'Celeste, please, come and sit down.' Eddie gestured to the sofa with the blanket she'd seen Quinn take out of the wardrobe earlier, rumpled and left in place. She wondered – had he slept at all before he'd come in to be with her?

Eddie had the heater switched on and moved it closer to them as he took the opposite sofa. 'Warm enough?' He had a jumper on and sweatpants, probably hastily grabbed when he heard the commotion coming from Quinn's room.

He shook his head at the offer of part of the blanket so Celeste pulled it across her lap and drew her knees into her body. The blanket smelt of Quinn: masculine, musty, and it reminded her of the man she saw as strong, the man she'd known before.

'What's going on with him, Eddie?'

He scratched the back of his neck. Celeste had seen Quinn do the same gesture. 'I'm going to deflect that with a question of my own.' Their voices were soft in the night against the low lamp light, the tired wallpaper, the square outline of where a picture or maybe a mirror had been removed from above the mantel. 'Are you and my brother close?'

'You know our history?'

Eddie looked at her properly rather than fiddling with the heater to make sure it was positioned properly for optimum warmth. 'He told me there was someone back then, when we came to the village before, but he never gave me a name and it didn't click until recently. And then it *really* clicked when he said you were up here tonight.' He sat back against the velvety material of the sofa. 'He's always played his cards pretty close to his chest.'

'That sounds like Quinn. Not that I know him all that well,
I'm starting to realise.'

'Are you and he... well, are you a thing now?'

'Together?' She shook her head. 'He's hinted that's what he'd
like but... well, it's complicated.'

'These things usually are.'

'So are you going to answer my question?'

He sat forwards, arms resting along his thighs. 'He has nightmares. Night terrors.'

'About what?'

'The things he's seen, the things that happened when he was
serving in the navy.' He was scratching at the back of his neck
again. 'I'm not sure whether I should be telling you anything. He
really should be the one to do that.'

'I'm not asking for details, Eddie. But one minute, we're
falling asleep next to each other and the next, it's as though all
hell has broken loose in the bedroom – it sounds dramatic but—'

'It doesn't. I've run in there enough times to know how terri-
fying it is. The first time I saw him like that, I tried to wake him
up and he freaked out; he went crazy, he upturned a table, threw
a lamp across the room. It took a long time to calm him down
and when he woke in the morning, he couldn't remember much
about it. Now it's a judgement call. Sometimes I stand back and
wait for it to pass; other times I know when to intervene.'

'Does it happen often?'

'Yes.'

Her heart sank. This Quinn, the one who'd done this tonight,
the man she'd seen wandering in the dark lane that night, this
was the man he was beneath the surface. Traumatised, in pain,
suffering. And she hadn't seen it. She hadn't realised and somehow, she thought perhaps she should have. 'Is he getting help?'

'I wish I could tell you he was. He needs help, I know that, and deep down, so does he. He needs to talk to someone who's better equipped to deal with this sort of thing than I am.'

'Does he tell you about what happens in these nightmares or night terrors?' Her fingers toyed with the frayed edge of the woollen blanket. 'Sorry, I'm not sure what to call them.'

'I think only Quinn could really define them. When he can remember them, that is. And I've said too much already, I don't like talking about him behind his back but it comes from a good place. And I didn't want you thinking my brother had totally lost it tonight; I didn't want you to keep your distance because of it.'

'I won't. And even though he isn't getting professional help, having you is better than not having anyone at all.' Looking at Eddie now, she could see how this might be taking its toll. He looked worn out, tense. 'Why don't you go and get some more sleep and I'll stay here until it's time for the bakery to open, sneak out then?'

'I think I will. Let me turn the heater off first.'

'I won't sleep; leave it on, I'll do it when I go.'

Passing her, Eddie put a hand on her shoulder. 'He's a good man.'

'I know he is,' she smiled.

An hour or so later, when Celeste crept out of the pub, closing the front door quietly behind her, she wondered whether the handsome, strong, confident Quinn McLeod had so much weight on his shoulders that he had no idea how to deal with it. No clue where to start.

All she wanted to do was see him get the help he needed. But if he wasn't listening to Eddie, he wasn't likely to listen to anyone else either.

And would he really thank her if she interfered?

22

Celeste didn't see Quinn for a couple of days after the night they'd shared a bed. She'd got her door at the cottage fixed and come clean with Jade about where she'd stayed, omitting anything about the nightmares, saying instead that Quinn and Eddie had put her up as though it was purely a favour in the context of friendship. Whether Jade believed her or not was another matter but for now, she wasn't asking any questions.

She'd thought about that night a lot since. She wondered whether Quinn remembered any of it, was he embarrassed, ashamed, wondering what to say to her when he saw her again?

She was still thinking about it today when Lois came into the bakery mid-afternoon. 'You've left Barney at home?'

'He's on snow-watch, willing it to fall from the skies again.' Since a couple of days ago and the start of what looked to be a decent snowfall, the white dusting and the occasional frost had been all they'd been graced with. 'But at least it means he's resting and inside in the warm.'

'That's good.'

'It's a relief. I wasn't sure how much he'd listen to me.' She took off her gloves and pulled out her purse from her bag. 'I think the hospital stay gave him quite the scare.'

'I'm sure it did.'

Lois peered into the glass-fronted cabinet. 'I knew I should've come this morning.'

'What are you after?'

'Six of your chocolate brownies.'

'Then you're in luck,' Celeste beamed. 'I made another batch but was waiting for the last two to go before I brought them out.'

She put the two in the cabinet into a box and went out the back to bring through the rest, four of which she lifted into the box.

'Wonderful,' Lois smiled.

'And you got your Christmas cake from Jade?'

'I most certainly did. It smells and looks out of this world.'

'I saw the cakes in progress, so it ought to.'

'My family arrived from Ireland this morning and they're going to love it.'

'Well, have a wonderful Christmas, all of you.'

But Lois dismissed the wish with her hand. 'I'll see you again before then.'

After she held the door open for Lois, who went on her way, she had an influx of half a dozen customers before Jade returned to relieve Celeste for lunch.

'How was the music party with Phoebe?' Jade and Linc had joined some of the parents for a party for all the kids who went to music group.

Jade made a face as she tied her apron on. 'Loud. Phoebe will sleep for a good couple of hours now, though, and I bet Linc will too.'

'I can imagine.' The word *sleep* reminded her of Quinn. Did the disturbed nights ever let up for long? Or was he always running on empty?

They busied themselves through the afternoon. Celeste rejected the suggestion she go out for a walk for lunch and instead made herself a ham and cheese roll on rye that she ate out back. The busier she was, the better. Less thinking time about the man who had come unexpectedly back into her life.

Every time the door to the bakery opened, the girls were reminded of the season and usually held the door for their customers as they left, mostly so they could make sure that nobody let it blow open.

The afternoon quietened down and Celeste refilled the glass-fronted cabinet now supplies had dwindled again. She adjusted one of the snowflake decorations on the bakery's window so that it would look perfect from the outside and as the day drew towards another close, she stared beyond the window and up at the ominous sky. She wondered what it had in store for them next. Rain? Snow? Hail or sleet? It didn't seem to be able to make up its mind lately.

'Celeste…' Jade's voice prompted from behind her.

'Sorry, did you ask me something?'

'A few times,' Jade laughed. 'What's going on with you?'

'Nothing.' She looked through the glass and up at the sky again. 'Do you think we'll get snow again soon?'

'I hope so. Did you have a think about cookies?'

'Cookies?'

'You said you were going to think of another festive recipe, try something out if you got the chance.'

'Completely slipped my mind.'

'No worries.' Jade had joined her at the window. 'I like it when the streets are quiet.'

'It's magical, isn't it? Quiet out there, quiet in here.'

'Oops, spoke too soon,' Jade laughed as, right on cue, Tracy, who ran the Heritage Inn with her husband Giles, came bundling in on the off chance they had a yule log left.

'We sure do.' Jade boxed one up for Tracy.

'Lifesaver. I promised my daughters they could host a little party with their friends and have a yule log – but guess who forgot to make or buy one.'

'Were you ever going to make it?' Celeste asked.

Tracy bellowed out a laugh. 'Not likely. Yours are too nice.'

Prompted by Tracy's jolly mood, Jade asked, 'Have you been at the pub?'

'Oh, no, you can tell?'

'I can smell mulled wine.'

'Caught red-handed. Benjamin's mulled wine recipe is the best and I was having a catch-up with Melissa – a long overdue catch-up.'

It made Celeste happy to know Melissa was seeing her friends, getting her head together, dealing with what was happening and finding her way. She and Tracy had been friends for years.

Celeste left Tracy with Jade while she went out back. She took down her notebook and flipped through for inspiration to try and come up with a new cookie recipe. She smiled to herself because Tracy was still chatting away at a volume in the bakery. Full of the Christmas spirit, the way Heritage Cove was itself.

'Now is there anything else I can get you, Tracy?' Jade's voice carried through to the back where Celeste had sat down on a stool while she thought about flavours.

'I'll have one of those if you have any going,' laughed Tracy.

'I don't know how to make those but anything behind the glass counter and it's yours,' Jade replied.

Curious, Celeste leaned out to see what Tracy could possibly have meant but she didn't time it too well because Quinn was standing close to the wall that separated the kitchen from the bakery.

'You hiding?' he asked her.

She held up the notebook. 'Working.' And she tried to ignore the pairs of eyes on them both right now.

'Enjoy that yule log,' Jade rallied, sensing Celeste might prefer to talk to her visitor without the audience.

Quinn turned around to check whether they were being closely watched before saying softly, 'I know we need to talk. I've been worried to face you since the other night. When you saw me at my best.'

'Don't do that… don't dismiss it.' When he didn't meet her eye, she knew how hard this had to be for him.

'I'd like the chance to explain if I may.' He scratched the back of his head in the same way Eddie had done in the middle of the night as he tried to find the right words for Celeste.

Jade made it clear she was coming towards them by clattering a couple of trays together. 'Why don't you go on a break.' She squeezed past Quinn to put the trays out back. 'I've got things here, we're quiet now, can't see there being a rush.'

'Are you sure?' Celeste put her notepad down.

'Of course. I'll call you if I need you.'

With Jade back in the bakery, Celeste suggested they head out to her cottage.

'I thought we might walk down to the cove.'

His suggestion met with a smile. 'It's dark and it's freezing.'

'I know,' he replied lightly.

'Okay, give me a few minutes to go back to my cottage, get some layers on and I'll meet you out front.' It wasn't like she needed to bundle up for her short commute so she'd need time to find a big scarf, a hat, a bigger coat than the jacket she'd thrown on to run the few steps from the door to the cottage to the back door of the bakery.

It wasn't long before she joined Quinn out front and found him, face ducked down into his coat as much as it could go. He looked up at her. 'You're right; it's bloody cold.'

'Want to rethink walking down to the water's edge?'

'I'm a tough guy; I don't want to back out. Unless you do.'

She shook her head and laughed when he revealed the bag slung over his shoulder contained two rather large and very warm blankets. 'Tough guy, eh?'

'Tough, not stupid,' he grinned, 'and I have a torch too. A big one.'

Despite the bitter temperature, they set off across the road, down the track that ran parallel to the chapel. They didn't talk much as they made their way down the path to the beach and the cove itself, Quinn shining the torch to help them out.

'I'd forgotten how beautiful it is here, even in the dark and on the harshest of days,' said Celeste, the wind almost taking her breath away as she let him take her hand when she stepped from the path onto the sands. They couldn't see much but the glow from the moonlight and the big torch was enough.

'Nature at its best,' he agreed, before leading them over to the rocks at the very back. 'Oddly enough, we're the only ones down here.' He laid one blanket on the sand.

'Funny, that.' She sat down and he sat next to her, covering them both with the second blanket.

'Suits you.' Celeste nodded to his beanie, a dark-grey number which covered his ears.

'Cheers.' But the smile didn't last long. He knew what they were here for.

'You've had those nightmares before, haven't you?' she began, warmed beneath the blanket from the material and his body

heat. She sensed he was struggling with how to start the conversation and she wanted to do whatever she could to make it easier
for him.

'Many times.'

'How long has it been going on?'

His breath puffed out a white cloud. 'Since before I left the
navy.'

She let his answer settle. Because that was a long time ago, a
long time to be dealing with what she'd seen the other night.

'It didn't happen all the time. Sometimes, I'd go a few nights,
even weeks without them, and I'd start to wonder whether I was
over it. Done.' He harrumphed. 'I'm proven wrong every time
they come back. It's like a reminder that I'm not winning at this.'

The soothing sounds of the waves crashed around them. 'Are
the nightmares about the things you saw when you were at sea?'

He didn't answer right away.

'I can't begin to imagine what it was like for you. We didn't
talk about it at all when we first met. Not the details, anyway.'

That evoked a smile from him, eyes misted with joy. 'We
didn't do all that much talking from what I remember.' He rested
the torch in front of them on the sand so that it shone across the
surface of the water, and he focused on the sea, on its volatility,
the depths you couldn't determine. 'Back then, I was on a high,
pretty much permanently; the adrenaline of my job was an
addiction. I chased it. I loved it.' Elbows resting on his knees, he
had fingers steepled together and rocked his hands back and
forth against his mouth.

'What happened to change all that?'

He shifted and realised the blanket had too. He readjusted it
so that she was covered up properly. 'Warm enough?'

'Stop worrying about me.'

'I like worrying about other people.' And then his expression changed. 'It's part of why I wanted to be in the navy but part of what made me leave.'

'You wanted a family.'

He turned to face her. 'I did want to be with family.'

'That isn't what I meant exactly.'

Confused, he said, 'I wanted to put down some roots, have my family around me when I felt my world had gone to shit.'

He'd missed her meaning, whether intentionally or not. But she didn't want to guide the conversation, not when he needed to put what was going on in his own words.

He watched the waves, closed his eyes more than once as he struggled either to remember or think of the right words. He pulled the blanket up higher. He must have felt her shiver.

'I don't know how you ever did such a difficult job.'

'Tough, that's me.' His voice had an edge that belied his attempt at a joke. 'My job was intense; it's part of what drew me to the career in the first place. I was part of a team on board ships which were responsible for keeping the maritime trade flowing and keeping out the bad guys.' He smiled. 'We were guardians of the sea, forces for good.' His smile didn't last. 'Keeping calm under pressure was a big ask but I did it. It never came easy; it took practice, it was always an achievement. But an achievement I managed. I bet you've seen war movies on the TV—'

'Not really my go-to choice of viewing,' she joked to make him feel more relaxed. And it did, for a moment, until he looked back at the water. He even emitted what sounded like a low laugh but the sound of the crashing waves, the wind around them and being bundled up in winter clothing made hearing every little noise a challenge.

'In the movies you see guns, violence, explosions, the characters are wounded, lose limbs, end up shell-shocked, lives ruined.

I'm lucky, my limbs are all intact... it's my head that's the problem. It's not in a good place and hasn't been for a while.'

'What happened?'

'It wasn't just one event, one trauma. Looking back, it's manifested over time. I started to feel the opposite of calm whenever I came under pressure. Even handling weapons, which was something I was confident in, became more real. That sounds weird, I know, but it's the only way I can explain it. I wondered whether perhaps it was because I was no longer in my twenties and I knew the consequences, the value of life and how precious it is, how tomorrow isn't guaranteed.

'Stopping drug traffickers was something I had experience in but rather than the buzz of stopping them, the sense of victory that we'd protected our country from criminal and terrorist gangs, I began to feel fear, fear that almost bowled me over. One day, a day that initially felt like a lot of others in my career, we ended up on board a ship to search for illegal cargo. The sea was particularly rough that day. It was dirty, dark, the helicopter hovering overhead to observe felt louder, more oppressive than ever. I found myself counting down until we found the drugs and got back on our own ship. And those drug searches often took hours. I lost my balance on deck a few times. It wasn't like me; my heart was pounding, I was sweating more than I ever had before. And I was scared. Scared of what was going on around me, scared of never making it out alive, and I was terrified I'd be seen as letting down the crew. I was putting others' safety as well as my own at risk when I wasn't operating at 100 per cent. It's not a job where there's much margin for error; you can't take five minutes to get your shit together before you carry on – five minutes can change everything, five minutes can cost a life.

'During that drug search, it was the first day I acknowledged that something inside of me had changed. And after that, it happened more and more, I came to expect the racing heart, the sweating, the headaches that came, the apprehensiveness and anxiety, sometimes anger that appeared out of nowhere. The lack of sleep was one of the worst things and it felt cumulative. I was going downhill and powerless to stop it.

'The way I am now, the nightmares, the PTSD took time to develop. It became next to impossible to detach from situations the way I once could.' Quinn looked at her so tenderly, as though it was she who needed the comfort and she wished she could do something to show him the same care. But she couldn't, and how could she possibly console him over events she'd never witnessed, things she'd never ever truly get? But he was opening up at last and down here all alone, just the two of them by the wine-glass-shaped cove, all she knew how to do was keep listening.

'I never thought I'd be one of those men,' he said.

'One of what men?'

'A man who couldn't cope, who is triggered so easily. I thought I was too strong, too tough, indestructible.'

'Nobody is indestructible. And you are strong, you are tough. You came out of the navy when you needed to. I'm thinking that wasn't easy.'

'It wasn't. It was all I'd known for a long time.' He gulped. 'Coming home was hard. I was worried how I'd adapt to a new life. And I was embarrassed, ashamed. Ashamed at what drove me to leave the navy behind, embarrassed that despite being a civilian, I couldn't put a stop to the nightmares and night terrors like the one you witnessed. It's bad having Eddie deal with them and now you but it was worse trying to hide when I was at sea. It's pretty hard to hide when you're sharing quarters with other men. It wakes Eddie in another room so you can imagine what it was like on the ship. They'd happen when I was deployed, when I was on leave, when I least expected them. They're the reminder that I can run but I can't hide. It's like all the conflicts and bad things I've ever experienced have been loaded onto a reel and once a switch is flipped, it replays in technicolour in my head and I've no idea how to switch them off. And then there's the finale...'

'Finale?'

'Yeah, the finale before my mind says, "Hey, Quinn, enough now, time to wake up".'

'What happens?' Celeste prompted when he didn't carry on.

'The navy provides humanitarian aid in times of disaster, whether those disasters are human-made or natural. They have the skills, the experience, the equipment. We were drafted in to help one year when the winter floods in the UK were at their worst.' He harrumphed. 'It wasn't a war zone, that's the crazy thing when you break it down, but the event left a mark on me that was bigger than anything else. It was what you'd call a natural disaster. The word *natural* makes it sound gentle, doesn't it? It sounds so much less than battling in a war, defending the seas, sending in the troops to fight.

'There were floods, terrible floods. I pulled bodies from the waters, too many bodies, some men, some women, some children. These people weren't on the front line fighting for their country, they weren't trying to do anything illegal on our seas; they were honest men, women and children going about their daily lives. And then that happens. I had to tell victims' families and friends that their loved ones were gone.'

Celeste was frozen in time, listening to Quinn explain what it had been like for him, what it was still like.

'Then there were the people you couldn't save.' His eyes had a sheen that threatened tears. 'Civilians who had, hours before the disaster, been cooking in their kitchen, watching television, cuddling their children, doing the housework. I'll never forget some of those faces. They stick in my mind more than anything else. I remember one guy trapped in his car, the car was carried along with the waters that high, he couldn't get out, we couldn't stop the car. I watched him drown, unable to do a thing about it.'

He closed his eyes. He pushed on. 'There were so many we couldn't save. There was yelling, panic, gushing water, crying, shouting; it was deafening. And I watched one elderly lady, Grace, run the opposite way to everyone else. She'd run back to the row of houses and I went after her. Everyone else was running for safety but she had water up to her waist and made for her own front door. I caught her and wrapped my arms around her. I knew the emotions people had, their possessions, the homes they'd lived in all their lives, disappearing before their very eyes. I pulled her away, she screamed but not out of fear or loss of her property and memories: at me for taking her away from it.'

Beneath the blanket, Celeste put her arm around his shoulders.

'Grace is the one I can't ever forget, Celeste.' He leaned his head against hers. 'I see her in my dreams, my nightmares, my waking thoughts.'

She had no words that could make it any better.

'Floodwaters were rising, we were doing everything we could – evacuating people, we built sandbag walls to protect properties and several times, we thought we were winning. Most people listened to us because they were terrified, but not Grace. She'd literally clung onto the doorframe of her home. It didn't matter how many times I told her she had to go; she kept hitting me. There was no strength behind it – she'd used any she had to try to cling onto her home – but eventually, I got her out of there. I was saving a life.'

'You were, Quinn. It was the right thing to do.'

'As the paramedics saw to her, she was wailing, telling me I should've left her in there. It was her home and it was my fault she'd lost it. She told me she wanted to die in her own home where her memories were, the spirit of her husband.'

Celeste turned her head and looked deep into his eyes. She saw the raw pain, the emotion. 'It wasn't your fault. She can't have meant that she wanted to die.'

'If I hadn't seen her, she would have stayed there; she would've got her wish. But I couldn't do it; I couldn't leave her there. I had to save her no matter whether she wanted me to or not. I heard a week later, she died in hospital. She didn't put up a fight to live. I knew she'd died in a place she didn't want to be; I'd heard her trying to refuse the hospital but too weak to get her way with the paramedics. They would've wanted to get her out of the danger zone, check her over at least. And all of that was because of me.'

'You saved a life. That was what you did. She lived because of you.'

'I never got over it: doing what she'd asked me not to. It was the final thing that broke me and made me realise I had to get out. I couldn't have that life any more.' His voice wavered. 'I didn't even know her, Celeste. But the feeling of that small body in my arms, the way she lashed out at me, the words she said, the wish that I'd just let her be.'

'You couldn't have done that.'

'I only ever told Eddie. My parents don't know. I'm ashamed, embarrassed at how broken I am. I feel like a failure. Weak and pathetic that I can't overcome it and be the man I was before.' He looked away, as though admitting out loud might make it more true.

'It wouldn't be right if you were, Quinn.' She watched the way he shifted awkwardly as though he still believed it true that he was any less of a man for reacting the way he had and still did now. 'Have you asked anyone for help? Aside from Eddie.'

'No. And my brother is fast running out of patience.'

'I doubt that. It wasn't the impression I got the other night, but I do know he's worried.'

A small smile appeared. 'Did you and he talk for long?'

'Only briefly – he told me the full story had to come from you.'

'He's loyal.'

'He's a nice guy; you both are. I think you should listen to him. But whatever you decide to do, I'm glad you told me.' She leaned against him and when she closed her eyes, she felt him kiss her gently on top of her head. 'Can I ask you something else?'

'Go on.'

'Did you make all that stuff up about leaving the navy because you wanted a family?' Her heart was in her mouth waiting for the reply. She almost couldn't breathe, anticipating what he might say.

'I like having a family, I appreciate them all; life is hard without one.'

'Yeah.'

'But that's not what you meant, is it?'

'No, not really.'

'Are you asking whether I want more?' Even near the rocks with some shelter and beneath the blanket, it was getting colder down here in a place so beautiful and special but no more able to battle the plummeting temperatures than anywhere else.

'I suppose I am.'

'I do,' he said. 'I want you.' He pulled back and took her in his arms, held her close. 'But for some reason you don't want me.'

'I do. But don't you want more?'

'I just said I did.'

'I'm talking about the whole deal: marriage, kids…'

He shrugged. 'I haven't thought about it, really.'

'So you don't want kids?'

'Didn't say that either.' His brow creased in confusion. 'Celeste, you're going to have to spell it out to me.'

Right, deep breath, it was time to be as honest with him as he was being with her.

She sat up straight, pulled away from him. 'I've never wanted children.'

'Okay…'

'No, I mean, never. I've never felt a tick tock of my biological clock like my sister, I've never felt the need to procreate, nurture, whatever you want to call it. And I know that makes me different to most women. Maybe that makes me cold, shallow.'

'You're neither of those things; I know that for certain. And different doesn't have to be a bad thing.'

'Quinn, what I'm telling you is that I don't want those things and I don't want to get in the way of someone who does.'

It took him seconds to realise what was going on here. 'This is why you've been pulling away from me? Because you don't want those things and you think that I do?'

'When we got together that summer, I asked you about what would make you leave the navy and I remember you saying that some day you want to put down roots, have more of a sense of family.'

'I don't really remember the conversation.'

'I do.' She gulped. 'And when you came back to Heritage Cove this time, it's what you told people.'

'Celeste, I was vocal so that people believed me. I didn't want them to know the real reason I'd left my career behind. I'm being truthful when I say I haven't thought about marriage and children much. I suppose I've had too much other stuff going on. I mean, I knew I didn't ever want to be in the position of some of those guys, away from their kids for months on end, watching them grow up from hundreds or thousands of miles away. But other than that, I didn't give much thought to what my own plan was long term.'

'I don't ever want to be responsible for taking away someone's dream. I've been in that situation before and the relationship ended because we didn't want the same things. When you were only here on leave, it was great – no promises to each other, no strings attached. But it's different now.'

'You should've just told me, been straight with me.'

'I could say the same.'

He met her gaze. 'How about from now on we try for a bit of honesty?'

'We could try.' She didn't want to get her hopes up, but was it worth the risk with Quinn?

'Okay, you ready for some more honesty?'

'Go on.'

'I'm so cold, I think parts of me are shrivelling up. Can we please go now?'

She stood up and held out her hand, the blanket falling from her shoulders to the ground. 'Ready. But this conversation isn't over.'

He stood, towering over her. 'I'm sure it isn't. Celeste, I—'

She reached up and put her hand across his lips. 'Not now – I need to get back to the bakery, you have the pub.'

She picked up one of the blankets and shook it while he did the other.

'When can I see you again?' he asked.

She hesitated. The problem between them still stood. He'd

lost a sense of his self; she didn't want to take away any more of
his happiness. She couldn't even meet his eye.

'Tomorrow too soon?' He crammed the blankets into the bag.

'I'll be in the bakery all day.'

'And I'll be working at the pub from midday, but I can sneak
out for a late lunch, like really late, say mid-afternoon.'

'I'll give Jade a long morning break and hopefully I can get
away too.' Her heartstrings were already being pulled in every
direction. Was this what she wanted? 'But I can't say for certain –
I have to play it by ear most days, we both do.'

'Fair enough.'

They walked, battling the wind that blew sand towards them.

Before they started up the path, Celeste stopped. 'I'm not sure
how this is going to work, Quinn. I don't want to hurt you.'

'And I don't want to hurt you either.' He pulled her into a hug
and she gladly leaned her head against the broad, strong chest
beneath his coat. 'But I'd like to give us a try.'

'I'd like that too.'

Although it still stood that she didn't want to take anything
away from Quinn. He deserved to have it all: the home, the wife
and the kids if that was what he wanted.

And she wondered whether it would be once he got his head
straight.

And if so, where did that leave her?

23

It was the day before Christmas Eve in the Star and Lantern and the boys were rushed off their feet, with plenty of bookings for lunches including a party of six from the loft conversion company Harvey still worked for when his own renovations business allowed. Another was a party of twelve, all teachers from the local high school, including Linc, who, when asked, said he'd had far too much champagne to pick up a guitar, let alone play any kind of tune the way he sometimes did here at the pub.

'I like it busy.' Eddie, umpteen glasses between his fingers, bustled back behind the bar where Quinn loaded a fourth pint of Guinness onto a tray once it had settled.

'That's Christmas for you,' Quinn agreed. Ever since he'd talked with Celeste the other day, it had been difficult to dampen his spirits, and even though they hadn't yet met up again because of their demanding work commitments, just the thought of seeing her at some point saw him through his days and he'd had a good few nights' sleep too. Although he was under no illusion that that would be it for the nightmares; they were lurking, waiting, and now Celeste knew, it gave him more impetus to do something about it. Not that he had yet.

Quinn took the pints of Guinness over to the teachers' table and on his way back, stopped to talk to Barney. 'You all right there?' He was in one of the chairs facing the fireplace. 'Not too noisy in here for you?'

Barney burst out laughing, as did the guy next to him – a relative of Lois's visiting from Ireland, if Quinn had overheard their conversation with Eddie earlier correctly.

'We're grand,' said the other man.

'We'll holler, loudly, if we need anything,' Barney assured Quinn.

Back behind the bar, Quinn gave the tray a quick wipe and put it on top of the others as he told Eddie, 'The pace over the past few days has been crazy.' They'd spoken to their parents earlier and suggested that perhaps next year, they come up and stay with the boys at the Star and Lantern. They'd stayed away this year with the brothers settling in, but they were more than excited at the prospect of being guests next time Christmas came around.

'Don't knock it.' Eddie wasn't; he was buzzing on the footfall since they'd taken over the pub.

'Wouldn't dare. I wonder what tomorrow will be like. Christmas Eve was always ridiculously busy at the old pub, wasn't it?'

'Fingers crossed it's the same here. Same as today would be great. Then there'll likely be a bit of a lull until New Year, or at least there won't be so many parties.'

They both looked over at the teachers' table. They were having a whale of a time.

When Barney came up to request a couple of toasted sandwiches, Eddie was quick to share the details he'd found out about a gin festival. 'I'm thinking around early March might be the right time for it,' Eddie suggested to Barney, as though he had an equal stake in the pub.

Barney was all for it. 'Just let me know the date and time and we'll be here to support you.'

When Barney went back to his companion, Quinn was still pondering Eddie's reaction. 'You didn't seem to mind running it by him.'

'I'm not really running it by him. But I am interested in what he thinks. I want him to like what we do here; it'd be nice if he was a part of it. And if there was a legitimate reason for us not doing an event, he might have inside knowledge before we go and waste time and money putting on something that is going to fail.'

'I've got a good feeling about this village.'

'Oh, you do, do you? That wouldn't have anything to do with your visitor the other night, would it? The damsel in distress?'

'Celeste is no damsel in distress, believe me.'

'No, I can tell she isn't. But she's part of why you wanted to be here.'

He didn't deny it. He couldn't. 'It wasn't the only reason, but I'll admit it was a bit of a sweetener.'

He missed Eddie's next comment because more champagne was requested at the teachers' table.

Quinn took over more alcohol and topped up glasses while Eddie served behind the bar, and after Eddie finished with his customer, their conversation continued.

'I've got a good feeling about the village too,' Eddie admitted.

'Well, that's good.'

'You didn't think I would?'

Quinn shrugged. 'I had wondered whether, despite the fact we bought the pub rather than leasing it, you'd want to increase turnover and then you'd be looking to move on again. Are you telling me you definitely don't want that?'

'For the first time since Claire left me, I finally feel as though I might want to stop moving on.'

Quinn patted his brother on the back. 'You don't know how much of a relief it is to hear that. The Star and Lantern is ours, Eddie. This is going to work.'

* * *

The pub didn't quieten down at all until late afternoon and it was then that Eddie suggested Quinn take a break before they got busy again.

'You can go first,' Quinn told him.

'I need to do some reordering so I'll do it on the laptop here, take a break later if I get a chance. If not, I'll have a coffee from my fancy machine and put my feet up between customers.'

'You sure?'

'If you don't take it now, I might change my mind.'

Quinn didn't need any more encouragement and as soon as he escaped into the rather fresh air, there was only one place he intended to go: the bakery.

He swore the temperature had dropped another five degrees since his run first thing when, according to the weather forecast, it had risen by two.

As Quinn approached the bakery, Gus was coming out and closed the little door behind him.

'What did you go for?' Quinn eyed the paper bag with the logo for the Twist and Turn Bakery emblazoned on it.

'Abigail's favourite: a pain aux raisins.'

'Lucky girl.'

'I spoil her a bit, but she deserves it.'

It reminded Quinn of Gus's comment at the stables about Abigail having had a tough time. But he was distracted when Celeste tapped on the window and held up her hand showing all five fingers before going back around the counter. They'd agreed that as soon as one of their schedules allowed, they'd go to the other one, who would do their best to get away. It hadn't happened the first day when Quinn came this way, nor last night when Celeste came into the pub. Hopefully, it would work today.

'I'm sure she does deserve it,' said Quinn. 'You mentioned the other day at the stables that she's had a tough time.'

'Yeah, so I guess I'm always looking out for how to keep her spirits up. I just hope I'm not going too far.'

'Never,' Quinn grinned. 'And you said that Denby helped her?'

'He did. She loves him. He belonged to our neighbour and after Abigail had a nasty accident, it was Abigail's time with our neighbour and with Denby that really turned her around.'

'The power of animals, and neighbours, of course.'

'Yeah.' But Gus turned serious then. 'Look, tell me it's none of my business if you like, but I've seen you on your morning runs a few times and you look like a man with stuff on your mind.'

'That means I've ignored you more than once,' Quinn laughed. Exercise had the power to make him zone out as much as he needed.

Gus's laughter pealed out down the street that had descended into winter darkness, its Christmas lights showing the way now. 'You did, but I've got a thick skin. I didn't take it personally.'

He thought he'd had that quality too, until he didn't.

'Don't tell me Barney's interference with the pub is getting to you?' Gus wondered. Without a specific response from Quinn, he'd begun to draw his own conclusions.

'No, it's nothing like that. It's... well, it's my past life rather than my present, if that makes sense.'

'You were in the navy, right?'

'Yeah.'

'You must have seen some things none of us could even imagine. I had a friend in the army; some of the stories he told were hair raising. I always thought he embellished, but maybe not.'

'Some of the guys did do that.' Quinn could remember some of the tales he'd overheard, especially when they docked and went out to bars and clubs and some of the single lads were doing their best to impress. But he, and plenty of others, avoided talking too much about the details. And besides, a lot of it they were duty-bound not to share.

'You did a tough job.'

'I loved it for a time.'

'But not now,' Gus said for him.

He gave Gus a brief recap of his departure from the navy, not the exact details, more of an overview of how the things he'd seen could mount up and before you knew it, they were in control of you rather than the other way round.

'Admitting you're having a hard time is a huge thing,' said Gus. 'Men have been discouraged from doing so for years; we're taught to be the strong ones, the ones who don't have to show emotion.'

'I made the excuse that I wanted to get out of the navy for family issues. It was true, my brother needed me for reasons I won't go into, but it was more than that.'

'You and your brother are close?'

'We are. And he's trying to help me.'

'You're still struggling?'

Quinn nodded. He found it easier to watch Celeste bagging

up items for her customer than focus on the man in front of him. 'But I'm getting there.'

'Would a certain young lady have something to do with that?'

He opened his mouth to deny it but decided it was obvious anyway, so what was the point? 'Celeste and I knew each other before.' His admission got the predicted eyebrow raise. 'I came here on holiday once with Eddie. I was on leave from the navy and we'd picked this little village for some time out. We were staying in a holiday house and Eddie had taken himself off fishing – I came here and wandered around. I stumbled into the bakery and the next thing I knew, this pastry came flying towards me.' At Gus's inquisitive look, he added, 'It's an original way to meet a girl.'

'You could say that. And now you both want to pick up where you left off?'

'I'd like to.' He thought about their conversation down by the water: the fact she asked him about kids, told him that wasn't what she wanted. He'd been truthful when he said he hadn't thought about it. There hadn't been room in his head for any of that.

Right now, all Quinn knew he wanted was one thing... her.

'So what's stopping you?' Gus asked.

Quinn rubbed his hands together in the cold. Despite the gloves, they were still chilly and after he'd warmed them a bit, he shoved them deep into his pockets. 'I've got some stuff I need to work through.'

'Counselling?'

He almost smiled at the directness. Men went one way or the other in his experience – either they were direct like Gus and said what was on their mind, or they bottled it all up the way he and plenty of others had. The danger with the latter was that at any point, the dam could burst and take everything else with it.

'I think that's the way to go, yeah. Know anyone?'

He'd been joking but Gus didn't take it that way. 'I'm afraid I don't. The only counsellors I know are of the four-legged equine variety.'

'That sounds interesting. I could head down to the Heritage View Stables and see whether any of the horses will listen to me.'

Gus chuckled. 'You'd be amazed at the healing power of animals. Although I'm a vet, I'm biased. You could always borrow Denby, have a ride, that might help.'

'Tell me you're joking,' said Quinn before he realised that's exactly what Gus was doing. 'I'm a terrible rider, awful. Abigail wouldn't let me within ten feet of her beloved horse. I think I'll stick to running or the gym.'

'I'm sure you're not that bad.'

'I'd rather not put it to the test.'

Gus contemplated something else. 'I might have something that's of interest to you. Stop by my veterinary practice any time after New Year's Day, I'll be back at work full-time by then.'

'Sounds mysterious.' Quinn turned as Gus waved to someone behind him.

'I'm serious: be sure to stop by.'

'I will. Thank you.' He left Gus handing over the pain aux raisins to Abigail, who'd arrived, linking arms with Hazel. He opened the door to the bakery, almost colliding with Celeste coming the other way.

Breathless as she pulled on her coat, she told him, 'I've got an hour.' But she registered the temperature. 'Whoa, it's freezing out here! Or maybe it's more that the bakery is super toasty.'

'No, you were right the first time,' he said, wanting to maintain the closeness now she'd pulled the door closed behind her and he hadn't even stepped back. It was a good job nobody was trying to get inside right now as they were blocking the entrance.

Celeste waved to Hazel, Gus and Abigail. 'I saw the pair of you talking; you're making friends.'

'I suppose I am.' But there was only one person he was interested in right now. 'Come on, with a whole hour to ourselves, where do you want to go?'

Celeste opened her mouth but as a big group of women came towards them, she pulled him to one side so they were in front of the window. 'Please don't, please don't, please don't...' Her eyes were closed. She opened one when she heard the bell to the bakery door tinkle.

'You have to go, don't you?' he concluded.

'I'm really sorry. But Jade still has a couple of yule logs to make and deliver. It's usually quiet at this time. I thought...'

But he silenced her by pressing his lips against hers, which did the trick.

'I have to go inside.'

He still had his hands on either side of her face, holding her there. 'Are you sure you're up for this?'

'For what?'

'Us.'

'You think I'm making excuses.' She looked through the door to the bakery. Jade glanced up more than once – it was the way Eddie got Quinn's attention when he needed help, like he was absolutely fine to anyone else watching but subtle enough that Quinn knew he needed a bit of a hand.

'I don't. But I have to check, Celeste. I'm a bit of a mess. Those nightmares – they terrify me when I'm aware or when Eddie tells me what happened during the night if I can't remember. You must've been scared. I wouldn't blame you if you needed to back off until I've sorted myself out a bit more.'

He'd looked away from her and it was her turn to put her gloved hand against his cheek to make sure he met her gaze. 'I'm up for this, whatever it entails. I will stand by you, be your friend. But after what I told you, are you sure you want anything more?' She stopped him answering. 'Just think about it. I mean it. I want you to have everything, you deserve it. But you need to think about whether I can give it to you.'

'I want you, Celeste.'

She looked into the bakery again. 'I have to go. Don't give me any answers now; let's keep it this way until after Christmas?'

'Hit pause for a bit, you mean.'

'Exactly.' She reached for his hands and took them both with hers. 'I want you to enjoy your first Christmas here in Heritage Cove. We'll see each other as friends. But promise me you'll think carefully before we take it any further.'

'It'll be hard to do, but I'll do it. For you. Promise.'

It almost broke his heart to let her go inside but he knew she was right. They'd leapt into a no-strings-attached relationship before because there were no consequences, nothing was permanent. But now it was.

And he wanted them both to make the right choice.

24

Christmas Eve in Heritage Cove started early, the same as any other day for Celeste and Jade in the Twist and Turn Bakery, but what was different was that today, Celeste had woken up knowing what she really wanted. She wanted Quinn. And it had been the most difficult thing she'd ever done to tell him to think about his choices, to consider whether he really saw a future with her when she might have a different vision to him of what that was going to be. She'd always felt selfish saying she didn't want to have children. It wasn't that she didn't like kids; she adored Phoebe. She just didn't want it for herself. And since breaking up with Julian at the law firm, it had put her off getting serious about anyone else ever again. Celeste loved her life the way it was: her ability to focus on the bakery and put all her efforts in there. But what she hadn't really told anyone, even her sister, was that she wouldn't mind sharing that life with a partner. With a man who wanted the same things in his future as she did.

But she had no idea which way Quinn was going to go. All she knew was that whatever way it was, she had to respect his decision.

When they finally closed the doors to the bakery at the end of the day and made their way to the pub to join other locals for celebrations of another festive season in the Cove, Celeste was excited but nervous.

'I wondered whether you'd be giving me space,' Quinn confided when he got a moment to come out from behind the bar. She'd gone to request another three glasses of mulled wine for herself, Jade and Melissa.

'I am, but we can still see each other,' she said softly. She just couldn't reach out and touch him in the way she wanted to. 'And we can still talk.'

'Just not about us.'

She nodded. 'Got it in one.'

'Well, I have other news.'

'Since we saw each other yesterday?'

He tilted his head in the direction of the kitchen and they went past the Christmas tree. They hovered in the corridor but against the wall enough that if Benjamin came flying through, he wouldn't crash into them.

'I made some calls.' He stood so close, he didn't have to speak too loudly.

'Calls?' She was watching his lips; she couldn't help it.

'About counselling.'

'I wasn't expecting you to say that today.'

'Neither was I.' He leant a hand against the wall behind her and his body hovered close. She wanted to tell him not to, but not when he was telling her something so monumental.

'Clearly I've picked a bad time with it being the holidays, but I still set up some sessions for the New Year.' His voice was soft, his eyes never left hers. 'Eddie already had some numbers for me for organisations who offer support to veterans and between us, we found a few others.'

'I'm glad.'

'Me too. And I really think talking to someone impartial will be a start. Talking to people who weren't there, who don't know me.'

The way he was looking at her had her insides all over the place.

'Until the New Year, I'll do my best to try to work through some of it myself. Eddie says he'll have things in hand here and he wouldn't listen to any argument on that.'

'He's a good brother.'

'He is. And I think taking time to work through my own thoughts might be a bit easier now you know.'

'I'm glad I've helped.'

'I told my parents too.'

'That makes me doubly glad.'

He was hovering so close and the only thing to break the moment was Benjamin coming out of the kitchen, making them both jump out of their loved-up trance.

'You two couldn't have picked a worse place to stand,' Benjamin tutted as he whizzed past with a tray of bowls of chips and condiments.

'Come on, let's go into the bar.' Quinn tilted his head in that direction. 'I'll get you those mulled wines.'

'Three, please,' she said, squeezing past Barney when they reached the bar. 'Almost Christmas, Barney, it's so good to have you home. Are you resting enough, though?' She put her arm around his shoulders.

'Of course I am, Lois insists on it. And I should go into hospital more often if I get all this attention.' His grey hair was freshly cut for Christmas – he'd told them earlier in the bakery that he liked to be smart for the festive season.

Lois came up behind them and overheard. 'Do not say that. I

like having you home.'

Quinn saw to the mulled wines and Eddie moved to the other end of the bar where Barney had gone too. She wondered what they were talking about.

'They're in cahoots about something,' said Quinn when he set down the tray with the mulled wines for Celeste.

'They are. Wonder what they're talking about.'

Quinn called down the bar to ask the question.

'We're helping,' Barney called back. 'It's what we do here.'

'Not sure I follow,' Quinn said, more to Celeste than anyone else.

Eddie went on the opposite side of him so they could keep the conversation just between the two of them and Celeste. Barney was busy discussing something with Lois now. 'Barney, like many others, saw the ad on the door for temporary help next week. He asked if we were both all right, I said we were but you had a few things you needed to do this week. Before I knew it, he'd leapt in, spread the word, and rather than one application for a temporary job, help we might not necessarily need but could end up paying for for a week, we've got a list of volunteers should I need it.'

Quinn's jaw dropped and Celeste hoped he wasn't annoyed that his brother had taken steps to cover the time Quinn was going to take to begin to talk with someone and sort his head out.

'You would've done the same for me,' Eddie added. 'I can't guarantee I'll be able to run this place solo for a week, but you need to take the time right now, now you've made a decision. I want you to do it for yourself, for us, for the future.'

Quinn faltered. 'I don't know what to say.'

'Thank me by getting the help you need,' said Eddie.

'I will.' He didn't say another word, just wiped down the bar top all the way to the other end as the knowledge settled.

'You okay there?' Celeste could tell he was processing what had just happened and perhaps he thought she'd already taken the mulled wines and gone back to her friends.

He looked up at last. 'Yeah.'

She leaned over the bar to talk quietly. 'Barney won't ask you the details, you know; he's not nosy. He'll assume it's important, that's all.'

'I can't believe people are helping us out when they barely know us.'

She shook her head, grinning. 'Quinn, welcome to Heritage Cove.' And with the tray in her hands, she turned back to look at him and added, 'You're gonna love it.'

* * *

Before the pub closed its doors for the evening, Quinn grabbed Celeste. 'Come outside with me.'

'Don't you have clearing up to do?' She'd already pulled on her coat and noticed that so had he.

'Clearing up can wait. Eddie promised he'd leave me my share.'

Celeste approved. 'Good to hear he's not totally bending over backwards for you.'

'I'd hate it if he made my life too easy.'

The pub had almost emptied apart from a few stragglers including Benjamin and his family, who looked like they were there for the duration. It had been another busy season at Mistletoe Gate Farm and they'd invited Eddie and Quinn to share Christmas Day dinner with them tomorrow when they could celebrate a break from their hard work all year. Not that it would stop for long, they'd told the boys. Having a Christmas tree farm was a year-round occupation, much to many people's disbelief.

'What are we doing out here?' Celeste wanted to know.

'You'll see.' He grabbed her hand and this time, she didn't protest. It was Christmas Eve, special, magical, a time for togetherness and it felt so right. It didn't mean he wasn't taking this seriously, wasn't thinking about what he really wanted.

'Where are we going?' she laughed.

'I have something to show you.'

He was holding her hand; he kept laughing as he pulled her along, running to the end of The Street as the lit-up sleigh hovering above with Father Christmas on top showed them the way. Then they turned down a road and he only stopped when they reached Gus's veterinary surgery.

'What's going on, Quinn?'

Quinn led her up the front path and although it was late, there was a light on. Gus opened up when Quinn knocked. And it seemed like he'd been expecting them.

'Quinn, what is this?'

Gus was definitely in on whatever this was because he told them to wait there in the reception and disappeared into one of the practice rooms.

'Quinn, what *is* going on?'

'I was supposed to wait until New Year to talk to Gus. I was supposed to wait until New Year to think about what you said. But I'm not a patient man, as it turns out.'

Celeste turned when she heard a sound. 'Who's this?' She crouched down when Gus emerged with a golden retriever on a lead. 'She's adorable.' Celeste fussed over the dog; she was beautiful, soft, happy, wagging her tail in enthusiasm.

'This is Bailey.' Gus handed the lead to Quinn. 'I'll give you guys a moment.'

'Is this the dog he's looking after, the one who'll be a Christmas gift?' Although right now, she wished the gift was going to her. This dog was gorgeous and seemed taken with her already, the way she was still wagging her tail and sniffing her forearm, getting as close as she could.

'No, this is another dog. When I got talking to Gus the other day, he told me how Abigail's recovery from what happened to her was aided by her horse Denby. When I came to see him earlier today when I couldn't wait any longer to find out what he wanted to share with me, he told me he was looking after Bailey. Her owner for whatever reason doesn't want to take her to Poland with them when they relocate. So she's under Gus's care for now. But now I have a decision to make.'

'Are you asking whether I think you should buy a dog?'

'I am.' He crouched down next to her to make just as big a fuss of Bailey as she was.

'Well, I'm in love with her already, so I say go for it.' Celeste couldn't leave the dog alone.

'Bailey here has been through some of the training as an assistance dog.'

'What's an assistance dog?'

He explained the condensed version he understood from Gus. 'A trained assistance dog can help people who have physical disabilities, medical conditions... anxiety, depression, PTSD.'

'And Gus thinks Bailey could help you?'

'Maybe. Bailey has done some of the training, still a long way to go, and it does cost. But whether I need an assistance dog or not, as soon as Gus told me about Bailey and introduced us, I could see me taking her home.'

'I can see it too.' Celeste couldn't stop smiling. 'Although I'm not sure about the pub.'

'No, that's something else to think about.'

'How much training has she had?'

'She's mastered a few of the basics. She's a work in progress.' He looked from Bailey to Celeste. 'Like me.'

Bailey's tongue hung out as she looked from Celeste to Quinn and back to Quinn again as though she wanted to know the outcome of this conversation.

'Aren't we all a work in progress?'

'I feel like I'm ending the year with a promise of a new start, Celeste.'

She felt comfort settle inside her. 'That makes me really happy.'

'I know that's what New Year is to a lot of people but this year, it feels really significant. Calling the helplines my brother found for me, I put the phone down three times before I dared to speak to anyone. But I know I'm on my way.'

'I can tell you that you are. I can see it in your eyes.' And she could hear it in his voice. He had his brother at his side; it seemed right now that he was capable of anything.

'I'm here in the Cove to stay,' he said as though she might doubt it.

Bailey nudged her hand and she fussed the dog around the ears. It was a distraction from Quinn, from not daring to get her hopes up. Just because they wanted each other didn't mean they were on the same path.

'I suppose what I need to know, Celeste, is whether you'd like to be a family. Me, you and Bailey, that is.'

When she looked at him, her heart melted. She wasn't sure she'd ever seen a man look so nervous.

'Quinn, you'd be giving up your chance to be a dad if you're with me.'

He shook his head. 'Family comes in all shapes and sizes.

And maybe this is the shape of ours. I can't see anything else I want more.'

'Really?'

'I think I've told you enough times. I'll tell you every single day if I have to. But I'd rather you just took me at my word.'

'Okay.' Had she said that out loud? Had the words left her lips? Everything felt surreal right now.

'Okay? So you're saying...'

'Yes. I'm saying yes.'

'So we're an item?'

'Yes.'

'So properly, not just friends?'

'Quinn, would you stop asking questions and just kiss me?'

He looked down at Bailey. 'Sorry, but this woman gets all my attention now. Have you any idea how long I've waited for this?'

He took her face in his hands and his lips crashed down on hers, sending her world spinning in all directions.

The only interruption was a giggle.

Quinn cleared his throat as they pulled apart. 'Hello, Abigail.'

'Dad's too scared to come out in case you two were kissing,' she giggled.

Quinn grabbed Celeste's hand. 'Thanks, Gus,' he called out and Gus poked his head out of the practice room. 'I'll be in touch. Look after Bailey for us.'

Gus emerged from his hiding place and raised a hand to wave to both of them.

'Back to your place?' Quinn asked Celeste the second they left.

'I thought Eddie told you he'd leave you the clearing up.'

'I can have another hour... or two.'

They ran hand in hand along The Street, past a few revellers tumbling from the pub and to a few calls of their names, no idea from who, and when they were almost at the cottage, Quinn lifted her up and slung her over his shoulder.

Celeste, upside down, was glad she'd only had a couple of mulled wines and plenty of food to soak it up. 'I wish you had your uniform on,' she squealed, 'this is very *An Officer and a Gentleman*.'

He set her down at the door to her cottage and pressed her against it. 'That can be arranged. I still have my uniform.'

'And the hat?' she asked when he took his lips from hers again.

He planted another kiss on her. 'And the hat. Now let us inside before we freeze.'

But before she did, she wrapped her arms around his neck and her legs around his waist as he lifted her up. 'Merry Christmas, Quinn.'

'Merry Christmas, Celeste.'

ACKNOWLEDGMENTS

It's an absolute pleasure to be a Boldwood author. A big thank you to the entire team; you are all fabulous and do such a brilliant job to get our books out on publication day in all formats all around the world.

Special thanks to my editor Rachel Faulkner-Willcocks for guiding me through the many stages to take a book from first draft to the polished version ready for my readers. Thank you also to Cecily my copy editor and Emily my proofreader, for your skills and direction. And of course to Jenna, who campaigns so passionately for my books to reach readers far and wide.

As always, I want to let my family know how important and wonderful it is to have them at my side and for respecting the closed study door – well, sometimes at least, especially when I put a post-it on to say *Please Do Not Disturb!*

And lastly, my huge heartfelt thanks to every reader who has picked up a copy of this book. I hope you love the story!

Helen x

ABOUT THE AUTHOR

Helen Rolfe is the author of many bestselling contemporary women's fiction titles, set in different locations from the Cotswolds to New York. She lives in Hertfordshire with her husband and children.

Sign up to Helen Rolfe's mailing list for news, competitions and updates on future books.

Visit Helen's website: www.helenjrolfe.com

Follow Helen on social media here:

facebook.com/helenjrolfewriter

twitter.com/hjrolfe

instagram.com/helen_j_rolfe

ALSO BY HELEN ROLFE

Heritage Cove Series

Coming Home to Heritage Cove

Christmas at the Little Waffle Shack

Winter at Mistletoe Gate Farm

Summer at the Twist and Turn Bakery

Finding Happiness at Heritage View

Christmas Nights at the Star and Lantern

New York Ever After Series

Snowflakes and Mistletoe at the Inglenook Inn

Christmas at the Little Knitting Box

Wedding Bells on Madison Avenue

Christmas Miracles at the Little Log Cabin

Moonlight and Mistletoe at the Christmas Wedding

Christmas Promises at the Garland Street Markets

Family Secrets at the Inglenook Inn

Little Woodville Cottage Series

Christmas at Snowdrop Cottage

Summer at Forget-Me-Not Cottage

Boldwood

Boldwood Books is an award-winning fiction publishing company seeking out the best stories from around the world.

Find out more at www.boldwoodbooks.com

Join our reader community for brilliant books, competitions and offers!

Follow us
@BoldwoodBooks
@TheBoldBookClub

Sign up to our weekly deals newsletter

https://bit.ly/BoldwoodBNewsletter

Printed in Great Britain
by Amazon

31454049R00165